Confessions of a Rain God

Robert Mayer

Confessions of a Rain God

Cover design: Rhonda Ward
Cover model: Malia Byrne
Model photo: Traci Hatico

ISBN-13: 978-1936404-33-9

Published by Combustoica, a prose project of About Comics.
www.Combustoica.com.

For rights inquiries, contact RIGHTS@ABOUTCOMICS.COM

Published December, 2012.

Books by Robert Mayer

Fiction

The Origin of Sorrow

Danse Macabre

The Ferret's Tale

I, JFK

The Search

Sweet Salt

The Grace of Shortstops

Midge and Decker

The Execution

Superfolks

Non-Fiction

The Dreams of Ada

Notes of a Baseball Dreamer
(First published as *Baseball and Men's Lives*)

Confessions
of a
Rain God

Translated from the Mayan

By Robert Mayer

There are still beings, no doubt, who can worship us; we shall make them capable of obedience. Now, do your duty; as for your flesh, it will be ground between teeth, so be it.

—Popul Vuh
Book One
Chapter II

To the Goddess
of the
Golden Butterflies

Even the stupid jungle knew that something was amiss: his hairy roots had clenched in scrotal fear. Amid crisping leaves the naked woodland shivered like a bride. Furry creatures of the night prowled in morning's blaze, vainly seeking shade for lidless eyes. Pumas, jaguars, coatimundi crept through burned brown brush in search of sustenance. Stoic deer, thin ribs carved like temple walls, staggered from the uplands, where drought had murdered the growing things; they tasted the jungle's fungus-ridden toes, and wretched. Warblers high in barren trees, who should have welcomed the dawn with gentle song, screeched instead from hoarse and coarsened throats. Secret snakes, shy iguanas exposed their breasts to glaring light in mass and massive sunlit suicides. Golden butterflies impaled their wings on the pointed beaks of birds. Every creature seemed to sense a potent rage about to assault the earth that day.
Every creature except the mortals.
    And the gods.

    —Lock up your daughters, Itzamna says.
    He is the mighty god of the sky.
    He's trying to be amusing. It doesn't suit.
    —Don't start that again, I say.
    An error of passion, it was. An over-reaction.
    It could happen to anyone.

    I am an old god with a long nose and stringy gray hair. I go by the name of Chac (it rhymes with mock.) My sculpted visage, carved in stone by fawning artists, once adorned the grandest temples, the proudest monuments. Now, when sweaty diggers disturb the temples, denude them of jungle clay, they find that from every sacred carving my great protruding nose has broken off. Thus have I been rudely tweaked by Time, by Fate.

I can't say I don't deserve it.

I used to be the rain god of the Mayas, worshipped and feared at once. Between us, my four frogs and I could whip up any temper of rain desired: a brief evening sprinkle to tamp the summer dust, a late afternoon downpour to slake the fields of corn, a seven-day torrent that would flood the jungle bottom, sending jaguars, pumas, iguanas, wild turkeys scurrying for higher ground, striking fear into the heart of the Lord Maya himself. A thousand different rains I could conjure.

Lately I haven't tried. My mortals are long gone. There's no one left to tremble, to applaud.

I have been implored by Itzamna to explain in what manner the finest civilization of its time, with its startling mathematics, its enduring architecture, its perfect observatories, its rock-hard calendars, disappeared when it did. The Mystery of the Mayas, you call it.

I confess. It was all my fault.

Itzamna's dull grey eyes suddenly sparkle in his oversized head. The sun flares brighter. Like sky gods everywhere, Itzamna bathes in praise; he insists upon it. But blame he does not suffer well.

She was a laughing girl. I see her running along the beach at the water's edge, splashing in the surf, holding the hem of her purple kub high across her thighs, with other boys and girls in pursuit, her breasts bobbing mangos, until she reaches the stone jetty at the curve of the lagoon, and stops, her laughter suddenly gone as she sees the violent waves pounding the jutting rocks.

She was a laughing girl, I see her fleeing, crashing through the jungle, grabbing the stalks of orchids or lianas as she stumbles, Kel in swift pursuit, Kel the best young athlete in the village, his smooth chest bare, unable to catch her, till she slows her pace to let him overtake, till she gives him a gift, a bouquet of purple orchids she has plucked: a gift that makes him smile, and blush.

She was a laughing girl, I see her head thrown back in joy, or a sly smile beneath her wild hair. I envy their flirtatious humor, though after nine long bakuns I cannot remember their jokes.

Kel was taller than most of the boys and men, with bronzed features well carved. Broad-shouldered, confident: a born leader, the elders said. Tika was swift, full-bodied, clever, sultry, wistful: her dark green eyes sad even while she was laughing, her lips hinting at secrets even when she was sad.

Their coming union will grace even the stars, the elders said of Tika and Kel.

That joke I remember.

See Tika as a child, sitting in dirt in front of her father's scraggly hut, smearing her face with juicy pulp while biting her tiny white teeth into a mango. A monkey lopes beside her, the family pet, grabs the mango from the startled child, begins to eat. The child looks down at her sticky, juice-covered hands, and stifles cries. Determined, she snatches at the fruit. Beside the hut a slave woman is watching. The monkey dances around the child, rolls the mango away in the dirt. The child scrambles after it, begins to giggle. Her baby laugh is musical.

Suddenly a great shadow falls upon them, cast by the towering hat of the Lord Maya himself. He is making a rare visit among the lower men. Beside him is the High Priest, whose high feathered hat throws a shadow almost as long. The Lord Maya stoops to admire the child. Laughing, she with her small dusky hand throws the sodden mango. It strikes the embroidered chest of the Lord Maya's sacred kub. Pulpy juice leaves a mark near his heart.

Outraged, the High Priest raises his sword, as if he would strike at once: the child, the monkey, the frightened slave. Remove a head or two. The Lord Maya stays his hand. Instead of striking out, the Lord caresses the child's dimpled cheek.

The two favored ones do not speak, instead remove their shadows. From beside the hut, trembling, the slave woman approaches, kneels, lifts the girl from the dirt.

—Time for a bath, she says.

High above, watching, Fate nudges her lover, Time, and points a crooked finger. Time, napping, opens his sleepy eyes.

—That one, Fate says, pointing, musing. Let's do something special with that one.

I did not dwell on portents, not then, not now. I pass the time throwing dice with Itzamna; with Ixchel, my former lover, now his wife; with a hoary fraud who claims he used to be Zeus. (He drools a lot.) We dwell in a quiet aerie (cynics say asylum) that floats above the mist, among the clouded stars, beyond the ken of man. There are more of us here than you might imagine: the place is bulging with gods who no longer have clients: Hun gods, Celtic gods, Kurdish ones, Greek and Roman, Neanderthal, Paleolithic, Norse, Aztec, Inca — I could go on and on. The Mayas alone, uncommonly clever, used to succor more than two hundred of us.

From time to time there are discussions about organizing, about warring to regain our former glory. Nothing will come of it. Disenfranchised gods live for the sound of their own threats. That's all they have to prove they still exist.

I do not believe in threats. I was a benign god (despite what happened.) I do not seek your pity, your sympathy.

All I seek is a little of your time, to hear my tale. Time, as the Mayas knew, is all there is.

Her full name was Ixtika. She was no different than a thousand mortal girls my abstract gaze, my stinging rain, touched each season. An ordinary human, all in all. But somehow, as she grew from laughing child to somber womanhood, as I watched her mature and darken and battle the sorrows of mortal life, her baby belly replaced by alluring lean, my heart became enchanted, my loins began to throb. This I do not deny. But Gods are forbidden to lie with humans. It's the first rule of the pantheon.

Why, I do not know. Why do we make such painful rules?

Why do you?

Your sacred codexes burst with them. What to eat, when to pray, whom to fondle.

The rules are needed to please the gods, you say.

Which of course is lizard-turd.

Ixchel I loved. No problem there. Ixchel was the goddess of women, the goddess of pregnancy. We were married for a thousand years (it was common-law.) She had large breasts and thick hair and a heart big as a manatee. She bore me four frogs (we were careful) who grew up to be my helpers. When we parted it was amicable; we're still good friends. Ixchel, as I have mentioned, later took up with Itzamna, god of the sky. The first god among equals, he likes to say. (We try to humor him.)

Ixtab also I loved, after a fashion. No problem there, she, too, was divine, the goddess of suicide. We had a wild affair that often found us writhing in moist and wrinkled sheets of gentle mist. Exploring the limits of ecstasy. Of which there are none.

I should have been satisfied. But I was not.

Tika lived in a village at the edge of the jungle, where the earth sloped away to the sea. The center of the village, the throbbing heart, was a maze of masonry: sturdy rock temples, markets, ball fields, pyramids. From three sides of the central plaza the huts of the villagers spread like arteries. To the east was a large communal well. To the north was an equally large well, at the end of a broad stone walk. This second well was not for slaking thirst. The mortals had declared it a sacred cenote, and used it only for human sacrifice: to give us gods a taste of innocent flesh, of mortal limbs, of streaming blood.

What can I tell you? They did not know us very well.

The village was a mortal construction in a land flowing with milk and beans. (We gods are adept at phrases.) The jungle near which the village stood, and the highland forests beyond, were rich with animals, with fruit. Deer, turkeys, enormous rabbits provided the mortals with meat; fields grew high with corn; lazy fish were thick along the beaches, as were turtles, iguanas, ducks, herons, egrets. The sea offered salt for preserving flesh. Tails of stingrays were useful saws with which to sever limbs. Occasional manatees, harpooned with sharpened bones, provided more belly-fill than a romp of white-horn deer. Cotton gave its life for cloth, cacao beans for chocolate, their favorite drink. Great swarms of bees, stingless, filled the hollows of trees with honey, from which the humans made a boozy drink called balche. Rock quarries were pregnant with sturdy stones: enough for them to construct with tools of flint more pyramids and temples than they knew how to properly assign.

In short, the mortals had enough of everything to last until the end of days.

Except fresh water.

There were no lakes, no rivers, nearby. Their very lives depended on my rain. Without it the animals on which they fed would die, the corn in their fields would wither, the people themselves would perish of hunger and thirst. It's not a pleasant way to go.

I granted them the rain they needed.

(Most of the time.)

How they adored me for it!

They worshipped Itzamna as the foremost of the gods, but privately they knew it was me they depended upon.

I did not question this. I did not make a stink. I was the essence of humility.

That is no small feat for a god.

Tika's father, Hunac, was a lower man, who worked in the communal fields by day, made weapons to trade at night, and followed the soldierly nacom into battle when invaders threatened the village. He worshipped, in ascending order, the nacoms, the High Priest, the sacred Lord Maya, and the gods. Perhaps that was Tika's subtle attraction for me: she was common.

Her stepmother, when not in the fields with Tika's father, wove cotton into cloth for mats, kubs, breechclouts; ground corn into meal for tortillas; raised deer, monkeys and coaties, which she often suckled at her breasts, and generally looked after the children. Like most Maya women she had breasts both large and firm, from the constant grinding of corn.

Of Tika's beginnings I remember mostly this: her father worked side by side in the fields with a ribald friend, Akbal. They shared with each other's families whatever game they caught or killed. Akbal's first-born was a son, whom he named Ahkel. Three years later, Hunac's wife gave birth to their first live child, a fine-looking baby girl. Hunac overcame his natural disappointment at not having a son. What choice did he have? The two men donned their finest breechclouts, and celebrated. Over gourds of balche they decided what a fine thing it would be for their families to be united. They drank to the sacred promise that the girl Ixtika and the boy Ahkel would be married to one another when they reached the proper age.

On the day of her betrothal, Tika was three days old. It was a marriage made by the gods, the drunken fathers proclaimed. We, of course, had nothing to do with it.

She was born in the rainy season. She struggled fiercely against her birth, as if she did not want to join the mortal world. The difficult labor, a painful birth, weakened her mother, Ixlu Chel, already chilled and unwell from weeks of damp. While the fathers celebrated, the mother never rose from her mat. A lung sickness was proclaimed. She was given turkey broth to drink, laced with the ashes of burned dog droppings.

The cure didn't work.

(It never has.)

Three months later she was dead.

Tika was nursed at the breasts of hired women, and cared for by Hunac's sisters. When she was five years of age her father married again, a shrew called Axix. More children were born through the years, but Tika often felt apart, closer to Kel than to her own half-siblings. The knowledge that she was her real mother's only child, that her mother had died because of her birth, lay buried inside her like the grit of a bitter root.

The only remembrance her mother left her were three painted pots, which she'd learned to create while she was heavy with Tika. Those and a legacy of blood unknown to all of them. Forgotten even by me.

Shunted like a borrowed thing from one aunt to another, Tika gave little voice to her spawning curiosities. Only when she was returned to live with her father and a stranger — his new wife — did she dare to voice her thoughts. One day, sitting cross-legged on a mat beside him, she asked her father to tell of her real mother. Hunac frowned. He told her that by dying, her mother had deserted both of them.

—There's no need to speak of her, he said. You have a new mother now.

Like all lower women, her stepmother, Axix, would cross the village each day to draw water from the communal well, water to use for cooking and a bath. Tika walked obediently at her stepmother's side, greeting neighbors, playing near the top of the well as her stepmother walked down the long curving steep stone stairs, arms laden with a heavy earthen pot. When she had filled the pot with water she would strain to carry it up the uneven steps. Tika was too small to help, but knew that when she grew older this would be her task, too. Unlike the other little girls, she did not find the prospect appealing.

It always surprised me that they never rigged up pulleys with which to raise the pots of water from the well, or carts on which to move the heavy jugs. Both would have saved much sweat. But the Mayas, who were brilliant architects, whose mathematics and astronomy surpassed all, and astounded even Itzamna, never bothered to invent the wheel. Mortals, it was clear, have as many blind spots as gods.

Often, Tika would sit for hours alone in the sun-warm thatched hut, gazing at the three lovely pots her mother had left behind. To her they were as grand as the vast pyramids built by the men, built to outlast time. Until one day, returning from play, she noticed that the stone ledge near the doorway, where the pots had always been kept, was naked.

—Where are Ixlu's pots? she asked.

—We traded them at the market, her father said, glancing at her stepmother's back. For provisions.

He didn't say what provisions. Tika didn't ask.

Two days later, straying further behind the hut than usual, she found broken shards from her mother's pots: blue, yellow, red — mere slivers, which had not been swept away, which had evaded the stiff branches of her stepmother's broom, a thatch whose trails were visible in the dirt. The hateful truth was clear even to the child. Axix has destroyed them, to rid the house of Ixlu's memory.

The smallest of the shards Tika, teary-eyed, slipped into the hem of her kub. She never spoke of her find to anyone. But to each new kub, as she grew thinner, taller, she transferred the bitter fruit.

Tika mourning her mother's pots is one of the few memories I have of her growing-up. Gods and children tend to ignore one another. And properly so: our selfish natures would clash. But there is one conversation between Kel and Tika that I clearly recollect.

—When we grow up I shall be a nobleman, Kel said one day, when he was ten years old and Tika nearly seven.

It was late afternoon, their fathers had gone from the fields to the communal sweat baths, the women were busy preparing posole laced with venison. The youngsters were sprawled on the hillock between the plaza and the sacred well. A blue and yellow parrot gazed at them from a tree on the jungle's edge.

—I shall be a noble, Kel continued, and you shall be a noble's wife.

—You can't become a noble, Tika said. You have to be born a noble.

—There is a way, Kel said. I shall be a noble before we marry.

She didn't ask him how. She had learned already that a boy was supposed to dream.

She watched a trio of ravens glide black against the deep blue sky, aroused by a scream from the jungle.

—Look how pretty the sky is, Tika said, chewing on her hair. I think I will live forever.

—You will be a noble's wife, and live in a fine new house, Kel said. But no one lives forever.

Spitting out the hair she drew a line in the dirt with a stone.

—Artists do, she said. The artists in the temples. They paint the faces of the gods. They carve the gods in stone. Through this sacred work they live forever.

Kel, frowning at her silliness, hugged his arms around his knees. She was still only a child, he was almost a man.

—Only boys can be artists, he told her. It's the law.

Tika held the stone in her fingers, her arms stretched in front of her, and stared at it as if to give it life.

—I know, she said. It isn't fair.

Kel did not understand what wasn't fair.

—Let's mix our blood, Tika said suddenly. As an offering to the gods. So you will become a noble. And I will live forever.

Kel grinned, nodded. He patted the ground until he found a rock with a sharp edge. Holding his breath, he slit a small cut in his finger, drawing bright blood. He took Tika's left hand in his. He drew the edge of the rock across her palm.

Nothing happened.

— You have to press harder, Tika said.

He looked at her innocent upturned face.

—It will hurt.

—I know, she said.

He hesitated, gazed at her dark eyes, at the courage they hinted at. Took her hand, tighter this time, and pressing hard managed to slice her palm. He dropped the rock and placed his own bleeding finger against her wound. Their two dark bloods commingled like merging streams. The parrot fled from its limb like a messenger.

—Now it's in the hands of the gods, Kel intoned.

What can I tell you? They were children. They hadn't yet learned the primary lesson of life: the gods have slippery fingers.

What the mortals — even the elders — never seemed to grasp, was this: the trait that most becomes a god is apathy.

Even so, from high above we had as many ways of viewing the Mayas as they had of viewing us. To Itzamna, the sky god, they were like precious children. He delighted in their every display of cleverness: their alphabet of glyphs, their arches and houses of stone, their temples and observatories. He would pull my sleeve sometimes to point out some particular new cleverness of theirs. (I always made a show of admiration.) For the same reason, he tended to flare in anger when they misbehaved, or acted stupidly. He favored strict discipline, the teaching of lessons. Of morals. And he liked a show of respect from time to time: a dance, a prayer, in honor of himself. (I always thought he was too involved.) When the men of the village had begun, a few years earlier, the construction of a mammoth new pyramid in the vast central plaza, Itzamna assumed — all of us assumed — it was for him.

To Ixchel, his wife, the mortals were less like children, more like beige or copper puppies. She found them infinitely amusing, if not downright cute: the way they played among themselves, their roughhousing and warlike growls, the seriousness with which they worried their mortal bones. She helped them with their litters, and when the women made pilgrimages to her shrine at Cozumel, to sing her praises, it was something like a favorite mutt rising up on hind legs to lick its master's face, tail wagging: it gave her a feeling of warmth, and cheap superiority: a sense, however simple, of being needed. Ixchel is big-hearted, as I've said. She gives her love and needs love in return.

Ixtab, goddess of suicide, was cynical. She was jealous of Ixchel, and I sometimes think she hated all the mortals. She viewed them as monkeys who could not even climb. As for their suicide, she refused to take it seriously. If mortal lives were insignificant, then so, too, were their deaths. The fact that the Mayas honored suicides was just a clever way of assuaging the guilt of the survivors.

When Itzamna suggested that this made them more astute than other mortals, Ixtab merely shrugged.

In light of what eventually happened, it will perhaps surprise you that of all the gods I was the most apathetic, apathy, as I've said, being a god's primal trait. The Mayas were short-snouted: they might have been so many rabbits, sniffing ineffectually, wrinkling what passed for noses in concern. They looked alike, were almost indistinguishable as they shuffled about their village like busy ants. They needed water to grow food, water to drink, water to wash away their excrement, so I provided the water. It was merely a task, a godly reason to exist.

Until I noticed Tika.

Why, among all the Maya girls, my gaze continued to alight upon her, I do not know. It's true that she had a violent habit of eating butterflies — alive — when she walked alone in the jungle. But this I didn't notice until later.

I am a romantic at heart. I think the first attraction was her breasts. The sweet mathematical ache of their upward arc.

I jest, it wasn't those. It was her gumption I admired, her rebel brain, wherein there grew a silent writhing jungle of its own. But who will believe that? Itzamna won't.

2.

In my early innocence the goal of my existence was to become the rain god of the giant turtles. I admired their stoic calm, the stolid way in which they plowed through time, the godlike way they endured for centuries. Imagine a rain-dance gathering of turtles: the stately, modest dignity. But the turtles needed rain far less than man. They drew back in their shells and kept their counsel. They supped and drank without a nod to Chac. They took my rain as if it was their due. Only the sea they worshipped, and never left her sight.

I soon succumbed to the frenzied pleadings of men: I agreed to be the rain god of the Mayas. You learn to compromise, or you go insane.

At once, however, I acquired an enemy.

The jungle that circumscribed their village was a hungry hairy beast. With his voracious appetite he could suck into his fetid innards the grandest stone conceits of the mortals. Even the mammoth tributes to us gods.

Though the mortals had hacked a large, flat clearing in which to live, the jungle constantly sought to reclaim it as his own. His dark roots gathered strength from rivers beneath the ground. Not a month went by when, shrieking with animal rage, he did not throw out new limbs, vines, greedy tentacles: a devious attempt to take back the clearing. Not a month went by but that the mortals, swinging heavy stone axes, beat back his approach. Like the dark, primitive side of their own mortal natures, the jungle kept trying to overwhelm: to claim for his own their round observatory with its clever spiral staircase, their timeless pyramids, their proud painted temples. No matter how bitterly they fought him, the jungle kept creeping back.

They worshipped me in their temples, they carved on their buildings elegant masks of my elaborate nose, masks the jealous jungle coveted. The mortals were my wards, I did not want to see the jungle bury them, but this created a conundrum within me, a conflict that is rare in godly sensibilities. Whenever I unleashed the rain that the mortals depended upon, the jungle used it to fuel his rapacious greed, to grow his lianas longer, to reach out and try to strangle the villagers. Try as I might, I could think of no solution. This may have been a precursor, an early indicator, of the central conflict of my devastating tale.

A pitiful characteristic of the mortals was that they worried about the future, something that does not concern us gods. Out of such concern they created an almost infinite calendar. In some abstruse way they calculated — don't ask me to explain, my specialties are limited to rain, fog, mist, dew, an occasional hurricane — the following: that the Great Cycle in which they were living had begun, to use your terms, the 11th day of August, 3114 BCE; that the Great Cycle would last 1,872,000 days; that therefore the cycle would end on the 21st day of December in the year 2012. This information they built into the walls and steps of their great pyramids, which lined up according to the angles of the sun. When I asked Itzamna how the mortals in their observatories had figured this out, he said it had to do with the wobbling of the earth. In other words, even the sky god did not know — but he said they were exactly correct.

—What does that mean? I asked him.

On that winter solstice, Itzamna said, another Great Cycle will begin.

—Meaning what?

—Meaning nothing.

Zeus, bored, has been listening in, wiping his drool on his arm.

—We could always party! he says.

To continue with my tale, I must indulge in a few words about mortal society: about the layers of class and influence that affect their destinies. To lay a proper foundation, as any good builder must. It was not much different than other mortal realms.

The supreme leader of the village was the Lord Maya. He went by the title of *halach uinic:* the one true man, the one real man. I suppose that was accurate enough: one real man per village (a far greater proportion than you have today.) He was also considered a demigod, for no reason I could fathom.

His position was hereditary. When the Lord Maya died he was succeeded by his son. (The system cut down on arguments.) The Lord Maya had one wife and many concubines. He dressed extravagantly in embroidered breechclouts and feathered headdresses that were often as tall as he. His head was flattened with a board from birth, his ears and nose pierced and hung with jewels, his teeth filed to points inlaid with jade, his body and face covered with tattoos. He was the fashion-setter. His foreskin was shredded until it looked like ribbons. (I wince, like you, at the thought.) He was sacred, treated with great respect.

A notch below the Lord Maya in respect was a symphony of priests, who dressed in white robes and through meditation in dark temples forbidden to laymen claimed to ascertain the will of the gods. (In fact, I never spoke to a priest in my life; I don't know any god who did.) By virtue of being holy, the priests did not have to fight beside the warriors or to work all day in the fields. It was an admirable scam.

My favorite of all the priests was the chilan, the soothsayer. Every village had one. The chilan of Tika's village had a long nose and stringy gray hair and looked a lot like me. (It was pure coincidence.) He had been banished from the temples years ago for some kind of moral turpitude, and he used to stand at the side of the dirt road leading in and out of the village, haranguing the people to mend their ways. I never knew what he was driving at. Neither did the people.

He liked to warn that the end of the world was at hand. I think it was only a guess.

Next in line of respect was the nacom. In time of war he was responsible for the defense of the village against other tribes, against foreign invaders. He personally led the villagers into battle, and he was very good. If he was killed, the other men, being only citizen-soldiers, tended to turn and flee. What you might call today an exit strategy. In time of peaceful tribulation, when human sacrifices were offered to the gods, the nacom cut open the breasts, tore out the throbbing hearts.

—Nice work if you can get it.

(This from my idiot half-brother Chac-Mool.)

The nacom in Tika's village also had a sideline. He trafficked in counterfeit cacao beans. After corn, which kept them alive, cacao was the most precious possession of the villagers. From it they made the chocolate drink they loved. (I've tasted it, it's a little sweet.) Cacao was so precious that it was also used for money. The beans could be swapped for all manner of goods in the marketplace. A good slave cost a hundred beans, a night with a whore cost eight.

The cacao grew on the far side of the jungle; the nacom was the importer. After trading for beans from distant merchants, he would have his slaves remove the thick cacao skins from some of the beans and fill them with sand. Then he would mix them in with the good beans. In the marketplace the smart stall-keepers pressed each bean with their fingers to make sure it was solid, not sand. The use of counterfeit beans led to many arguments that had to be settled by the courts, and many a trader was put to death — by having a large rock dropped on his head — for using counterfeit beans.

None dared blame the nacom. During ceremonies he was often carried about on a litter with great pomp, to the cheers of the crowds. He went about his fraudulent business beyond the reach of criticism; he was considered vital to the defense of the village.

On closer observation, I noticed that actually there were two nacoms. Sometimes I confused the two. The war chief, who was in charge of defense and led the villagers into battle, was one nacom. He was elected for three years, and during that time was treated with deference. The other nacom was a priest, whose position was hereditary. It was this nacom who slashed open people's chests, tore out their beating hearts. Though he was considered necessary, the people didn't like him much. Why the soldier and the priest were both given the same title, nacom, I do not know. Unless it was because they killed equally well. The Maya brain was subtle at times.

A vision of the next Great Cycle, in the mind of the chilan as he squats in his rags on the outskirts of the village.

All nations have put down their arms. Turned their swords into plowshares. Food is distributed to all. Disease has vanished from the earth. Love blooms as commonly, as sweetly, as flowers. Carpets of blossoms, upon which lovers play in nature's nakedness, cover the earth.

I have heard him shout this to sniggering crowds from atop a towering stela near the main road exiting the village. The people whisper that he's insane.

When they are gone, he rolls himself in the dirt, and drools. Not unlike Zeus, in fact.

Between the priests and the lower men were the nobles, who apportioned the taxes and the captured slaves, oversaw the marketplace, directed the artists at their work. They lived in fine houses not far from the central plaza. They didn't work in the fields. Like the Lord Maya himself they wore large hats — not quite as gauche — ablaze with plumes and feathers of every size and color. The larger the hat, the more important the noble.

The great working mass of the rest were lower men. They supported with their labor the nobles and the priests. They fought the wars with spears in their hands, they built the massive temples with their sweat, they tilled the fields of corn on which the entire village lived. They acknowledged more than the others their total dependence on Chac.

It is the lower men — the vast majority of the Mayans — whom your snobbish diggers ignore in their learned texts. And their women as well. Think about it. It is ever thus.

I remind you, perhaps, of those mottled old men who sit on park benches, listening to the wiry white hairs growing in their ears, eager to impose on any stranger the tale of whom they were in the half-remembered days when they were young. I shall endeavor not to be as tiresome as they. I will not omit the sex, the violence. Being boring is the only vice that ill becomes a god.

One day the sweating boys were playing pok-a-tok, racing north and south across the ball field, swatting at the rubber ball with straw guards on their arms. The girls were watching, cheering, from the grassy knoll above, seated demurely with their arms across their knees, holding down the hems of their kubs so as not to distract the boys below. After only two hours — it was one of the smaller, easier courts of the seven in the village — the girls leaped to their feet with hurrahs. The ball had gone through the high stone hoop on the wall. The game was over.

As usual, it was Kel who had scored. He was the best player in the village.

The boys straggled off the field, breathing heavily. The girls hurried down beside them. Together they walked in a group, chattering their adolescent chatter, until as if on signal they broke into a run, beyond the walls, across the open fields, toward the jungle. They split into pairs, almost randomly, it seemed, and disappeared into the thickets, beneath the fronds of palm. I'd given them a taste of sweet spring rain the night before, the jungle was thick with steam and orchid smells in the afternoon sun, the jungle earth was still a soft mud: but they didn't seem to mind. Kubs and breechclouts flew onto low branches, hanging like banners in the filtered light. Beneath, beside, behind these flags the naked couples, without talk, almost without breath, fell at once to greedy grappling, to rhythmic copulation. All except Kel and Tika. They had run with the others toward the jungle, but as they neared his edge they slowed to a gentle stroll. They lagged behind as the others disappeared into the trees, into the scraggly bush. Now they were walking hand in hand along the brush that rimmed the field before it erupted into jungle vines. Both seemed awash in thought. From amongst the steaming trees came passionate cries. Handsome Kel, lovely Tika, paused, searched for each other's eyes, walked their quiet walk across the fading afternoon.

That was the first time since she'd grown into adolescence that I really looked at her. She had black hair that she didn't bind but allowed to flow off her shoulders wildly, in a torrent. Her eyes, brown or black, depending on the light, glowed with intensity, burned with pride. Her nose was long enough for a mortal, her unsharpened teeth flashed in her light copper face, her down-turned lips wore the luscious pout of lust delayed, and the innocent pout of secrets. Beneath her kub her ample breasts were trembling invitations. Her limbs were short as most Maya limbs, but she evinced the illusion of shrinking in size, or stretching tall, depending on her mood.

On all her body there was not a single tattoo. When her stepmother, or her friends, chided her about this, she dismissed them with precocious certainty.

—The gods made me this way, she said. I imagine that I'm pretty enough for them.

Such a darling she was. And only twelve.

—Besides, I'd heard her add once, Kel likes me this way.

Him I didn't like from the start.

The next day, as if by chance, I glimpsed Tika at her bath. She pulled her green kub gracefully over her head and stood naked in the sunlight behind her father's house. From a gourd of water — water born as my rain — she filled a smaller bowl and poured it over herself. Droplets skittered down her breasts like explorers, followed her body's natural creases, hung like gleaming beetles from her nether hairs. With soap berry root she rubbed on her skin a lather, and with her fingers caressed her every part, with the unselfconsciousness of the unobserved. She inhaled with satisfaction the fragrance of her nipples, knelt and lifted the bowl and poured the water over her head, splashed it on her shoulders, her belly's fragile arc. The water, shaping into fingers of its own, washed away the suds. She dried her skin with a cloth before she dressed.

I have an acquaintance who used to be the rain god of the Teutons. In his former land, he says, the mortals in need of rain used to pour water over a naked girl. This was their signal to him. Their supplication. How delightful that would have been. How direct, and sweet. How difficult to refuse! But the complex Mayas never thought of such a simple entreaty. Nor did I.

The naked-girl gimmick didn't save the Teutons. But they didn't perish, my friend assures me, from lack of rain.

When we were not occupied making rain, I was greatly amused by my frogs. They perched on my shoulders or my knees, or played endless games of leapfrog around my feet. They went by the names of Cib, Ahau, Ben and Enik. Enik was the smallest. He had a lame leg that made him land on his shoulder with a tiny thud every time he leaped. His favorite perch was midway down my sloping nose.

When I began to notice Tika, I was afraid the frogs might be jealous. Frogs and ladies often don't get along. But the frogs were as taken with Tika as was I.

—I'd like to perch on her perches, Ahau said.

—Don't talk smut, I chastised, and the frogs, as always, obeyed. They spoke of her often after that, always with respect (though a certain lascivious gleam never left Ahau's eyes.)

Sometimes, when she had completed her chores for her stepmother, when the boys were busy playing ball and the girls were acting silly, Tika would walk to the north side of the plaza, where the great new pyramid was being built, and she would watch the artists at work, carving into the stone facades the portraits of the gods: of yours truly of course, of Itzamna, Ixchel, Ixtab, of the young god of corn, Yum Kaxx, of the skeletal god of death, Ahpuch. Of many others whose aid they might need some day. All of the artists were men, and as Tika watched them chipping the blocks with their hard stone chisels — sometimes chewing on her thumbnail as she watched — it was easy to see what she was thinking: she would like to be an artist, like them. She pestered the artists with questions about why they had done this or that. At first they were annoyed by this interruption of their work, but she was so open in her admiration, in her desire to know and learn, that they soon came to welcome it. Only one kind of question annoyed them: when she would ask how they knew that such-and-such god looked like that.

—How do you know that Yum Kaxx is so young? How do you know that Chac has a long nose?

To such questions they would always answer: Because everyone knows. Because it has been taught that way.

She would make a doubting face at the answer, and the artists would turn back to their work, scowling and upset, because she had inflamed a nerve. The truth was, they didn't know; they could not be sure; no mortal could. This doubt plagued them night and day: that perhaps they were wrong: that perhaps their work was false and meritless. Because of this most of the artists drank a lot of balche.

As it happens, they were correct more often than not. Yum Kaxx was very young. Of my own nose you already know.

Steeped in creation, the artists viewed themselves as minor gods. But one vital distinction between us they never understood. The artists took their creations seriously.

One god of whom I do not like to speak is my idiot half-brother, Chac-Mool. He is fat-cheeked, pot-bellied and practically brainless. It is difficult to say what god he is: he has been given no responsibilities. He does naught all day but sleep and eat. Perhaps he is the god of happiness.

Chac-Mool is kept alive by his ravens. They feast on carrion from the jungle, and drop large quantities into his bowl. Whatever they deposit he scoops into his mouth and swallows: blood, bones, fur, flesh, feathers. Then he grins his stupid grin.

One day, seeking cruel amusement, Chac-Mool ordered his ravens to attack my frogs. He did this when I was away at a meeting of the Circle. (Chac-Mool was the only god who did not have to attend.) His ravens, with their powerful beaks and grasping claws, descended on my frogs without warning. Green frog blood was spilled, frog throats croaked in pain during the initial assault. Then Ahau, leaping free, managed to reach his gourd and splash it over the ravens, who cannot bear to have their feathers wet; they dropped their intended victims to shake out their soggy wings. This enabled the other three frogs to reach their gourds: to empty them during a second attack. Alerted by the flapping, the frantic croaking, the raven screams, the splashing to the earth of unspecified rain, I hurried back from the Circle. When I had dispersed the ravens with simple swipes of my arms, and the frogs were washing their wounds, I found, in a pool of water murky with green blood and black feathers, the punctured, almost lifeless body of little Enik. My favorite frog. From the corner of the mist Chac-Mool, grinning his stupid grin, reached out and tried to grab Enik. I stomped with all my strength on his fingers. I kicked him in the nose.

It is a terrible thing to hate your retarded half-brother: he doesn't know any better. I hate him nonetheless.

Enik lay motionless, his frog blood draining from his wounds. I didn't know what to do: it was a problem I had never encountered. I cradled his body in my hands.

—What should I do? I asked Ixtab, who had come up behind me and was looking on, pale and thin. Ixtab merely shrugged; the goddess of suicide is very smart, but she's not much good in a crisis.

—Itzamna will know! I said, and hurried back to the almost empty Circle, my hands cupped together, Enik comatose in my palms. Itzamna was alone, lounging in his grand chair.

—My frog is dying, I lamented. He was attacked by Chac-Mool's ravens.

Itzamna peered at the helper in my hands and nodded in sympathy.

—You've got to save him, I said.

—Me? I'm the god of the sky. What do you expect me to do?

—I don't know. I thought you would know something.

—It seems to me you need the god of healing.

—Of course! The god of healing! I should have thought of that myself. I hesitated. Who is the god of healing?

Itzamna leaned back in his kingly chair and thought about it. He scratched his head and stroked his chin. He is a master of elemental gestures.

—I don't think there is one, he said.

—What! How can there not be a god of healing? What kind of Circle are we running?

—What are you shouting at me for? Itzamna said. You've got the mortals to blame.

I was glad the humans would never know of this scene. Except for Chac-Mool, we didn't usually act that stupid. But the problem of a dying helper was unique.

The one way mortals excel gods is in dealing with death. It comes from practice.

With Enik losing more of his green every minute, turning a putrid olive, I hurried to find Ixchel in her lair. She picked up Enik and looked at him kindly. But she didn't know what to do any more than I.

—He was always the runt of our litter, she said.

—Don't say was! I shrieked. I'm not going to let him die. You have to help him. When the mortals are sick they offer you burnt dog droppings.

—But it doesn't help them.

She had a point.

—Maybe Ahpuch will know, she said.

—The god of death? That crazy ringer of bells?

—He knows more than he lets on.

I had heard that before. I hurried off, not sure if Enik was alive or dead in my palms. I found Ahpuch where he dwells, in a crevice behind the moon. With skinless bony hands he was shaking his bells. The same old tune.

—I've got to save my frog, I said. You've got to tell me how.

The creepy fellow, all teeth and bones, was unconcerned.

—Gods don't die, he said. He continued to make his eerie, shivering noise.

—He's dying, I said. Look at him. Are helpers really gods, technically?

Like a mad musician Ahpuch kept riffling his bells, even when he spoke.

—It's an interesting point. The question hasn't arisen before.

—Well, answer it now, I said. Is it your decision, or what?

—Just take him back to the mist and let him be, Ahpuch said. We'll have to watch what happens. A test case.

—A test case! You act like he's a mortal or something. He's my frog!

Ahpuch shrugged. He lost himself in a wild riff. It's no wonder the mortals fear death. At times he's quite insane.

There was nothing more I would learn from him. Hopeless and helpless, I carried Enik home.

The next day he began to stir in his sleep. In a week he was eating flies. In two weeks he was green as ever, and perching on my nose. He's a gritty little frog, that Enik.

A conversation comes back to me — this was years before — when Tika's father Hunac was teaching her the gods.

—The most important is Chac, he said (a dear man he was, and a true farmer, too) because Chac brings us the rain that grows the corn.

—I like corn, Tika said. I like Chac, too.

—There are four Chacs, her father said. (Not that again, I thought.) A red Chac, a blue Chac, a yellow Chac, a black Chac. One for each direction.

—Which one brings the rain?

Her father, hesitating only for an instant, said,

— They all do. The four Chacs are really only one. All four are really the same.

Tika frowned the way only a child can.

—Well, I like the one with the funny long nose, she said.

It was their standard teaching: this inexplicable confusion of me with my frogs (all of whom are green, in any case.) Whenever the mortals discussed us gods, rational men began to trip over their own contradictions, their own uncertainties. It was passing strange, their confusion, since we dwelled so large in their minds.

Tika liked to climb with her friends in the rock quarries by moonlight when the slaves and the workmen had gone. With sure legs, agile arms, bobbing breasts, they leaped from rock to rock, daring each other with longer jumps. One night Tika, slightly off her mark, twisted an ankle as she landed, and crashed hard to the rough surface between two towering blocks of limestone already hewn and ready for the hauling. She lay face down over a smaller rock, motionless, all breath gone. For a moment I felt a strange uncertainty; I discerned a murmur in the ticking of the stars. Until her friends turned her over, her eyes began to blink, the breath returned to her chest. From a cut on her chin, bright blood was dripping, staining the breast of her kub. But for the rest she seemed unhurt. She sat between the rocks for a moment, a silhouette between the moon-washed stones. Then she said she was fine. She soon rejoined the others at their game.

A short time later, as Tika and her friends followed the S-curved road back to the village, rain began to fall. A brief and gentle shower it was. Tenderly I washed the blood from her chin.

My feelings upon Enik's recovery were a new sensation. I had brushed against the sense of loss, a sense unheard of — a sense barely comprehended in the Circle. It softened my emotions, it made me more sensitive to the youthful charms of Tika, who, being mortal, could die at any time.

The thought frightened me. Somehow Tika's life was beginning to assume importance, though it shouldn't have counted a fig to a god. Importance is not a trait that clings to mortals, except in their own imaginings.

3.

The jungle was not a member of the Circle. Of him the mortals didn't make a god. In his entrails roosted the meat and fowl they devoured, the balche they drank and the honey they ate, the fronds that sheltered their huts from sun and rain, the hemp for their ropes, the wood for their spears, the fiber for their kubs and mats. Surely he'd have been worthy. But they seemed to make gods only of that which they could not control, and the jungle they believed they had mastered. So the priests enumerated the gods, the artists made representations in stone and paint, attempting to make real and visible the faces they couldn't see, while the jungle glowered around them, green and yellow with envy, screeching and screaming in the night, chafing, relentless, picking at the scabs of his unsightly machete wounds. Biding his time.

In the afternoons, when the day's harvesting was done, Tika liked to stroll in the jungle shade, her hair bound with a fiber so as not to snare on groping branches. I watched her one day as she smiled in merry communion with the spider monkeys cavorting in the trees, as she sidestepped with barely a glance a sleeping snake. I pondered her innocent beauty as she gazed at a dark bush on which were lit with folded wings a dozen black-tipped golden butterflies. She seemed entranced by their purity, even as I was by hers. Until suddenly her hands darted forth and she trapped in the cage of her fingers a single butterfly, while the rest took flight in a golden rush. Enthralled, I watched her peek at the fluttering wings between the loose net of her fingers. I saw her close her eyes, as if the better to feel the powdery caress of the frantic, struggling wings against her palms. When, after a time, she opened her eyes, I waited for her to release her delicate prisoner, to watch it spin away. Instead, with sudden savagery, she popped the lacey creature into her mouth. She filled her mouth with air, she seemed to be savoring the flutter of the wings on the moist interior of her cheeks. Her chest was heaving, as if her heart was beating in rhythm with the frantic wings.

Curious, intrigued, I waited for her to release it: to part her lips and let the butterfly issue alive from her mouth in a rather strange and no doubt symbolic rite, a sacrament unknown to me. But just as I was certain she could imprison such fragile beauty no longer — that she could be so cruel no longer — she crunched her teeth: she chewed, and chewed again. Then, not content with expectorating butterfly elixir, she swallowed all: let it trickle like morning chocolate down her throat. I was amazed, staggered. In my three thousand years I had never once seen a mortal devour a butterfly: not man nor woman nor child.

Day after day I watched her do it. I do not know how she acquired the habit. Soon it became clear that no one knew of it, not her parents or her sisters and brothers, not even Kel. It was a secret of her being, the dark lust of innocent lips. At first I was horrified. Soon I was merely tantalized. She was never a glutton about it. She never ate more than one.

Time has washed the Maya temples, even as it washes history. They gleam now in pure white limestone against the stark green of the trees. Thus do they appear in the excavations of the diggers. But such was not the case in Tika's day. The brightest reds, yellows, blues were the mortals' daily feast. Their village was a peacock's tail, a child's garden of colored building blocks. Which color was where, which temple red, which yellow, which blue, I don't recall; the dyes have long since faded to nothingness. Only my image of Tika remains in full color: wild hair black, pale eyes green, bright teeth white as the caps of waves, skin a pale copper dust, clothed mostly in purple kubs: a sinuous orchid among the brooding blocks. That was my perception of her, whatever she was doing at the time: whether planting corn seed in the fields with a sharp stick, or helping to harvest the grain that was taller than she, or weaving mats in the failing light of her father's hut, or walking in the evening with her betrothed, or watching a masked drama danced on the Platform of the Skulls, eager face flickering in the fires, or struggling to mold clay pots as beautiful as her mother's, in the end always smashing them in frustration at their lack of perfection. This was my image of her until a certain moonlit night cast upon her the dye of a shroud.

Tika and Kel were walking alone in the fields. They teased and laughed, as young lovers do, till they came to the building known as the Nunnery — it housed the younger priests — looming dark and silent in the night. If you've never seen the Nunnery, you should, it is the masterpiece of Maya art. It is sculpted row after row on its facade, tier after tier, with charming, identical masks of the god of rain. Of Chac. They are rather good likenesses of me. The execution of the artists almost equaled their taste.

In the moonless shadows of the Nunnery wall Kel and Tika kissed, as if to mock the sleeping celibate priests. They encircled one another with their arms and kissed again. A raven glided high above, lost in the black sky. Kel's tongue found Tika's open mouth, they gasped with commingled breath, as humans do. He pressed against her, hungrily. Tika, losing her balance, reached out, grabbed hold of a promontory for support.

It was my nose. My nose curled eighteen inches from the wall. None of my noses was broken off then.

Their bodies warmed, one touch stoking the next, frantic tongues now darting like lizards in each other's mouths, now twisting like eager snakes. Kel pressed his body forward. Tika leaned back in supple, yearning, teasing encouragement. And all the while her left hand clung to my nose, squeezing it in her passion, pressing moist palm sweat onto stone. Kel's hand foraged for her breasts beneath the stiff cloth of her kub. He pressed the hanging cloth of his breechclout between her legs.

All the while her left hand held, squeezed, stroked my solid nose. Their mutual passion was threefold as I watched, as I, too, breathed ungodly breaths. Kel reached between her knees, tried to raise her kub. Tika, hot moist face pressed into his neck, shook her head no, held her kub in place. The boy somehow obeyed her resistance, respected her innocence — I think he'd have been upset if she gave in — pressed his loins against her cloth, spent his seed that way.

My brain was in turmoil as I watched them straighten their clothes, watched them stroll away from my masks, walk past the Temple of the Magician, back through the fields in the night. It had been mere chance, I warned myself, she was merely grasping for support to the nearest promontory. Yet why had they chosen the wall of the Nunnery? Hadn't Tika ever so subtly guided him in that direction? Was she really as off balance as she seemed? Could she have been a temptress, inventing an excuse for reaching out? Could she, secretly admired each day while passing my masks, have come to fancy a wise old god over a handsome but callow youth?

Such is the delirium, the self-deception, of a brain on the brink of love. Mortal or divine, that part's the same.

From that day forth I had a sacred new purpose: to ennoble young Tika with my eyes: to delight in her every motion, her every gesture, her every word. I had the notion that for twelve years she had been growing to womanhood, like a precious flower, right here under my noses, just for me. How she could be just for me I didn't understand. Union between god and mortal was not only forbidden, it was quite impossible. Everyone knows that. Still, I listed sunrise with the day's first sight of her. I ransomed her with my eyes.

I was aware of the truth, of course. I cannot cauterize my brain as humans can. I knew that in time — a very short time — her flesh would sag, her fluids would leak, her bones would rot and stink, the luscious package called Tika would be mud. It is the prime equation of mortals: life plus time equals death. And yet the Mayas, despite this doom implanted firmly in their beings, had devised a mathematics, a calendar, an astronomy, that could calculate across a span of ninety million years. Faced with such touching and stoic generosity, I followed their lead. I cast aside all doubts, all grim realities, all knowledge of the misery that must follow love as the day follows night.

—In short, you played the fool, Itzamna says.

He still gets pissed with me, after all these years.
I do not apologize. I loved, therefore I am.

And Tika?
She drank the cool droplets I poured for her, she bathed in my gentlest vapors, she anointed her inmost parts with my offerings.

I knew the truth, of course. It was all so much rain to her.

For more than a year after she teased my nose not a day went by when I did not gaze at her. I admired, as I might the pattern on a bowl, the curve of her purple kub as she helped her father pluck the corn from the fields; the stubbornly sultry way her hair, brushed haphazardly with an orange lobster claw, had of masking her eye; the equally sultry way she had of tossing her head to fling it back in place. I watched her swim naked in the bay, on her back, her lean limbs gliding through the green creating barely a ripple, the sun gleaming off her upturned body as if he, too, knew she was a gift for the gods. Often, while grappling out of habit with Ixtab, I was thinking of Tika; afterward I'd be ashamed. But it was not only her body upon which I dwelled. I was enchanted with a sparkle in her eye that was at once both coy and determined; with the perhaps carefully calculated innocence with which she questioned and provoked the artists. (How do you know that Chac has a long nose?) With her outward grace that seemed a gilded mask, barely concealing an inner mischief, perhaps even a destructive cast, of which in her adolescence she was not fully aware. She was not a farmer, she hardly cared that the rain god existed. Yet I came to feel she needed me — or at least would need my help one day. That is a more powerful attraction than you might think.

The mortal need for rain was commonplace, it no longer gratified me. But in Tika I sensed — or onto her I projected — a need more personal. Perhaps that was the key: with a goddess you rarely feel needed. Out of my own boredom, my own longing, I wove a mystical link between us. Simply by being there, for me to watch on her daily rounds, eating, sleeping, working, walking alone in the jungle (I began to watch her very carefully there) she made me feel young again.

Itzamna says I was obsessed. It's all the same.

4.

From Tika's village, stone roads built on causeways ran north and south along the coast, and west around the edge of the jungle to the mountainous highlands beyond. The roads connected the village with other large Maya towns. Along these roads the merchants traveled from village to village, bringing cacao beans and sacred quetzal feathers, trading them for stingray claws and tortoise shells from the coastal villages, or handmade kubs and breechclouts of dyed cotton. The traders brought with them, as well, news and gossip from the other villages, and it was about this time that tales first were heard, in the marketplace of Tika's village, about small bands of foreign invaders that had begun to attack Maya villages hundreds of miles to the south. According to these tales the invaders did not tattoo their faces, but wore beards instead. They called themselves Spaniards, and came from far across the sea in large boats fitted with weapons of war so powerful they could knock down walls. Maybe temples.

Here I must offer an aside. The investigations of your diggers into the disappearance of the brilliant Mayas has led to a major error. Not only do they not know the happenstance, they have gravely misdated the time. It was many bakuns later than they reckon. The cataclysm did not occur until after the arrival of these Spaniards with their curious beasts and their maddening priests and their cloth-powered boats. This I know for certain. I was there.

—He was there, Itzamna agrees.

And adds a sigh both ill-tempered and fake, in the form of a weak gray tornado over a desert. Unobserved, therefore unnecessary.

With each passing season, the tales of these bearded, costumed invaders grew more difficult to believe. Some said they had brought with them in their enormous boats animals larger than anyone had ever seen — huge creatures called horse-beasts, that could do the hauling work of three women. It was said that a man could sit on the back of one of these beasts and be carried across the village without the use of his legs. Other tales said that these Spaniards did not worship the gods — or rather, that they worshipped only one god, a god of peace and love, and that they killed with fire-shooting sticks, or worse, anyone who did not agree to worship this loving god. The Lord Maya and the high priest heard of these tales and held frequent councils with the nacom. They were considered with a certain bemusement, like the stories of a child, because they contained so many contradictions. One faction wanted to begin immediately the construction of a defensive wall around the entire village. But it was pointed out that this would be useless if the invaders really had weapons that could knock down walls. Since the nearest sightings of the invaders were hundreds of miles to the south, the Lord Maya decided to take no action until more information was known. The nacom assured the priests that he would lay in a full supply of spears, enough to defend the village against all enemies.

By comparing notes with other abandoned gods, I've discovered that most wars among mortals have been waged by peoples who favored only that one god, and wanted to force him on others. With few exceptions, tribes that believed in many gods, like the Mayas, were content to live and let others live. What this proves I have no idea. It's only scholarship.

The oldest joke in the world — quite literally — is that being a god leaves little room for advancement. A more serious source of godly depression — our primal suffering as eternal beings — is the shortage of emotional reward. The other gods, with roughly equal, if different, powers of their own, pay very little attention as we go about our tasks. The obsequies of the mortals below may satisfy for half a day, but little more. This leads from time to time to the need to assert one's godly powers, to have some real effect, to watch what happens, for instance, if you withhold your rain. A habitat where it rained each afternoon would pay scant attention to Chac: he might atrophy from neglect. So every so often you withhold your grace, you make them suffer, for no greater reason than to remind them that you're around. (Yahweh, the god of the Jews, is the master at this.) So it had been with me a few centuries before, long before Tika, in the aftermath of my life with good-natured Ixchel. We parted amicably and are now good friends, but when, soon after, she took up with mighty Itzamna, I was forlorn. Wallowing in the sloth of self-pity, I realized that what I needed was a prolonged dry spell. I would use my sovereign powers, I would make the mortals suffer and beg. I would interact. This period of therapeutic self-help is known to the Maya priests and Lords as The Dreadful Three-Year Drought.

Creating it was simple enough. I impounded the gourds, I sent my frogs on holiday; there would be no more rain for a while. This caused little comment in the Circle; nobody cared. But the Mayas down below were sore annoyed. They looked at the sky and pleaded and cajoled, and danced and stamped their feet. It seems I had chosen to begin the drought at the start of their planting season.

As the year progressed, the corn in the Maya fields, bereft of water, couldn't live. The grasses withered, the earth became parched. This led the Mayas down the spiritual road from annoyance to hunger to fear. They took to throwing slaves, then captured Mexicans, then some of their own pretty maidens, down into their sacred well, in the mistaken belief that this would make it rain. Why they believed such a thing clouds the mind. Gifts to Chac, they called these human sacrifices. But what they thought I would do with a bleached and shriveled human, any more than with a festering coati, I have no idea. I didn't touch them, of course, I left them there at the bottom of the well, to turn in time to bony skeletons. My lovely drought continued.

With each passing season the Mayas grew more unhappy. The grain in their storerooms, despite being rationed, soon vanished. When tossing people to the bottom of the well proved ineffective in summoning rain, they began to spread-eagle fellow mortals on a curved stone, rip open their chests with a sharp rock, tear out their hearts by the roots and place them, still pulsing and dripping blood, in the stone bowl of my idiot half-brother Chac-Mool. Being all teeth and no brain, Chac-Mool devoured the hearts. Why they thought he could make it rain is another Maya mystery. He is only a heavenly accident, a god of nil, the patron saint of imbeciles; he does absolutely nothing; a miserable atheist might call him a placebo. Perhaps they thought Chac-Mool had brotherly influence. (Fat chance!) Whatever the reason, this butchery was so bloody, so pointless, I could hardly watch.

—Why do they do that? I once asked Ixtab, the goddess of suicide, when we for the first time were sprawled together on my rumpled bed of cloud. Ixtab has dark tresses and pointy incisors and a seductive smile. Her breasts are small, unlike Ixchel's, but there is about her a forthright lustiness.

—What do you expect them to do? she replied. You've destroyed their grain, you've driven away their game, you've left them starving and weak. (She said this not in judgment, merely as observable fact.) They see death beckoning, and they're afraid. They're thinking: why is Chac doing this? What did we do wrong? What does he want from us, blood? So they've given blood. They do that all the time in smaller ways, by fraying their fingers, by piercing their penises. When that doesn't work, they give more blood, by hacking open chests and wrenching out hearts. Religion, they call it. Granted, it doesn't work, but nobody ever said mortals were smart.

—But it's murder.

—Of course it's murder. So what are you, a weak-kneed lily? They're trying to save their village.

—I suppose.

—Who started their trouble, anyway? Ixtab said. Who created the drought?

I didn't answer. I had never asked to be a god.

(Of the giant turtles, maybe.)

We gabbed into the night about everything under the stars. It was the first time we had really talked. I knew I could never love her — she was a bit too sharp for my taste, a bit too tart — but by morning her pointy incisors were nibbling my nose.

Down below, the mortals were parading their suffering like flags of surrender. They left their parched cities and moved into the jungles, to feed on the bark of trees. The old people were left behind to die of thirst in the huts and temples and ball courts, and on the sides of the roads. Hundreds, nay, thousands, lined up for Ixtab's blessing: to gain the honor of the sacred death of suicide. But Ixtab rejected them.

—Suicide in the face of starvation, she ruled, is not an honor. It is merely an evasion.

Her tongue was licking my ear. We made love without pause for seven months. (Being a god has certain perks.) All during our torrid antics, the suffering, dying Mayas in the jungle were sending emissaries back to the village, to try yet another sacrifice: in the sacred well, or on the bloody stone. With no effect, of course.

Eventually I felt much better. Whether this was because of my drought, which renewed my faith in my powers, or whether it was because of my affair with Ixtab, who looks you in the eye every moment, I cannot say. Perhaps it was both. In any case, one autumn afternoon I decided to make it rain. Ixtab had her time of the month, I had nothing better to do. I called in the frogs, and we let 'er rip.

That very morning the surviving Mayas had tossed one of their comeliest maidens into the well. Her name was Ixki Chel. While the lower men and women went into a frenzy of dancing and drinking and cavorting in the rain (some day I have to try that) the high priest made a note of her name and of her clan in the sacred book of Maya. She became a part of Maya legend, her name passed down from priest to priest, from High Lord to High Lord, her blood descendants listed in the secret codices, generation after generation.

In truth, of course, this Ixki Chel they killed had nothing to do with making it rain. She was just in the right place at the right time.

The diggers have noticed that above my broken-off noses I have a tearstained countenance. This, they say, was probably symbolic of rain.

The diggers are much too concerned with symbols. They don't know anything.

Tika came of age on a bright day capped by a royal blue sky, which the priest said augured well. The plaza in front of the main temple was swept clean, and was layered with fronds of palm. Four venerable old men sat at the corners of a square, holding a rope to form an enclosure. Inside the rope stood the three boys and three girls who were to come of age that day. The priest — it was one of the lower ones, I think — sprinkled the six children with water from the holy well. He then made a speech to them, about their duties to their parents, their duties to the village. The usual stuff. All this time my eyes were fast on Tika. Her fresh-scrubbed skin seemed to glow with the moist excitement of becoming, at last, a woman. As I watched — all the mothers and fathers were watching with pride from outside the squared rope — I actually felt a certain solemnity. I had the sense that bawdy Fate and haughty Time were watching, too.

When the priest had done with his tendentious advice and his tedious prayers, the mothers of the three boys stepped inside the rope and removed from their children's heads the small white beads that had been affixed in their hair since birth as a symbol of purity. Then the mothers of the girls ducked into the square — in Tika's case, her stepmother. They knelt before their daughters, reached under the white kubs of the girls, removed from a string that hung at their navels the bright red shells that had dangled there from infancy, and which no man had dared to touch — the fragile seashell tokens of their honor. I watched Tika closely as her stepmother removed the shell. A smile split Tika's face, a smile both shy and not, a glimpse of white teeth between her lips. I thought I saw Fate wink. (She's not so blind as mortals think.) When the six mothers held the beads and shells in the air, the onlookers filled the square with cheers. The children leaped the ropes, ran to hug their families, their friends. Tika hugged her father, her half-brothers, her half- sisters. Then she turned to Kel and took his hand.

All that afternoon I trembled. Now she could do it. Now, with her father's blessing, she could marry. Now she could give herself to her betrothed, wedding or not.

I followed her every move that day. I sweated at her every word. In the evening, after dinner, they went for their walk.

—We will marry when I am a noble, Kel said.

—But. . . She turned to face him.

—Trust me, Kel said. It has all been set in motion. By the end of the autumn harvest it shall be done.

—But how?

—Trust me, Kel said again.

(Personally, I didn't think I would.)

They arrived beneath the stars at the Nunnery. Kel tried to guide her to the ground, but she refused.

—I want to wait until we're married, Tika whispered.

—But Tika!

—It's what I want, she said.

Kel began to sulk like a sick frog. Tika tickled his ear to bring him around. She kissed him hard on the lips, right there under my nose. She led him by the hand along the wall, and kissed him again and again. She kissed him, as if by design, under every one of my noses.

What was I to make of that?

What would you have made of that?

Returning early from the Circle one day soon after, I found my frogs at play, at a game I had never seen. Ben and Cib were side by side, about six inches apart. Little Enik was in the center, a little below them. Ahau was also in the center, somewhat below Enik. They seemed embarrassed, taken aback, when I arrived.

—What's going on? I asked.

None of them wanted to answer. Finally Enik piped up.

—We're playing a game, he said.

—What kind of game? Go ahead and play.

They looked from one to the other, uncertain.

—Go ahead, I insisted. What do I care about your games?

Again they looked from one to the other. Finally they started to play. Ben and Cib, side by side, puffed themselves up large and round. Enik made himself small in the middle. Ahau opened his mouth in a wide slit, began to throb his neck like a tremulous muscle. I waited for something to happen, but there was nothing more. I couldn't make head nor tail of it.

They all seemed disappointed at my puzzlement. I prepared to turn away.

—It's a game we made up, cute little Enik piped.

—Oh?

—It's called . . . He looked to the others for support. It's called Tika.

Still puzzled, I looked at them again, at Ben and Cib large and round, at Enik, at Ahau's open mouth, his throbbing neck.

—You rascals! I blurted.

With a fierce expression I swiped at them with my hands. Making sure to narrowly miss. They hopped away, out of reach, chirping merrily.

I scowled at them darkly, and shook a crooked finger.

They knew it was a pose.

Soon after they came of age, the mortal boys and girls began to get tattooed. Their arms were tattooed all around, their bodies above the waist, except for the breasts of the girls. Pictures were cut into their skin with knives, and were smeared with colored paints, which the skin soon absorbed. It looked quite painful to me. I knew I would wince for her when Tika's turn came. But it never did. Tika refused to have it done.

—Kel likes me this way, she told the others.

It was a lie. Kel the unimaginative, Kel the sturdy athlete, Kel the traditionalist, wanted her tattooed like all the rest. But somehow she'd divined my taste: it was Chac who liked her that way.

In my idleness, I project. I am a butterfly, black-tipped, gold-winged, asleep on a jungle bush, fragile wings folded, at rest. Suddenly, mortal fingers snatch me up. The fingers form a cage in which I'm trapped. The supple, pliant fingers of Tika. Frantic and afraid I flap my wings. They beat against her palms, which smell of female sweat and soapberry root. My wings beat faster, losing their vital dust to her skin. I begin to inhale the end of my own life. The cage of fingers swings upward, she is about to set me free. Instead I'm hurled to the back of her own mouth. (Is this relief I feel, at not being allowed to fly away?) Her jaws close on darkness, my beating wings are sticking, clinging, to the insides of her cheeks. The more I struggle the quicker I lose my strength. Losing my life in a mortal woman's mouth.

Her jaws begin to part. There is a crack of light, a last slim chance to escape. Then her teeth crunch down, an avalanche of falling rocks. The first crunch severs my body from my wings. The second cuts my torso in two. The third makes goo of my head. Saliva flushes me down her throat. Dark wet passages of Tika. Stomach acids eat the lacework from my wings. Swirling acids of nil.

What have I become?

A semiotic fantasy:
I am the blood and the body of Tika.
My frog Ben is smirking.
—You mean a semi-erotic fantasy, he says.
Tie your tongue! I well know what I mean!
Semiotic.
I am the blood and the body of Tika
I am the beauty and the breasts of Tika.
I am the sacred triangle of Tika.
Amen.
A semiotic lust. Only words.

I know. I know. I am also the shit of Tika.

Do you known why mortals shit? To remind themselves each day that they are mortal. It covers, even excuses, the stench of failure.
We gods don't have to shit.
Sometimes we fail nonetheless.

Work on the great new pyramid was continuing. Some of the hauling and mounting of the large stones was done by slaves, under the direction of the artists. Much of it was done by the lower men when they were not occupied with planting or harvesting. The stones were hauled from the quarries to the pyramid site on logs that were dragged across the countryside with hemp ropes. The brilliant Mayas, as I've mentioned, had neglected to invent the wheel.

Perhaps because of my interest in Tika, I became curious for the first time about the whys and wherefores of mortal concerns. Why, for instance, did they spend so many years, so much labor, constructing these buildings, pyramids, observatories? They seemed to have all they required to meet their needs: ample and tasty foods from the jungle and from the sea, easy shelter in their stone huts and thatched roofs, all the sex they desired, both within their marriages and without, ample supplies of water most of the time. Despite all this, they went about forever unfulfilled. Out of this frustration, this ceaseless search for something more that they never would attain, seemed to grow their clever 20-unit mathematical system, their accurate astronomy, their impressive architecture, their alphabet of glyphs.

What was missing, I suppose — what they were always searching for — was the sense of completeness that is inherent only in gods. If so, it was a dubious quest. Being complete, we gods tend to be a rather dull group. Your average god is not very original, not even very creative once the initial inspiration has passed. Perhaps, I began to think, by our very completeness we gods were also lacking something: the constant, fearful thrust into the unknown that spices mortal life. As gods we cannot truly take risks, because we have nothing to lose.

One night as I gazed at Tika, calm in the repose of sleep, her kub drawn up to her shoulders, veiled starlight filtering through the door, I saw her features contort, her lips draw tight, as if she wanted to cry out in the dark. Sounds, tormented grunts, issued from deep within her, as if from a stuttering mute. Suddenly she sat upright, her dark green eyes yellow with fright. Her father, her stepmother, her brothers and sisters, asleep in the same large room, accustomed to these sounds, stirred, shifted position, rolled over on their mats, resumed almost at once their even breathing. Tika alone remained awake, sitting in the dark, her kub fallen to her waist, breathing rapidly. I wanted to offer comfort, but didn't know how.

I don't understand mortal dreams. The phenomenon has never been explained to me in any way that I can comprehend. How can creatures of their own imagining wake and frighten them so?

I've heard them discuss their dreams. They dream of priests who fly through the air like birds; of trees turning into stones; of deer that rise from the sea with men on their backs and trample children beneath. They dream of flowers whose tangled roots topple temples; of snakes that swallow skulls; of pots giving birth to rainbows; of dwarfs riding turtleback. They dream they are drowning, they dream they are falling, they dream they are flying backward through the entrails of Time. They dream they talk with death, or copulate with Fate. They dream of poisoned wells, and saviors.

I don't know what it's for. We gods don't dream.

Unless the mortals themselves are a dream.

Whenever she could, Tika made time to watch the artists at work. She worshipped the dexterity with which they carved solid limestone into the delicacy of lace. Only once did I see her concern herself with the skies, walk to the other side of the village, where the round observatory reflected the brilliant sun, and ask one of the nobles why he spent his nights peering through a hole in the roof.

—The stars tell us many things, the friendly noble said. They tell us how to count time, and the seasons. They tell us when to plant, and when to reap. They tell us the times of the year, and the years of the people.

Tika listened without comprehending. So, too, did I. With a feeling of escape she recrossed the village, to watch the artists carving gods.

I did not believe this noble. I've tried many times to talk to the stars. They do not speak.

Sometimes I think they are dumb, or have nothing to say. Other times they seem not alive at all.

Perhaps the stars are assistants, like my frogs. Perhaps they serve Time or Fate the way my frogs serve Chac. But that won't explain their silence. My frogs never shut up, and are very smart.

The noble must have been lying, as nobles often do.

She did not want to marry Ahkel!

She loved him, perhaps, but like a brother. Growing up so close, that was only natural.

She moaned and huffed and puffed, as was the custom, and with real enjoyment. She had a young woman's juices, after all. But see how she stopped him where she could! She didn't want him in a husbandly way!

She would go through with the marriage. She would not dishonor her father. She would not end a betrothal of fourteen years. She would not make of Kel a laughingstock. But only out of duty, not out of desire, would she marry! She longed, in a young woman's way, for something more, though none of this did she understand herself.

Thus did I interpret her actions at the Nunnery.

It was plain as the noses on my faces.

Beautiful butterfly-eater!

5.

The mortals took their ball games seriously. Boys learned the rudiments of pok-a-tok almost as soon as they could walk. On feast days they were given as presents small rubber balls, and miniature arm baskets, with which to practice. As they grew older they played scrimmage games almost every afternoon on the smaller courts of the village, me and my frogs permitting. Talent scouts among the lesser priests watched these scrimmages with interest. Every Sunday there were games in the central court between the finest teams in the village. These games were the subject of discussion the entire week before. Men argued the merits of the respective teams, and wagered cacao beans on the outcome. During the games themselves, all productive toil stopped, and the entire village, including the Lord Maya, came to watch.

—Such preoccupation with children's games is the sign of a decadent society, the long-nosed chilan warned from the outskirts of the village. But nobody paid attention.

Once every five years, the games took on a special religious nature. These were games against other villages, some as far as fifty miles away. The games were arranged far in advance. Tournaments were held to determine the best team in each village, who would then compete. These games were played in the plaza court, by far the largest of the seven. The Lord Maya would watch from his throne at one end of the ball field, the High Priest from his throne at the other end, both wearing their most outlandish hats. The vertical hoop on this field was so small and so high — 35 feet from the ground — that scoring was extremely difficult. Sometimes these games went on for days, even for weeks, without a winning score.

These inter village games were dedicated to us gods. They were preceded by music, by dances, by offerings. To emphasize their sacred nature, special rules were in effect. At the conclusion of each game, the captain of the winning team was decreed a nobleman, right there on the field, in front of the cheering village. The captain of each losing team lost his head to the sword.

—An overemphasis on athletics, the chilan scolded. Nobody wanted to hear.

It was this risky path that Kel, supremely confident, envisioned as his road to nobility.

The priests did not fail to note his athletic prowess. On a spring afternoon, when the work in the fields was done, one of them took him aside and gave him advance word: the following autumn, at the conclusion of the harvest — the time when wars were usually fought — a great festival would be held for Itzamna. The focus of the festival would be the largest pok-a-tok tournament ever held. Every village in Mayadom was expected to send a team, to compete right there in the plaza court. All summer long, the priest told Kel, games would be held among the villagers. The team that won the most matches during the summer would represent the village at the sacred Games of Itzamna.

Preening and confident, Kel thanked the priest for this advance knowledge. The next day he went to the highlands by himself, his bow slung over his shoulder, and killed a deer. He sliced open its chest with a flint knife and left the carcass there, as an offering to one of us. I forget who, I forget who they thought was in charge of games back then; it wasn't me. When he returned, he spoke one at a time to the best young athletes in the village. He was a persuasive young man. He convinced all he chose to band together, to form a team that could stoutly defend the honor of the village. Every afternoon when the work in the fields was done they practiced together. Soon there was an official announcement of the Games from by the Lord Maya himself. Many teams were formed. But Kel already had gathered the best boys. When the practice games began, no team could match his. Week after week, Kel's team won easy victories. By summer's end they hadn't lost a single game. The choice of the priests was unanimous. Kel's team would represent the village in the sacred Games.

Tika, who liked to swim for hours, with long, graceful strokes, back and forth across the crystalline bay, and who liked to run in the jungle or on the highlands, otherwise did not care much for sports. She watched Kel play each Sunday and cheered him on because it made him happy, because it was so important to him. But she was oblivious to the implications of each successive victory, and Kel never mentioned where it was leading. He didn't want to worry her.

When the autumn harvest arrived, and the Games were only a few weeks away, they became the talk of the village. Preparations were visible everywhere. Scores of thatched dormitories were being constructed to house the visiting teams. Huge stores of food were being prepared. Tall and handsome Kel, the captain of the team, who was almost seventeen then, was a celebrity throughout the village, followed by small boys wherever he went. Men clapped his back and told him of the wagers they planned to lay on his team. He decided at last that he could keep the truth from Tika no longer, lest she hear it from someone else. It was an unspoken truth, the fate of the loser: to mention it was considered bad luck. But he was afraid she might overhear it nonetheless. He felt she had to be prepared.

—You know, he said, as they sat one evening in the middle of a field, when the sacred Games are done, I will be a noble, as I have always promised. Then we can be wed. I think we should marry seven days after the games.

Tika smiled into his eyes, an open, honest smile.

—You know I don't care if you're a noble, she said. I never have.

—I know. It's me who cared. And soon it will be so.

Tika squeezed his hand, squeezed his knee.

—How can you be so sure? she said, a bit of tease in her voice.

—It has already been written, Kel said, by the Lord Maya himself. I am the captain of the team. When we win the Games for the village, I shall be made a nobleman, on the spot. Then we will be married.

—And if you don't win the Games? Can't we marry anyway?

Kel's eyes hid his pain as he searched her face. She truly didn't understand.

—I'll win the games, he said. You'll see.

Tika kissed his cheek.

—I know you'll win the games, she said. But if you don't, can't we marry quickly anyway?

Kel looked at the ground where they were seated. He scuffed at the dirt with his sandal. Patiently she waited for his reply. At last he faced her. He smoothed a strand of her hair into place

—If I don't win the games, he said, speaking slowly, you'll be free to marry someone else.

Surprisingly, the boy had a delicate way with words.

Tika's head recoiled as if she'd been bitten in the face by a snake. She couldn't believe what he'd said. For more than fourteen years they'd been betrothed.

—Free? she said. I'll be free?

She wanted to punch his shoulder, she wanted to scream at him. But her fist lost its force before it touched him, her mouth opened wide without a sound. She'd been very young the last time sacred Games were held in the village; she had not remembered. Only slowly was the vision coming back: an understanding that drained her will.

Her hands fell useless to her lap. As she looked at the ground in the fading light her head seemed to loll on her neck, like a puppet's on the Platform of the Skulls. Neither of them was able to speak. Finally she took a deep breath, filled her chest with the humid night air, as if imbibing spirits. She tried to summon strength, but still her words were weak.

—You would do that? she asked. You would risk . . . everything? Just to be a noble?

Her face was still toward the ground, her chin balanced almost on her chest. Kel touched her cheek, gently. When still she did not look at him he dropped his hand.

—I was chosen by the priests, he said. It's for the honor of the village. It's for the honor of the gods.

Tika's eyes lifted. They began to roam slowly over his face. His fingers on her cheek had ignited her like a flame, had filled her anew with strength, had turned her will to a simmering rage.

—I hate the priests, she said.

She rose to her knees, shaky in her anger.

—I hate the village.

She was speaking louder now, her voice rising with every word.

—And I hate you, too.

—But Tika, he said, starting to rise. The gods . . .

She stood, almost falling on buckling legs.

—Damn the gods! she screamed. She turned and took two steps away, beginning to run. She stumbled, stopped, screamed the words again, over her shoulder, her voice piercing the night:

—Damn the goddamn gods!

Stunned by her blasphemy, Kel made no move to follow as she ran, stumbling at first, then surer of foot, across the brambly field, away through the night, toward the jungle, looking for something unknown to swallow her up.

—Blast the bastard gods!

I imagine that she loved him after all.

For three days she refused to speak to him. She avoided him in the fields and in the village. When he came to call at her father's house, turned her back. Alone with her stepmother, desperate to confide her feelings, she lamented her situation. She felt as if she'd been betrayed.

—The men make the rules, her stepmother said. The gods made the world for men.

Which was nonsense, of course; it was a lot more complicated than that. Besides which, it was Kel who'd be risking his life.

Disappointed as usual, fingering the small shards in her kub, Tika sought out her father. She spoke with hesitation, but found him understanding.

—Do you love Kel? he asked.

—I think so.

—Well, think of him, then, instead of yourself. He's the best player in the village. He's the captain of the team, chosen by the priests themselves. What would you have him say? That he cannot play in the Games, because his nervous future bride fears for his life? Suppose he said that, and some other boy took his place; suppose the village lost the Games, and the other boy lost his life. What would Kel's position be then? Do you think he could continue to live in the village? He'd be the object of scorn and derision wherever he went. There would be no place for him in all of Mayadom. Nor for you, either.

She took in her father's words. They entered her being like pointed pins into her nipples.

His voice was gentle as he added: Women, too, must be brave.

Tika knelt beside him on his mat. She touched her lips to his cheek. Then, without a word she stood and walked out of the house, walked off alone toward the jungle.

For all of her life she'd felt her betrothal to Kel was a blessing. Now, for the first time, she felt that loving him was a curse.

Such is often the case with athletes' wives.

The mortals often spoke of the soul. They pondered where it went after they died. They entrusted it to the gods. Personally, I have seen more bloody throbbing hearts than I care to, but I have never seen a soul. If souls, in fact, exist, I have no idea where they go, or what they do there. I don't know why the mortals thought the gods would be concerned with surplus human equipment. As if we had a junkyard up here. Such souls, if they do exist, must be the province of Time. Or Fate.

In an underground cave deep within the jungle was a turquoise-studded human skull with eyes of jade. The skull rested on a carved pedestal, carved by unknown forces: carved perhaps by the hands of the underground river. Around this skull in the jungle cave swirled hundreds and hundreds of golden butterflies. In great circles and small, in ovals, in S-shaped curves, in all manner of patterns the butterflies fluttered in a nonstop jamboree, never pausing to rest their tired wings. In the pale light within the cave the butterflies displayed almost no color at all. But I know they glowed bright gold by the light of a simple fire. It may be that these butterflies — or the turquoise-studded skull — or the skull and the butterflies together — were the jungle's soul.

On the other hand, they may have been only his heart.

None of the mortals knew of this cave, I think, except perhaps the chilan. The chilan was like Ahpuch, the god of death. Very often he knew more than he said.

In the late afternoon, to escape from Kel, Tika prowled the jungle by herself. Normally she was amused by the antics of the monkeys in the trees, but now she scarcely noticed them. She tried to accept without reservation her father's wisdom, because she knew it was correct.

She had to set aside her fears; she had to show her faith in her betrothed; she had to erase all thoughts of his possible death. There would be time enough to face that if it happened.

She ate a butterfly to give her resolve.

On the third afternoon of such solitary walks, she realized what she must do. She found a way to demonstrate to Kel — to all the village — her faith that he would triumph, that he would live, that they would marry. She hurried from the jungle to tell him her plan.

At the jungle's edge she heard a wild flapping just above her head. She stopped short as a sacred quetzal bird, hundreds of miles from its normal home in the highlands, fell in a motionless heap at her feet, its green and gold feathers bent and broken.

Her hand sought her mouth. She bit the back of her fist. It was a portent, she felt: a portent of death.

I saw the fear on her face. I wanted to speak with her, to offer comfort. There are no such things as portents, I wanted to tell her. Whatever happens, happens. Nothing portends in advance. Omens are the cheap invention of dramatists.

I wanted to tell her but there was no way she could hear. To the mortals Chac has no tongue.

Tika knelt beside the bird to see if it was dead, to see if it had been struck by an arrow, or a stone: to kill a quetzal was a sacred offense, and could be punished by death. As soon as she touched it, the battered bird flapped its feathers, struggled to right itself. It hopped away for several steps through the grass. Then it took off in uncertain flight, wobbling through the air.

Tika closed her eyes, breathed deeply, trying to calm herself. When she looked again the bird was gone.

As she resumed walking she tried to convince herself it had never been there, that it was only an illusion, had only been her fears taking a shape. But she did not succeed. She hurried to find Kel and the comfort of his sturdy chest.

She found him in the plaza ball court, alone, practicing by himself in the dying light. Over and over he swatted the ball toward the high stone hoop. From where she stood the ball and the hoop were both invisible in the quick-falling dark. It was as if he were playing with phantoms. He would run to retrieve the ball, swat it high, run to retrieve it again. All she could see was his white breechclout moving in the night.

She was overcome with admiration, and jealousy. She loved his dedication to perfection — how he stayed here long after the others had gone to eat, to drink, to carouse. Only among the artists had she seen such dedication to their craft. She was jealous that, unlike them, unlike him, she had no skill to which to give her life.

Silently she trod down the long stone stairs, walked across the field toward where Kel was. Only the sound of the ball as it hit the wall proved that there was indeed a ball, that he had not gone insane and lapsed into a twilight pantomime. She waited, watching him, until an errant ball bounced in her direction, until Kel, come to retrieve it, noticed her in the dark, and stopped. He looked at her as at an apparition.

—Have you been standing there long?

—I didn't want to disturb your practice.

She gazed at him in silence, as in a drama on the Platform of the Skulls. She went to him and leaned her head on his chest.

—I'm sorry, she said.

His arms encircled her, one with the sporting basket still attached.

—I was wrong, she said. I want you to play in the Games. You have to play, for the honor of the village.

He tilted her small face upward toward his. I could see a remnant of pain in her eyes.

—I know you'll win, she said.

He kissed her on the lips. Tight and hard they kissed in the dark of the court, his practicing forgotten.

—And we will do what you want, she said. We'll marry seven days after the games.

Kel smiled and stroked her hair, removed from it a petal from a jealous jungle vine.

—And to show my faith, she said into his shoulder, you'll take me to Cozumel Island the week before the Games. To the shrine of Ixchel. So I'll be prepared for marriage.

A moment's darkness furrowed Kel's forehead. She did not notice it in the night. She might not have noticed it at noon. He stroked the thick strands of her tangled hair.

—We can go after the Games, he said. The week before the wedding. That will satisfy the gods.

She pulled away and held his strong hands within her softer ones.

—But that won't show my faith in your victory, she said. I want to go before the Games.

—I know your faith, he replied. You were only upset. You don't have to prove your faith.

—I do, she said. If not to you then to the village.

—Who cares what the village thinks?

—I do.

A confused smile crossed her lips. She had the curious notion that their words were somehow being reversed by the acoustics of the court. It was Kel, not her, who always cared what the village thought. I could see in her eyes the truth of it: she had to prove her faith to herself.

—That's not a good time for us to go, Kel said.

—Sure it is. A voyage on the bay, some fishing while the women pray. It will give you a chance to relax, take your mind off the Games. It's just the thing you need.

—I'm not sure the priests will allow it.

Screw the priests, she thought, but did not say it.
She snuggled into his chest. He could feel her heartbeat
in her perfect breast. How could any man resist. (How
could any god?) She murmured, Do the priests have to
know?

His nose was pressed to her hair, imbibing the smell
of soapberry root. His eyes were on the blank wall of
the court. Above them a bank of clouds had covered the
village. The lovers were invisible.

His voice was vague and distant as he spoke.

—Perhaps they don't, he said.

Which I suspect surprised her as much as it did me.

6.

The corn was harvested with sprightly vigor that year.
The entire village seemed to shimmer with pleasure over
the forthcoming Games. Men laid wagers of balche or
beans on the outcome. Headdresses were sewn with new
feathers. Hunters roamed the highlands and brought
back vast quantities of deer, tapirs, turkeys, pheasant.
Soon the athletes began to arrive from the other villages,
accompanied always by priests, in some cases by the
halach uinics themselves. Welcomed with great honor,
the athletes were put up in the new dormitories, the
priests and Lord Mayas in the sacred temples.

The days before the Games were a lively spectacle
of color, music, dance and feasting. Vast tables of food
were laid for the athletes. They were entertained at night
in the central plaza with dramas in praise of us gods.

The convening Lord Mayas used the occasion to
discuss the problem of the Spanish invaders, who
reportedly had attacked a village further to the north
than ever before. Terrible stories had traveled from

village to village about how the Spaniards had brought with them bloodhound dogs that attacked the Maya warriors and ate out their warm entrails. If mere dogs could be so horrid, the people worried, imagine what the horsebeasts could do. Reports told of the multiple raping of women, accompanied by Spanish laughter. But no decisions were taken by the Lords. The problem still lay far down the coast. The Games were a time for celebration, for play.

At the outskirts of the village, the outcast chilan continued to wail against the Games as a distraction from the true business of life. But he was largely ignored by the throngs who passed on the road: visiting merchants intent on a quick profit in the festive atmosphere, athletes seeking whores in the gaming establishments, villagers caught up in the excitement, too restless to stay at home. The one exception, who sought out the chilan in private, was Tika. She had lain awake for several nights, wrestling with the thought, after the notion had come to her: the chilan perhaps could foretell the outcome of the matches.

But did she really want to know?

She decided in the night that it would be a bad idea to visit the chilan. But by day she could not stop herself. Late one afternoon, when he had removed himself from his roadside stone to a shaded patch of grass, to rest, she approached him, and pressed a cacao bean to his wrinkled palm.

—Who will win the Games? she asked.

The chilan looked down his long nose at her, his watery eyes barely visible in his wrinkled face.

—Do you plan to lay a wager?

—No, Tika said, I will not bet. I promise. I only need to know if Ahkel's team will win.

The chilan put the bean in the pocket of his earth-stained, once-white robe, and studied her face as if it were a rare, dark blossom, and he a botanist. Beyond them on the road, noisy, drinking crowds were passing.

—Ahkel's team will not lose the games, he assured her.

Relieved for only an instant, Tika with her quick intelligence became suspicious of his phrasing. She pondered his use of the negative. But the chilan was not done.

—Nor will Ahkel's team win the Games.

It was a riddle. She looked at him in puzzlement.

—That is no answer, she said.

The chilan reached into his robe, offered her back the bean. She didn't take it. She turned and walked away, more frustrated than before.

—Let the old fool have his bean, she muttered as she joined the passing throng. He was a fraud, as most people said. She had hoped it wasn't so.

At the same hour, Kel was at the opposite end of the village, being ushered by a priestly assistant into the presence of the high priest, in his private quarters behind the sacred temple, a dark room lit by torches that scattered leaping ghosts across the walls.

—I would like permission, Kel said to the priest when they were alone, to go tomorrow to Cozumel Island with my team.

The priest frowned; the creases in his face resembling in the firelight deep black arrow scars.

—That would be foolhardy, he said, in a crackling voice. Even dangerous. The Games are but three days away.

—With your permission, Kel replied confidently, the danger lies here. Look around the village. The visiting athletes are feasting, drinking, indulging themselves with women. I have warned my players to stay at home, to save their celebrations till after we win the Games. But carousing with the others is a sore temptation.

At Cozumel they will have rest and quiet, far from the noisy, drinking crowds. We will return in two days more fit to win than the teams that are debauching.

The priest lay down a feather with which he'd been writing in a worn and well-thumbed codex.

—Your request is highly unusual, he said.

—My betrothed, Ixtika Chel Chek, wants to visit the shrine this holy month. So do other women. We shall escort them there, and bring back a catch of fish. There is nothing unusual in that. It will hardly be noted.

—The seas are calm?

—The seas are calm, the skies are clear in every vista.

The priest stood and gathered his clean white robe and came around from behind his hewn table and paced the small, flickering room. He looked less imposing than usual without his monstrous hat to hide his naked scalp.

—You think it will help you to win?

—I'm sure of it, Kel lied.

The priest nodded and pursed his long lips. He fingered a secret Codex that lay closed on the table. Kel pondered for a moment what it would be like to know how to read. As a noble he would have the leisure to learn.

—You are the captain, the priest said at last.

The priests had a way of making every decision sound momentous. I think that was the secret to their holiness.

—Thus far your play has been flawless, Ah Kel, as has been your choice of players.

He scratched his jutting chin, as if not wanting to continue. But he did.

—I shall bow to your judgment in this.

I must admit I was surprised. I didn't think he'd let him go.

—Thank you, Kel said quietly.

He was anxious to be dismissed before the priest changed his mind. The priest returned to his seat at the table, a simple wooden chair without the snakes and carved quetzal birds of the Lord Maya's chair. He seemed to forget the boy was waiting. But he had not. In time he looked up.

—You have my private blessing for the voyage, the priest said. But not my public approval. Do you understand my meaning?

Already this was becoming its own art form. Deniability.

—Yes, Kel said. As captain, the responsibility is mine alone.

—Then go with the gods, the priest said, and waved his fingers, but not his hand.

When Kel had left, the priest took up his quill. Of the hundreds of sacred books the Mayas stored in the libraries of their Nunneries, in which they told the history of the world, with more or less accuracy, only three still exist. One of them is the diary of this priest.

Here is what he wrote that day, in a neat hand of tiny glyphs:

The captain of the sacred team is having woman trouble. I have granted him permission to visit Cozumel before the Games. He will not win the Games unless his mind is at rest. A calm sea is no threat beside a stormy woman.

It was the first time I was ever impressed with him.

Having unburdened himself, he felt relieved. He knew that no one would see the diary until he was dead.

And what of Kel, leaving the priest's quarters, threading his way among the boisterous villagers in search of Tika, to tell her they would leave for Cozumel in the morning? What was his attitude toward the fast-approaching Games? He thought he would win, of course. He was accustomed to winning, he almost always won. And if he lost? Was he prepared to meet his death with quiet pride under the terrible sword of the nacom? He was. He was a soldier on the eve of battle, prepared to do what must be done: prepared to give his life for his village.

No man can have a better end. It is an outlook much to be admired. I'm sure that I would share it if I were mortal. But he didn't think he would die, not really. He thought he would win the Games. He thought the gods would see to it that he did.

There was a problem with this thinking, however. The captains of the other teams were also were placing their faith in the gods. And we were the same gods.

This much was certain: all but one of the captains would soon be sore annoyed.

They gathered on the beach at dawn the following day: Kel and his six teammates, Tika and five other women — two were maidens like herself, three were young wives who had never made the trip before — and ten slaves that Kel had borrowed to do the rowing. The sea was polished smooth as they climbed into the large canoe. The oars of the rowers dipping into the licking waves made no more sound than a man dipping a ladle into a pot. The gray sky unrolled yellow, then white, then blue as Itzamna's sun engulfed the horizon. It climbed over the sea and warmed them. For the most part they sat in silence, except for the rhythmic grunts of the rowers. The women were shy and kept their eyes cast down, as befits those on a sacred pilgrimage. The young athletes were equally shy and on their best behavior in the presence of these women who were soon to visit their female god. It was as if the vast sea, the vast outdoors itself, had been transformed into a temple, as happens at the best of times.

The misty outline of Cozumel was pale gray on the horizon. With the passing hours as the sun climbed higher and sweat dripped off the rowers the island sharpened from gray to green. In early afternoon they beached the canoe on the silent island sands. Hardly a word had been spoken during the long, smooth voyage.

If Kel still had reservations about the journey he did not let them show. He told Tika to lead the women to their shrine. The men would rest on the beach, he said, and then go out to sea for a catch of fish. They would return in the hour before dark.

Kel and Tika touched fingers; they were too embarrassed to kiss in front of the others. They said goodbye and Tika, apprehensive at her sudden position of leadership — it came from being Kel's betrothed — led the women from the beach to the narrow path through the woods, the path to the ancient shrine of Ixchel.

I do not know why women need a god of fertility. They are so fecund that one day their fetal droppings will choke the earth, will cover it like jungle parasites, four-limbed lianas everywhere entwined. But I'm glad the Mayas needed Ixchel. We had many good years together (not to mention my frogs.)

The female gods did not seem to require enormous temples that climbed toward the sky in adulation. Their strength was internal, and needed no display. The shrine of Ixchel was among the most sacred in Mayadom, but was only a small statue hidden in a grotto in a simple clearing in the woods. I never heard her complain.

Within the walls of the grotto Tika and the other women lighted fires, chanted secret chants to Ixchel, made offerings of pollen from corn. They sat for many hours. The details of their obsequies I did not observe. It was women's business.

When they were through, according to the cherished custom, Tika was fit to be wed.

The sun was still high in the sky when they finished their prayers. Instead of simply retracing their path through the woods they sought adventure, taking a denser route, pushing aside hanging branches that sought their faces, their eyes, and they emerged from the trees on the far side of the island. There, on a pristine beach with the ocean flat and blue to the horizon they removed their kubs and sandals and dove into the sea and swam. Afterward, with salt speckling their nakedness, sparkling in the sun like crystals, they emerged and sat on the white sand, a tableau for the ages, six lovely bronze maids, Tika the loveliest of all. Only the ages could see them. And me.

Soon they sang songs, played games, splashed in the surf, emerged, exquisite chests heaving, until Tika and two friends knelt on the sand, curious, at a place on the beach that was scuffed with lines of indentations, circular and deep.

—It's rounder than any sandal, one of them said.

—And larger than any man's.

Tika moved among the marks, following them from the trees to the water's edge. She knelt and examined them closer, smaller marks among the larger ones, measuring with her fingers, as she had seen the artists do.

—Some of these marks are men's, she said, pointing. Men who don't wear sandals, but square and heavy heels.

The other women, dripping delightfully, joined them to look.

—What kind of men do not wear sandals?

They looked at one another in a fearful silence, on the dread brink of understanding.

—And the big ones?

None of them wanted to say it. All had heard the tales. Only Tika dared speak.

—It can only be the horsebeasts. There is nothing in the jungle like this. Not in the jungle and not in the sea.

They all seemed to shiver at the word. In their nakedness they grew cold, their skin erupting in tiny bumps. They looked about in every direction. There was nothing to see but the seas, the sand, the trees and the distant blue.

Nearby they found a long deep trough at the water's edge.

—They came in a boat, Tika said. Men and horsebeasts both. Then they left again.

Fear shuddered their breasts, their loins. Some of the strange men, some of the strange beasts, might still be on the island, might be spying on them even now.

They sputtered different plans.

—We've got to warn the village!

—We've got to hide in the trees!

—Let's go to the beach and wait for the men!

So they ran. They ran to their kubs and sandals and put them on and scurried into the shelter of the woods. When they came to Ixchel's grotto they stopped as one, and hid inside. Their years dropped away as they trembled, until they were children again.

The fishing expedition of the men was alive with raucous talk. Much of it was directed at Kel and his impending marriage. The other players rarely had occasion to tease their serious captain.

—How many times have you popped her?

—Is she as small below as she is large above?

—He wouldn't know, they just hold hands.

All this Kel accepted without response, despite the grinning of the slaves. He was standing at the prow of the boat, his back to the men and the rowers, looking out to sea. A hint of roiled waters in the distance commanded his attention. But I was annoyed. How could he let them speak of her in such a slovenly way?

Soon he responded, speaking over his shoulder.

—You can all find out soon enough. You're all invited to partake of her on my wedding night.

What???

That was all I could think as a great cheer rose from all the men except the slaves, who grinned slyly behind their hands.

What???

I was near to apoplectic.

It was an ancient custom, to be sure. All change was evil to the mortals. Marriage was change, and therefore fraught with evil possibilities. In the old days, friends, neighbors, even fathers-in-law had been invited to sleep with the bride the first few nights, so the groom would not be alone in facing the danger. But the practice was barbaric, more Aztec, really, than Maya, and no longer was considered necessary. To think that stupid Kel would subject lovely Tika to that! To these drooling adolescents! Because of some superstitious fear! The scurvy dog! The coward! I couldn't think of enough epithets to hurl upon his head. Him standing there so proudly in the prow, staring over the rising seas at a large dot across the bay.

It never occurred to me that he was joking.

I followed his squinting gaze. I started. The looming dot on the sea was a large sloop of war. Giant sails were propelling it toward the coast at a rapid rate. A hundred pairs of oars churned the waters. Ten heavy guns protruded from the sides. It was the Spanish busybodies, who'd been poking along the coast for years. Their purpose now was clear: to conquer Tika's village, raping, enslaving, destroying, for no good purpose. All in the name of their sickly sweet god who liked to walk upon the earth like a man, turning cheeks. Whom they claimed could walk upon the water. Not even Chac can walk upon the water! Not even Itzamna!

—Heave to! Kel cried. Turn the boat around. Head back to the island. There's a sloop of war out there, much too strong for us.

Toward the island! Where the women would be discovered should the Spaniards choose to follow! It was more than I could bear. First the obscene invitation to his wedding night. Now these busybodies, who, given the chance, would deny my very being. I had nothing planned for the afternoon, but now my visage darkened with fearsome rage. Gray clouds hid the sun (I didn't want witnesses.) Waves ripped higher and higher under the sloop of the Spaniards, and under the tilting boat. My thickest rain began to pound the throbbing seas.

I was angry, and my frogs could see it. Wind whipped the sails of the sloop, tore the oars from the hands of the rowers. They pitched and yawed in the swelling seas, the sloop and the canoe. They began to take on water. Men shouted instructions in a panic. In the hold of the sloop fifty horses tugged at their ropes, neighed wildly, kicked at the inners of the sloop, kicking holes in the wood. Sweating men untied some of the horses so they wouldn't kick the ship apart, but they couldn't get close to many, who turned their backs and kicked at the wooden sidings with their powerful hind legs. A hundred slaves remained below decks, chained to their oars as the horses kicked the sloop apart and the heavy seas pounded in.

Wind and rain attacked all. The looping dugout pitched men overboard. Then it overturned. The sloop listed on its side, filling with water. Men were in the seas everywhere, and horses, men trying to swim toward the shore, men trying to cling to their crafts. The sloop sank beneath the waves, dragging with it the shackled, screaming slaves. The overturned dugout spun like a stick. My rain poured down on the swimmers, further swelling the seas. I tossed in streaks of lightning, just for the effect. By their flare I enjoyed the show.

Kel in particular I watched. In my rage our enmity had clarified. He was my rival for Tika's love.

She did not want to marry him, not really. She would be grateful to me.

Six times by flashes in the sky I saw the head of Kel sink beneath the foam. Six times it reappeared, spitting water. The rain fell harder still, the hungry seas roared. Kel disappeared a seventh time. This time he did not rise.

Even the best athletes drown, if you persist.

It was all very efficient. Soon only two heads bobbed alive in the water, both of them helpless Spaniards, drifting toward the shore. I paid them no mind. The rest — the men, the horses — were dead.

I was feeling good. Tika was safe, safe from the raping Spaniards, safe from Kel. Few impulsive storms of mine have been so inspired. Even Ixtab, watching, admired my rare display of anger. Surveying the calming sea afloat with drowned beasts and mortal corpses, Maya and Spaniard alike, I felt a godly pride. Only the horses I regretted. Them I kind of liked.

7.

The frightened women huddled in the grotto, silent, listening for the voices of men, wondering what a horsebeast sounded like. All they heard were their own hearts beating, their own chests breathing. When the sun began to redden, absorbing the day's blood (this the women did not know of, this the mortals rarely understood — where every day's spilt blood goes. When the sun began to sink like a giant sponge into the cardinal sea, they trekked in single file through the trees to the edge of the wood and the slope of the pink beach, to await, still hidden, the return of the canoe, of Kel and his fellow players. At the sight of my dark clouds far out over the bay Tika shuddered, then tried to shred her thoughts, still believing , in her youth, that this was possible. When night at last blanketed the beach the women became less fearful. There were no Spaniards on the island, they decided, or their fires would be visible, fires of the men or fires of the huge horsebeasts. Tucking their kubs beneath them, they sat on the cooling night sand, chanted chants in low voices, waited for the canoe. With the passing hours they made up consoling stories: the boat had been delayed by a storm, but it soon would arrive; the boat had been blocked by the storm and could not return to the island, but had put in to the safety of the coast; it would return to fetch them in the morning. Every possibility they conjectured aloud, except the one truth they feared in their hearts. This was a curious trait of the mortals: they believed unuttered truths would cease to be.

When more dark hours passed without the whisper of approaching oars, the women returned to the hiding ground of the trees, to sleep; surely a boat would come at dawn. All except Tika, who felt responsible: the expedition had been her idea. She sat on her heels on the beach, staring across the moon-splattered sea, her stoic face a stone, a mask, hardened by the salt of unborn tears. She looked quite beautiful, but I suppose she must always seem so, the widow for whom you have killed.

At break of day she crept to the cool of the trees where the others lay, and fell asleep. She shook and kicked her legs from time to time with rocking dreams. In late afternoon, a boat did appear on the horizon, coming to fetch them home. But it was not the craft of Kel. That sad canoe had washed up broken on the village coast, dragging in its stern only one, the shark-riven bones of a slave.

My pleasure at the carnage did not endure for long. In my rage, I realized, I had given little thought to Tika's feelings. She might well be upset when she learned I'd killed her betrothed.

Indeed, she seemed to be. She cried. She moaned. She fell to the ground in a faint. She recovered and screamed a wild scream, and wept again. Paroxysms shook her body. She scratched her arms bloody with her nails, and tore at her hair, and had to be restrained.

I told myself she was faking, for sympathy. But it soon became clear that she was not. She actually had liked the handsome prig.

I felt remorse for her grief — just a little. Then I salved my guilt the way all gods do. I told myself her loss would strengthen her character.

My saddened frogs didn't buy it. They crouched before me with wondering eyes.

—Why did you make us do it? Ahau asked.

For days there was tension between us. They moped about sullenly. They gave up all their games.

—All right, I shouted finally. I lost my head, okay? I should have stayed out of it. I should have let Kel be tortured and killed by the Spaniards. Let Tika be raped by a hundred men. Is that what you would have liked?

They hopped about, chagrinned. They knew I had a point.

(I suppose I could have drowned only the Spaniards. But in the face of my rage they did not think of that.)

—Tika will get over it, I said. And so will you. The sooner the better.

I did not say I was sorry. Gods rarely do.

The beach near the village was littered with corpses that swam out of the sea in indecent procession: athletes, Spaniards, horses, slaves. Ravens flew from the trees like famished leaves; six at least died of gluttony, their bulging bellies bursting on the beach. The athletes, those that could be deciphered, were borne away and buried beneath their homes, as was the custom. For the rest a large funeral pyre was lighted on the beach, to destroy the stench that was hanging over the village, threatening to spoil the Games. For two moons night hardly came, the fire on the beach burned so bright

Towards me the mortals had mixed reactions. They cursed the storm that took the lives of Kel and his team. But they blessed the storm that saved them from the guns, the spears, the horsebeasts of the Spaniards. The Spanish intentions they learned by questioning at the point of spears the two warriors who had reached the coast alive. Public outcry favored the immediate sacrifice of these soldiers to the gods, lest further calamity strike. The gods, they said, clearly were angry over something. But the Lord Maya ruled that the gods were gorged with blood just now. He made the two soldiers slaves of the village, and set them to work in the lines, hauling rock for the rising new pyramid.

The Games themselves, after priestly debate, were held on schedule. Too many athletes, too many priests, had traveled too many miles for them to be canceled over the loss of a few lives. A team was chosen to replace brave Kel's. The Lord Maya decided that should this team lose, the captain's life would not be forfeit; the team had little chance to prepare, and the gods (again) were gorged on blood.

If you looked at Chac-Mool, sick to his protruding belly, surrounded by retching ravens, you'd say the Lord was right. As for me, I cared nothing for their Games, I never have. Nor did Itzamna, to whom they were dedicated. The huge new pyramid rising slowly on the plaza, the grandest in the land: that was Itzamna's pride.

It's curious, the way the mortals stink when they die. Alive, they are no worse than any jungle beast. A fair maid like Tika, fresh scrubbed with soapberry suds, is even an aromatic delight. But once dead they become quite unbearable. I think their shit, wherein their mortality lies, backs up into their veins, replacing their blood. That would explain their stiffness as well as their stench.

But enough of mortal science. My concern here is loyalty, passion, lust, despair, the fall of civilizations.

—The usual crap, Itzamna says.

The week of the Games was a terrible time for Tika. She seemed to have aged many years in the few short days of her bereavement. She forced herself to attend the Games, out of respect for Kel and the others who were lost at sea. She sat in a special section provided by the Lord Maya for the families of the dead players. But her blood trembled in her veins despite the balche she drank to keep it still. Mourning with the other bereaved, accepting the sympathy of the village, she felt herself a fraud, a murderer, the cause of the deaths of seven young men. Kel had not wanted to go. Kel had sensed danger. If only she hadn't twisted him around, as she always could.

On the green field below, living players from every village swam before her eyes with the dead. The new local team won mighty plaudits when unexpectedly it won its first two games, before being defeated and dropping out. All this Tika registered without comprehending. What she felt were thousands of eyes crawling on her skin like bugs, as if the entire village knew. What she felt were the eyes of the high priest piercing her breast like knives, as if the high priest knew.

She forced herself to attend, day after day, her hair knotted behind her, chaste and sedate. Night after night she sat alone in her father's hut amid the drunken orgy of the Games. She felt as if her young life was over. No matter how long she lived there would be no way to redeem what she had done.

Soon the Games were complete. The distant travelers left. The life of the village returned to normal. Tika didn't know who won the Games. Nor did I. Week after week her mind seemed eaten away by her guilt. Though the marriage had never taken place she felt as unclean as a widow. She kept to herself for many months, as all widows do. But when the time came for her to rejoin village life, she refused. She refused to work in the corn fields with the others, fearing she would make the corn itself unclean. When she left her father's hut she would walk to the edge of the village and into the jungle, her young slave girl Ixtel trailing her like a coati. Birds would take flight, monkeys would screech and swing away through the trees, iguanas would slither from underfoot at her passing, as if the jungle creatures, too, resented her.

—It's not your fault, her little slave Ixtel said to her once, tears in her eyes, her thin arms around Tika's neck as Tika, uncaring now about cleanliness, sat in the soggy mulch of the jungle floor.

Tika wiped her eyes but shook her head.

—It is my fault, she said.

—You can't be unclean forever, Ixtel said, in her childish innocence.

—Perhaps if they had found his body, Tika said, musing more to herself than to the child. Perhaps then it would be all right. Then we could observe the rituals. We could wrap him in his manta. We could place corn in his mouth. We could give him jade beads, so he won't go hungry in the other life. We could bury him under his house, with food and drink, with his fishing lines and the ball he loved. Perhaps, after a time, it would be all right. But this way, with his body in the sea, being eaten by fish . . .

She didn't finish. Instead she choked, then screamed — a wild scream that set the jungle in motion all around as coatis, pumas, jaguars, wild turkeys all went crashing away through the leaves. Frightened by the scream, Ixtel broke into tears, turned, ran. Tika stood and ran after her through the jungle, slipping, sliding, and caught her near the edge, from where they could see the houses of the village. She took her in her arms and soothed her, caressed her, pressed face to cheek and smoothed her hair.

—I'm sorry, I'm sorry, Tika said. I didn't mean to frighten you. Will you stay with me, Tel, always? Will you stay with me no matter what?

The child nodded, clung to Tika's waist.

—If you let me, she said.

Tika kissed her fingers one by one.

Always, she said.

I don't know why she was carrying on so. What had occurred was clearly my doing, not hers.

But if that's all she wants, I thought: the body. . .

I scanned the sea in all directions. I poured fresh rain to clear the murky waters. I beat the leaves off the bushes along the coast, in case he had been washed up underneath and now lay hidden from view. It shouldn't be difficult to find a body.

But I couldn't find him. Not one stinking limb. A couple of rower slaves turned up, still lashed to planks of wood. But not Kel. The sharks must have hated him, too.

The misery of mortals is pointless. It dulls their will, it saps their energy. As emotions go, it's a failure. It achieves nothing, it should never have been devised.

But still they indulge, they seem to have a craving for it: the dark brooding chocolate of the spirit.

At least it is a private vice. Is Tika miserable? The market is still crowded with people buying and selling wares. Is Tika miserable? The chilan still harangues from the side of the road. Is Tika upset? The great new pyramid continues to rise on the plaza, the stones hauled into place by the slaves, the hammers of the artists ringing through the village day after day, month after month, like the slow eternal ticking of the stars.

Does Tika weep? Only those who truly love her care.

Sometimes, when she stirred herself out of her father's house, I would watch as she walked the road leading north from the village, till she came near to the chilan as he preached, or ate, or rested beside the road. She never approached him close. She looked at him from behind a tree, her face blank, a stela not yet carved. But it was easy to read her thoughts.

Ahkel's team will not lose the Games. Neither will it win the Games.

The chilan had seen the future. His riddle had come true.

She tried to understand how this could be. She was too awed to approach him, afraid of what else he knew. But mostly she was puzzled, and didn't know what to think.

I was puzzled, too. He was the best guesser I ever saw.

The mere effort of living seemed to tire her. In her father's house she would lie on her mat in the corner, try like the iguanas to sleep in the middle of the day.

—Enough of this nonsense, her father said to her after many months. Enough of this sulking around. It's time you thought of getting married.

—I am married, Tika said, staring dully at his eyes.

—Kel is dead, her father said. Besides, you never were married to him.

Tika, braiding her hair absently, lowered her gaze.

—I've spoken to the matchmaker, her father said. Something will soon be arranged.

Tika's eyes flashed for a moment. She glared at him. Her mouth opened as if she would speak. But she didn't. She whirled, all petulance, and faced the wall. Her face had turned as pale as mist.

My own face, I admit, was paler still.

Soon after, she left her father's house. At the edge of the village, not far from the encroaching jungle, stood a vacant hut, half hidden by tensile weeds. A family had lived there, but when three of them died within six months and were buried under the floor the family moved to another house. To this unwanted hut Tika moved, taking with her only a few possessions: her mat, her bowl, her weaving, some soapberry branches, and Ixtel. Her father let her go without a word. If he could no longer command her, if she no longer obeyed, then it was best she left his roof. Perhaps in time she would regain her filial senses, and return. Till then he had no daughter.

The move stirred Tika to further action. With the child's help she cut or pulled the weeds that had entangled the barren hut like snakes. She turned the earth at the rear and planted corn, squash, pumpkins. Farming was man's work mostly, but she had no man, and wanted none. At night she did her weaving, making mats, kubs, breechclouts, for herself and Tel and to sell in the marketplace. She dined alone with Tel, on posole and tortillas. She didn't know how to hunt animals in the jungle. She didn't care to learn. After dinner she sat or walked behind the hut, gazing at the moon and the stars, as if she would question them. But she never did. If people stopped by to visit, to inquire after her health, she ignored them. She sat in silence until they left. She made of herself an outcast. The offended villagers began to say she was mad.

Mortal company had become a threat to her, human chatter a bore. Yet she was so lonely she wanted to weep, and she often did. She began to question the reason for her existence. Her chest was a hollow cave of hunger, but she was hungry for she knew not what. She was a mass of yearning, unrequited, unrequitable. All around her life went on as usual, men, women, children working and laughing, not burdened by her questions, her doubts. Unafraid. She heard the gossip of the village. She agreed she was going insane.

8.

A few hundred paces from the edge of the village, at the opposite end from the sacred well, stood a whitewashed house of many rooms, where single men came each night to play. They played dice and cards and beans, drank balche or acrid chocolate, grew boisterous and disappeared into the back rooms where they could have their way with whores for a price of eight beans. The whores were mostly freed slaves, or wanderers from other villages. About this time there appeared at the brothel a new young whore. She wore a simple brown mask with T-shaped eyes in the image of Ixtab, the goddess of suicide. This had never been heard of before, a whore with a mask, but this one said she would never remove the mask in sight of man.

The earthen room is cool. Her kub lies in a heap in one corner. Cross-legged, naked, she sits on the mat, waiting. On her head is the mask, which she had fashioned from dried papyrus, earthen dyes and mud.

Beneath the mask her face is warm. Her mouth is dry. The T-shaped eyes do not admit much light.

The first night she sits that way, motionless, for hours. No one comes. Twice she urinates in the corner (she is afraid to leave the little room) and resumes her place on the mat. Her arms tremble, her knees tremble. From her breast she has tried to blot all feeling, but she is filled with fear.

Through the eye-slits she sees the doorway begin to lighten. Quickly she tries to pull on the kub, but it will not pass over her mask. She dares not remove the mask. She disentangles the kub, folds it under her arm, slips into the corridor, hurries past the other rooms, out the side door into the night, the sound of drinking and laughter trailing her steps.

She runs till she stumbles into the jungle's edge. She can hardly see. She feels her way among vines and trees and thick scratchy brambles. Not till she is deep within the darkness does she remove the mask.

She carries it in her hand like a severed head, till in the wakening light she can see the shape of her own hut through the trees. She hides the mask under a berry bush, emerges from the jungle still naked, feels like a thief as she hurries to the hut. Tel is still asleep. She lies on her mat and pulls the kub over her. The blood is alive in her arms, her legs. She can't believe what she has done. Yet nothing, she thinks, has happened. She has spent the night in a gaming house, but she has not been touched.

Her eyes stare vacantly at the earthen wall. She wants to cry, but no tears come. She is not sure why she wants to cry — because no one wanted her, or because tomorrow someone might.

She thinks of Kel. She is doing this for him, she tells herself: and she knows this is both true and not. Mucous fills her nose. This thought, that something can be both true and not true, is somehow too large, too disturbing. She thinks of his dark hair, his broad chest, the sight of him on the ball field — how happy he always was there — and she sniffles into her shoulder, sniffles till she falls asleep.

All that day, in the fields, she is distracted. Her head is as large as the universe. As large as the mask. Inside it, twisting, flapping, is the waiting bird of night.

After dark, when the slave child once more is asleep, she threads her way again through the jungle. A voice inside her is screaming, warning her not to go. Beside the berry bush she slips off her kub and dons again the mask of suicide; she walks in the dark of the absent moon. With the mask hiding her face she is no longer Tika, she believes: she is a long-limbed jaguar who can do whatever she will. But this feeling vanishes at the jungle's edge, in sight of the gaming house. Once more she is atremble, younger even than her fifteen years. She does not want to proceed. But still she goes, to the side of the house and quickly down the corridor to the room assigned to her.

From the other rooms she hears moaning, whimpers, cries. The sounds of passion. She has never known completed passion, she wonders what it is like. For her it had drowned in the sea. The smell of chocolate reaches her, and balche. She hears the men being noisy at their gambling games. At first the noise frightens her. Then she picks out voices, voices that she knows, and she is less afraid.

No one comes to her. She wonders why. Perhaps it is the mask, she thinks. If she removed the mask, if she walked out naked among them, then surely one would follow. But she dares not remove the mask. Perhaps if she were a different god, she thinks. But the twisting bird in her head, the naked quetzal, which told her to do this, had told her precisely which mask. Ixtab it must be, no other mask would do. She does not know why, she knows only what the quetzal said.

The second night passes like the first. No one comes. She slips away before dawn, feeling useless as a lizard in the sun.

Walking through the dark of the jungle she is more detached from her family, her friends, than ever before. She feels akin to the wild beasts, she feels without purpose, nonexistent. She is no longer Maya, no longer one of a people. She is flesh and bones only, a whim of nature, a one-eyed owl in a tree. In a tree, she imagines, she ought to dwell.

Returning to the gaming house the next night, still masked, with her kub held tight around her, she speaks to the proprietor. Her price no longer is eight beans, she says. Her price is two beans. That is all she is worth.

The proprietor, a cousin of the nacom, looks at her and shrugs.

—One of them still goes to me, he says.

Tika nods her mask. The proprietor spreads the word. In the little room she huddles in a corner, her kub pulled around her against the chill. For half an hour she huddles that way, until there is a lurching in the entryway and a stocky young man stumbles in. He staggers half drunk against the wall.

—I've come to screw the goddess of the night, he says.

Tika is terrified, her heart beats like a rabbit's when you hold it tight. She doesn't know what to do. She is relieved when the boy holds out his fist. She sticks out her hand, accepts the two cacao beans, places them on a ledge. She does not even think to squeeze them, to make cure that they are real. She drops the kub at her feet. She sees the boy's eyes grow wide, his mouth drop open at the sight of her. She feels herself flush in the dim light. She is glad he is more boy than man. Her knees are beginning to tremble. She waits for the boy to command her, but he doesn't. She kneels on the mat so she won't fall. Then she curls on her side, as if she is going to sleep. She hopes he will take back his beans and leave.

She wishes it were only a dream. She closes her eyes inside the mask — and hears him shuffling about, removing his breechclout. He is on the mat beside her, gently rubbing her arm. So long she has been without companionship, besides the child. His hand is soft.

Slowly she relaxes. Slowly she turns on her back. His hand caresses her breast. His mouth follows it, he begins to suck on her nipple. She feels her nipple grow hard in his mouth. She feels a warm stirring between her legs. She feels his hand there and spreads her thighs. She raises her knees and feels him climb upon her, feels his thickness pressing on her belly, then pulling back and with a quick sloshing sound slip inside. She cries out at a spasm of pain. He is heaving upon her, in and out, this boy — this Kel — and she shudders at the pain of it, then relaxes, realizing there is no more pain. She clutches him tight, this boy she doesn't know, this Kel, while tears wet her cheeks inside her mask.

When he is done he puts on his breechclout and leaves quickly. She would like to talk with him now, find out who he is, this first one. But speech is difficult inside the mask. Silently she watches him go.

She washes herself with water from the pot in the corner. She goes to the ledge and looks at the two beans. She is afraid to touch them, to see if they are real. She doesn't really care.

She squeezes them, and they are real.

She is seated on the mat when the next boy comes. He isn't much older than the first. Beneath the mask she is crying, thinking of Kel, seeing him disappear into the foam. When the boy holds out two beans she doesn't rise, she doesn't take them, she merely nods to the whitewashed ledge. The boy places them there and drops his cloth. He is already thick. She does not lie down as he approaches, but takes it in her hand. To look at it. To learn.

The second time is easier. She no longer fears. She closes her eyes and tells herself it is Kel.

Three more come that night. She begins to squeeze the cacao beans before doing business.

When one of the boys fails to arouse her at all, she cries out anyway, to make him glad.

Before dawn's first light she hurries off. Half the beans she clutches in her hand. The other five she leaves on the ledge for the proprietor. She runs through the jungle giddily, his lecherous vines grabbing at her arms, her legs, caressing her breasts. She feels a draining away inside her, the beginning of a cleansing. As if she is paying some necessary debt. In her hut she goes to sleep beside the child. When she awakes she is still tired. In the afternoon she naps.

The next day, and in the days that follow, word of the new girl spreads through the village. The young men began to fill the bordello each night to see what she is like. They come away both satisfied and not: satisfied with the pleasure of her quickly improved delights; not satisfied because they want to rip off her mask, see if her face is as comely as the rest. No sooner has their immediate need been sated than her mystery makes them mad again with desire.

Word spreads through the village of this angel of the night, who perversely wears the mask of suicide while purveying her delights. Married men begin to seek her. One teaches her new things, with which she enchants the next, who in turn teaches her other new ways. She is growing wise in the ways of passion.

—Where do you go in the night? Ixtel asks her. The child has become more like a little sister than a slave.

—I go to visit Kel.'

—But Kel was drowned in the sea.

—Yes, she replies.

The child looks at her queerly, then goes about her work.

It's a lie, Tika tells herself. I go not for Kel but for myself.

This silent admission makes her shudder, turns her skin cold, raises goose bumps. But soon she sheds this skin like a snake. Within it she finds new strength. That night she takes a small basket with her to the gaming house. She tells the nacom's cousin her price is going up.

—Eight beans? he asks. Or should we start with six?

—Ten beans, masked Tika says.

The proprietor laughs.

—Ten beans? There isn't a whore in Mayadom who commands ten beans. Eight beans, like all the others.

—Ten beans,'Tika says.

She goes off to her room. She places her basket on the ledge. She drops her kub and pinches her nipples so they will be erect when the first one arrives. She thinks: a fortnight ago I was a child. Now I am more than a woman.

If she will miss the usual years in between, she doesn't think of that now.

At first there is a long wait. Then one man comes, with ten beans. Then another, to see that body, that mask. Seven come that night, at ten beans. More are men than boys. It is they, not she, who tremble.

I thought I would hate her for it. I who had drowned young Kel before they could marry. I should have killed all who came to the brothel, and her the first. But I didn't. I didn't hate her. Instead I was intrigued all the more. Was this to her another form of eating butterflies? Was this to her a new and braver form of suicide, where you continue to live afterward? Or was it merely further punishment for her guilt-ridden brain?

—Who's that slut impersonating me? Ixtab asked one night, following my gaze.

I pretended not to know.

—She does a good job of it, I said.

I was, however, beginning to feel a certain jealousy. It's a most unseemly vice, it gnaws at the gut like a hungry puma. The cause was not the men who bought her body. I was no more jealous of them than I had been of young Kel (the late lamented.) No, it was the jungle. Him I began to fear. Him I began to hate. Him I decided was after Tika's bones.

Not a hundred yards lay between her hut and the jungle's grasp. And every day the distance was getting less. Tika didn't notice, but I did. New sprouts, new vines, rapacious tentacles, were inching day by day across the empty field. The leering jungle swelling in her direction. Planning the time he could trap her, pounce on her, bind her with lianas, have his way.

Miserably I watched the jungle sneak closer, while Tika remained oblivious. To and from the brothel each night she followed a jungle path, so as not to be seen by the villagers. Night after night she crept between his vines. I feared at any moment she'd be grabbed.

I began to wish they'd made of the jungle a god. Then he couldn't have her, no more than I. Each night I watched with apprehension until she was safely home.

To calm my churning gut I tried not to focus on Tika. I sought out the two Spanish warriors who had survived the storm the day I killed Ahkel, the two who had floated up on the beach like flotsam. I hadn't spared them with intent, they were no different to me than the hundred men who drowned. But now I wondered: perhaps Time or Fate had some intent in sparing them.

One of them was short and swarthy, with a dark beard and an odd circle of baldness atop his head. He called himself Aguilar, and answered to no other name. He had thick arms and legs and a perpetual scowl on his face, as if he was ever expecting deliverance by an arriving sloop. He hacked and hauled the stones as he was told, but only then. Every few minutes he looked toward the sea.

The other was tall and fair, with a blond beard and curly hair bleached by the sun. He said his name was Guerrero, but when the others called him Spaniard he didn't mind. For the first few weeks he looked toward the cove, like his compatriot. But soon his attitude changed. During breaks for food, sitting in the shade drinking posole, he tried to converse with the Mayas. He tried to learn how they spoke. When work was done, unlike his friend he liked to roam the village, admiring the bright colored temples. To practice the new tongue he began to speak without distinction to the artists and the slaves, the nobles and the lower men. He soon became surprisingly popular throughout the village, this Spaniard. This tall blond figure who walked among them with unlikely ease. This slave.

The Spaniard had been many places, had seen many things that were unknown to the Mayas. Sometimes he spoke of them. But none was more beautiful, more wondrous, he told them, than the massive temples they had built at the jungle's edge. Word of his words soon reached the priests, and then the Lord Maya himself. The Lord summoned the Spaniard to his chambers, to hear his stories of the lands beyond the jungle, the great lands across the sea.

For his audience with the Lord Maya, the Spaniard scraped off his beard. This pleased the Lord considerably; it was viewed as a sign of allegiance, a bowing to the local ways. Many times after that the Lord Maya summoned the slave Spaniard to tell his tales of the outer world. It did not sound like a world that was better, just different, the Lord Maya said. The tall Spaniard agreed.

He continued to work as a slave with the others, his muscles rippling, his bare chest shining with sweat as he hauled huge rocks for the new pyramid. Rumors soon blew like a sea breeze up and down the hauling lines: one day soon this Spaniard would no longer be a slave.

But at night my gaze returned to masked Tika. Watching from the mist I got eunuchs' erections. I was passion's fool.

Why didn't I take her myself, you ask? Take her as a swan, perhaps, as Zeus took Leda? Take her as a puma, a lizard, a snake.

I lacked Zeus's imagination. More important, I lacked his power. Zeus had tricks of which a rain god can only dream.

Fat lot they do him now.

One night a burly man came to Tika's room half-drunk, placed ten beans in her basket — half of them spilled to the earth — and dropped his cloth. When he came near, Tika nearly retched from the foul smell of him. He stunk of sweat, of urine, and worse. She struggled from his arms and drew away.

—Go, she said. Leave me alone.

—What? I paid my ten beans. I'll do with you as I please.

—You smell, she said. You stink like a dead fish. Go home and take a bath.

—You slut! he shouted, and he slapped with his hand. Tika blocked the blow with her arm and swung her knee into his testicles. The man dropped with a groan, clutching himself heavily. The angel of the night grabbed her kub and ran from the room. She returned with the proprietor and a guard. The drunk had barely struggled to his feet.

—What the trouble here? the proprietor asked.

—This whore tried to throw me out. I'll break her neck.

—He stinks, Tika said.

The man lunged at her. The guard stepped between. The nacom's cousin moved closer.

—She's right, he said. You smell like a dung pile.

—They'll show respect or they won't come near me, Tika said.

The proprietor followed as the guard roughly escorted the man out of the building, out into the night.

—You take a bath and come back tomorrow, he told the man. I run a clean establishment.

The proprietor laughed to himself. That notion had never occurred to him before.

She began to awaken earlier in the afternoons. After Tel had prepared her breakfast and helped her bathe, she would walk alone in the jungle. I watched them carefully. But it wasn't the jungle she wanted. It was the black-tipped golden butterflies. She still was eating them. I think she was eating more than ever.

Other times she walked to the new pyramid and watched it rise ever higher, thanks to the strong arms of the slaves.

9.

Intrigued with Tika in her Ixtab mask, I was neglecting Ixtab herself. Until one night, when I returned from a game of dice near the Circle, I found her perched seductively on Chac-Mool's lap. In a rage I grabbed her arm and yanked her away from him. She rubbed her wrist and glared at me.

—He asked me to, she said. He's so pathetic. He's never touched a woman.

I looked at Chac-Mool. His oversized, sloping head was wet with perspiration. As always he was grinning his stupid grin.

—And you wanted to be the one? I shouted at Ixtab. You'd better leave.

She made no move to go, until I advanced on her. Then she hurried away. Chac-Mool's stupid grin did not change, as if it were carved in stone.

Word soon spread through the Circle that the affair was over between Ixtab and me. My ego was slightly bruised. I played the wronged lover stoically. Secretly I was thrilled. Now I was free. Free to bask in my obsessive fantasy.

—That's what he calls free! Itzamna says.

She was a madwoman. That was the opinion of the village. Harmless, perhaps, but mad. She no longer tended the fields behind her house; the corn, the pumpkins, the avocados wrinkled liked old men's faces, and died. She bought what she needed at the market with precious beans. If people wondered where she got the beans, they dared not ask. From her father, they must have assumed, though she and her father never spoke. Slowly, surreptitiously, the jungle advanced across the fields. She didn't seem to notice, she didn't seem to care. She was more at ease with the jungle than with the people. She walked alone among lianas every day. Or sat by the rising pyramid, watching the slaves haul stones, watching the artists carve gods. She spoke to no one except Tel. Her hair grew wilder, her kubs went unmended, though the child made sure they were clean. She was a madwoman. Her mind had drowned in the sea with her betrothed.

They didn't despise her for it. They remembered who she was — or who she had been. They remembered pretty young Tika, the laughing girl. They kept away because it made them sad. Or perhaps because it made them afraid. One day it might happen to them.

They didn't guess at her other life. So many whores came and went, from one village to the next as the men grew tired of them. None connected Tika with the masked artist of love. None connected Tika with the angel of the night.

Maybe that's why she acted so: to throw them off.

Or perhaps she was truly mad.

I watched her eat the butterflies, and couldn't tell.

I had no idea where my foolish infatuation would lead. No good could come of it, that much I knew. But for the moment it made me happy. It kept me occupied.

Happiness, alas, does not live long, not even within a god.

Assistants, it turned out, could die.

One day Chac-Mool ate my frog.

Chac-Mool ate little Enik.

It happened while I was ensconced in a meeting of the Circle. Chac-Mool grabbed him from behind, popped him into his stupid fat grinning mouth, distorted now with rage — or so the other frogs described it later — chewed him up without a moment's thought, his head, his little body, his legs, green frog blood running from my brother's mouth, running down his chin like drool, chewed him up and swallowed him and spit out only his feet.

The feet were there when I returned from the Circle: two disembodied frog feet, one of them turned on its side, like sandals beside a mat. And his brother frogs, Cib, Ben, Ahau rolling on the floor of the mist, covering their eyes, wailing at the pain of it. In the far corner of the mist lolled Chac-Mool, grinning, the stains of Enik's blood on his chest.

I lost my breath at the sight of it. I didn't weep — not then. I didn't rage or scream. I felt drained, empty, weary. I stared in silence at the little feet. I hugged the other frogs, I tried to comfort them. I looked across the mist at the idiot and said nothing. What was there to say, to do?

I couldn't kill him. Gods, unlike assistants, really do not die. To attack him, to beat him — what was the use now? He was an idiot. He could not make connections. Enik was already digesting in his belly. A beating now would resolve nothing.

Still, I stared at him. I couldn't take my eyes from his stupid grin.

I knew why he had done it, of course. Revenge. I knew this was the reason even if he did not. Revenge for the way I'd pulled Ixtab from his lap. Revenge for my destroying his lascivious fantasy.

She wouldn't have done it with him, of course: she had too much style. She was using him to get my attention. But Chac-Mool couldn't comprehend this. I'd snatched away the female meat he'd hoped would bring relief to his loins. I'd snatched away his suddenly beloved. And so he ate my frog.

It was the first death.

I did not want to finish the thought. The thought completed itself in my brain. It was the first death resulting from my attention to Tika.

Not counting Kel, his six teammates, two hundred Spaniards, a hundred slaves and fifty horses.

For the horses, and now for Enik, I repented.

My prolonged grief I shall not render. How could one replace little Enik? Enough to say that I mourned. I mourn still.

To forget my grief I projected. I wallowed in fantasy.

I became a nipple of Tika.

I am pinkish brown in color, the color of dried blood. I ride her heaving breast with pride and daring, like a boat on swelling seas. Day is night to me and night is day. In day I dwell in secret dark beneath her kub, all ripe potentiality, asleep. A marker waiting for play. Inhaling the light sweat and soapberry drift of her.

Twilight comes. The sun leers golden over the painted temples. Tika behind her hut is bathing. I tighten at the rush of cold water. I stiffen more, I swell, I bloom at Tika's touch. I redden, I reach for the sky. Her swirling fingers draw me to ecstasy.

Then it is night. I ride her bobbing breast through the jungle, lashed by hanging vines, evading the lewd leaves of lianas. As she reclines on her mat I crown her breast like a ruby. Rough hands coarsen me, and tongues, and teeth. I pretend it is not a man. I pretend the hands are Tika's own, the tongue, too, and the teeth.

I adorn the kingdom of Tika. I exude the power of Tika. I share the glory of Tika. Amen.

So I grieved for Enik. I fantasized. What was that phrase I used earlier? Not erotic. Semiotic. A semiotic fantasy. All words.

And Tika?

Tika did not know of Enik. When not snatching butterflies in the jungle she sat more and more by the rising pyramid, watching the artists carve gods. Watching the tall Spaniard haul stones.

Itzamna was beginning to preen. The great new pyramid was nearly complete and he could hardly wait for the dedication. He reveled (I think I've mentioned this) in the abject worship of the mortals.

As God of the sky he liked to be called Chief. But we all had our sovereign powers, which he couldn't countermand. He merely chaired the Circle. Someone had to.

We all were puzzled when the top of the pyramid was not finished off with a point, like the others. Instead the mortals created a level top. Then on this huge platform that towered over the trees, over the jungle, over the entire village, they began to build a temple in the sky. Itzamna strutted and pranced. The Mayas were ingenious. What better place to honor the sky god? He declared it the most beautiful monument in all of Mayadom.

As for myself, I found it neither here nor there.

About this time I received a surprise offer. I was recruited by the giant turtles.

They had met in a secret conclave whose aggregate turtle wisdom totaled several million years. They decided it was time they had a god.

They'd decided they would start with one god only. They wanted their god to be Chac.

I was flattered. Excited, too, though this I tried to conceal. The grandest wish of my youth was being offered to me now!

Chac: god of the turtles. With sovereignty in every sphere!

(Rain alone at times gets tiresome)

I watched them below, gathered on the beach at the water's edge, awaiting my response. An admirable race they were, these giant turtles. Solid, dependable, stoic. Not given to weeping, to tearing of hair. Stately, almost godlike. Not nearly as frantic, as insecure, as men.

Chac, god of the turtles. It had a ring to it!

I looked down at the mortals — at their temples gleaming in the sun, at their liquid bodies moving through the village like so many squishy lizards. These in an instant would disappear from my brain, and I from theirs. Gone would be their god of rain. (—I can handle it, Itzamna said.) Gone would be Tika from my protection, my fantasies.

I looked down at the madwoman, seated quietly in her usual place, watching the Spanish slave hauling stones.

I told the turtles no. Reluctantly they accepted my regrets. I stayed on as the rain god of the Mayas. The turtles said they'd find someone else.

I don't know if they did. Me they never asked again.

The blandishments of the turtles had a fortuitous result, however. With the murder of Enik I was short-frogged. I had an empty gourd to fill. For a light sprinkle, one frog was enough, or two. But for a heavy downpour of the kind I liked best, all four gourds were essential. So I'd been thinking about how to replace Enik. Begetting another with Ixchel was out of the question, she dwelled with Itzamna now. And Ixtab I'd hurled from the mist. (I think she may have been barren, anyway.) But talking with the turtles, I had an idea that perhaps I could adopt.

Enik's death had proved that assistants were not immortal, they were somewhere between mortals and gods. And so, too, I'd always felt, were the turtles, whose godlike grace endured for bakuns. I made some inquiries. A bargain was quickly struck. The turtles would choose one of their number to be ambassador to the court of Chac.

Itzamna said it was highly irregular, and he was correct. But he agreed the experiment would be useful, now that we knew our assistants could be killed. For he, too, had assistants: eight bright yellow prancing jaguars who helped him lug the heavy sun across the sky.

A few evenings later my adopted turtle arrived. He went by the name of Jag, and a fine turtle he was: calm, unassuming, a bit clumsy on the uptake at first but a clever, solid worker once he learned the gourds. Ben, Cib and Ahau welcomed him to the family as best, in their bereavement, they could. He had one feature especially that they could not help but admire: that solid shell of his. There was no way Chac-Mool could do him harm. (The others did not fear Chac-Mool, they were much too agile for him; it was only Enik's lameness that had done him in.)

We tried some practice rains, my three remaining frogs and my adopted turtle. They soaked the mortal lands just fine. Solid Jag replaced little Enik.

But never, ever in my heart.

It was some time before we discovered, quite by accident, that Jag was a she. With that race you can't always tell. She hadn't let on, she hadn't wanted special privileges. But gradually her inner sweetness shown through her outer shell like a gentle blush.

Ben and Cib hopped about in a frantic war for her affections, ignoring the fact that, like gods and mortals, frogs and turtles cannot mix. Only Ahau remained above this battle. He was content to be her confidante, a caring older brother. Like me, his lustful eyes sought Tika.

—Like father, like frog, Itzamna quipped.

Itzamna thinks he's funnier than he is.

At first the Spanish slave at his work did not seem to notice Tika. Until one afternoon their eyes chanced to meet. Quickly they both glanced away, as if burned by fire. When, the next day, their eyes met again, the Spaniard kept looking a moment longer. Only Tika turned away. Across the bustling road they soon held one another's gaze like offerings. I realized at once what I was watching: the mating dance of the mortals.

Soon Tika brought with her a gourd. She sat for a time shading it with her hands to keep it cool. When the workers were given a rest, she stood and crossed the road. She approached the Spaniard and held out the gourd. Without a word he took it, raised it to his cracking lips, leaned back his head and drank. When he had drunk his fill he wiped his mouth with his hand and handed the near-empty gourd back to her. Tika took it and left without a word.

I watched as she traversed the village to her hut, hardly twenty steps now from the jungle's grasp. Her beauty was as promising and as wild as ever, and yet with a new leanness to it, which seemed to call attention to the bones of her face instead of to the flesh. She strode now more with womanly dignity than with girlish bounce, though her body, still young, was firm as ever. There was something queenly about her. The woman she was becoming was beggaring even the girl.

The next day she brought to the work site not a gourd but a pot. When the workers had their break she approached the Spaniard and offered it to him. He was aware that the other slaves, the other workers, some artists, even some passersby, were watching. What did the madwoman want with the Spanish slave?

—I can't' he said, looking around, and gently pushed the pot away.

She pressed the ladle into his hand, pressed his fingers around it.

—Drink, she said.

It was the first word she had spoken to him.

The Spaniard looked into her eyes. He dipped the ladle into the pot and tasted the posole. Ladle after ladle he drank that way, till the pot was almost empty. As he drank, his gaze hardly left her face.

The onlookers turned away, whispered among themselves. If the poor madwoman had been so shameless with anyone else they might have taunted her. But not so with the tall blond Spaniard. He was liked throughout the village, the rumor was everywhere that one day soon he would be freed.

In any case, they told themselves, nothing would come of the mad feeding the hungry. They had sane daughters aplenty to thrust upon the Spaniard when he was free. To turn his head from Tika.

Myself, I'd seen his eyes. I was not sure.

I was a butterfly impaled in her mouth. I was the thatch between her legs. Such were my fantasies.

Imagine the dreams I could have dreamed, if I could dream.

"Drink."

That was the only word she'd said to him. Yet that night there was consternation in the brothel. The masked artist of love did not appear. Nor did she appear the next night. Or the night after that. The customers complained. The proprietor shrugged.

—The whores are free women, he said. I don't keep them in chains. Maybe you weren't tipping her enough. Maybe she got bored.

—We weren't done with her yet, a drunken voice shouted.

—Maybe she was done with you,'a sober voice replied.

Some of the regulars made inquiries of the merchants in the plaza, asked whether in their travels they had heard tell of a special new whore in another village, a whore who wore the mask of Ixtab, a whore who people called the artist of the night. The answer always was no. She seemed to have disappeared.

In due course the inquiries stopped. But the whore was not forgotten. She became something of a legend in the village, boasted about fondly by those who had known her — and wistfully by many who had not. While in the jungle, not far from the village, the pieces of a mask, sliced apart like a mango, lay scattered beside a berry bush, until a steady rain began to fall and buried them in the mud.

10.

When the Spaniard was given his freedom none of the villagers knew which day it happened, because he continued hauling stones for the rising pyramid as if he were still a slave.

He had been summoned to the Lord Maya's chambers. The Lord was wearing one of his loftier hats, and held in his right hand the scepter that symbolized his power.

—Alfonse Luis Guerrero, the Lord Maya said (he must have looked it up), you have served this village well. If you are granted your freedom, where will you go?

—I shall remain here, the Spaniard replied.

—And what will you do?

—I will continue to haul stones for the completion of the great pyramid, while I build a hut for myself, clear a field, find. . .

—Find what?

—Find a woman, the Spaniard said.

—If you are freed, you are at liberty to leave. To go anywhere in that large world of yours.

—I will stay. I am Maya now.

The Lord Maya did not exactly smile — I don't think I ever saw him smile — but I got the idea he was pleased by the answer. He laid his scepter on the earth, the sign that the Spaniard was now a free man.

—Go with the gods, he said.

The Spaniard merely nodded. For me, the pointless phrase had an echo. The last time I'd heard it said was by the High Priest, when the boy Kel splashed off for Cozumel.

What would happen next seemed obvious. The Spaniard and Tika would come together as husband and wife. Why this should be so was another question. Was it the attraction of two outcasts, who needed to cling in an alien world?

I thought not. Tika was indeed an outcast, by her own choosing, by her own behavior. But the Spaniard was not. Straight away upon gaining his freedom he had his ears pierced and hung with jade rings, he had a snake and a quetzal tattooed upon his chest, as was the custom. He was the tallest man by far in the village, and the fairest, but it was hard to doubt the truth of what he had said. He was Maya now. The village was pleased to take him at his word.

But if the two of them were not aliens who would soon huddle together like children in the dark, what then? Could they be 'soul mates' (the favorite phrase of the adolescent girls) who eerily had found one another from half way across the earth? I think not. If there were such a phenomenon as soul mates, it was my understanding that each person had only one. Tika was already spoken for.

What to do with this intruding Spaniard was a problem that loomed on the horizon (a felicitous phrase, don't you think?) He seemed a sincere fellow, as mortals go, and I didn't know what attitude to adopt toward him. I was pondering this question when I overheard my three frogs and my adopted turtle discussing the very same point. Like a curious parent, I listened, unseen.

—What do you think he's going to do with him? (That was Ben speaking.)

—With who?

—The Spaniard, of course.

—He's going to kill him. (Cib.)

—Again? Like he did with that ballplayer?

—Why not?'

—The ballplayer? (A softer, gentler voice: Jag.) I thought he said the ballplayer accidentally drowned.

—He's trying to tweak history. It was cold-blooded murder.

—Maybe hot-blooded. (Ahau's wise voice, for the first time.)

—What's the difference?

—Murder in the heat of passion. Of jealousy. Murder on impulse. Some say that's excusable.

—So that's what he'll do to the Spaniard?. Another hot-blooded murder.?

—I don't think you can do that twice.

—He's a god. He can do whatever he wants.

—We know he can do it. It's a question of morals. He's got to live with himself — for a long time.

That thought seemed to sober them. It sobered me. There was silence for a time. Then Cib resumed.

—I think he'll kill him anyway. He's gone bananas over that girl. He'll invent some excuse.

—Woman.

—What?

—Woman. (Ahau speaking.) She's a woman now, not a girl. That's why I don't think he'll kill him.

—Because she's a woman?

—Look what he did to her the last time. Killed her boyfriend, and it nearly drove her mad. I don't think he'll make her suffer again.

Another pause, and the sound of muted crunching. They were snacking on their afternoon flies. Till Ben spoke, with his mouth full.

—I don't know what he sees in her now. She's rather daft.

—Tits and twat, Cib said.

—There's hundreds of females down there, Ahau responded. He's only nuts for this one. Give him credit for that. He's faithful in his fantasies.

—What's the attraction, then? Her mind? Her butterflies?

—What is it ever? It just happens.

—You know what I think?

I could sense them all turning toward Jag's sweet voice.

—What? (Ben.)

—What? (Cib.)

—I think it's mathematical.

—How so? (Ahau.)

—She's a frustrated artist — a job forbidden to women. That's clear from the way she sits by the pyramid, watching. I think Chac is attracted to that. It reflects his own frustration over being forbidden to have a mortal.

—And?

—He's idealized her, placed her in a symmetrical equation. An equation that necessitates his passion.

Already she was over the heads of Ben and Cib, her suitors. Ahau must have been struggling to follow her argument. The turtles were deep thinkers.

—What's the equation? Ahau asked.

—It's simple. Tika pines for the perfection of the artist. The artist pines for the perfection of the god. So the god pines . . .'

—For the perfection of Tika!

—Exactly!

—A perfect circle!

—Of frustration.

—Which is the essence of life, both mortal and divine.

—It's like those butterflies in that cave in the jungle. They go around and around that useless skull, in circles. Trying to entice it back to life. Which will never happen.

—The same ones she eats!

—It all fits together.

In the background I heard rhythmic breathing. Ben and Cib had fallen asleep. Jag and Ahau were tremulous with excitement. I'd have bet my nose a romance had just begun.

—It all fits together, but I don't know what it means, not really, Jag admitted.

—Neither do I, Ahau said.

I waited to hear more. There was none. I dared not go into the mist, I didn't know what I might be interrupting. Instead I pondered Jag's equation. Tika despairs for the perfection of the artist, the artist despairs for the perfection of the god, the god despairs for the perfection of Tika.

It was lovely. Even if it meant nothing at all. It was one of those sly jokes of Time. Of Fate. Practical joke number one in the Sacred Codex: The Unquenchable Desire for the Unattainable. (Subsection A: forbidden love.)

Which reminded me of the original question they'd been discussing: was their father about to murder again? I'd often wondered what they talked about while I was gone. Do your children fear the same thing?

I will not keep you in suspense. I didn't murder him.

At times there is honor even among gods.

Not very often, I'll admit.

The Spaniard, who could be quite loquacious when telling his tales of the outside world, was strong but laconic around Tika. They seemed to communicate without words. One cloudy day, when he finished drinking the posole she had brought to the pyramid, he simply walked home beside her. Seeing where she lived, in the hut near the jungle's edge, he turned without a word and went back to his work. Toward evening, when his work was done, he strode across the village in the lowering sun to her hut. She seemed to be expecting him. She had a supper of corn meal and venison prepared. They ate in silence, speaking only with unreadable eyes.

After the meal he strode behind the hut and looked about.

—Tomorrow I will come, he said, neither gruffly nor excessively gentle, more as simple confirmation of a fact she already knew. It was the first full sentence to pass between them, as near as I could tell, and he left without another.

The next day he quit work early. He was a free man and could leave whenever he pleased, though he did not make a point of either telling this or concealing it, to Tika or anyone else. He carried with him a sharp stone ax. He paused only a moment in the hut, to watch Tika weaving a mat in the same design as her own. Then he carried the ax behind the hut, surveyed what had once been a field of corn and squash a hundred feet long, recently claimed by the jungle. He began to hack off green and grasping arms, which were groping lewdly only yards from Tika's bathing place. Again and again he swung the heavy ax, grunting louder and louder as he did, the sweat running down the muscles of his neck, his back, with the chunk and chock of his attack, the jungle arms falling without bleeding, the jungle himself retreating without screaming. In several hours he pushed him back seven feet at least. It was clear he intended to continue his assault day after day until the jungle turned and ran.

If my resolve to spare his life was less than certain, his attack on the jungle strengthened it. What a perceptive mortal he was, to recognize at once the jungle's leer, to see how he coveted her, to discern his plan of attack and cut it off. By routing the jungle he freed me from a deeper jealousy, and for this alone the man deserved to live.

For four days the Spaniard returned each afternoon to hack off jungle limbs. He slashed with powerful arms until the jungle, bleeding all manner of tropical juices now, retreated into himself to lick his wounds. When the small massacre was done and the field was littered with the corpses of tentacles, with severed vines and jungle arteries, with orchid petals strewn about as on the graves of warriors, the Spaniard set fire to it all. He burned the dead limbs to black coal, then with a forked stick spread the smoking blackness over the field, to enrich the earth for the seeds he soon would plant.

Each day when he was done, and stinking from the work, Tika would have a bath prepared for him. She would help him bathe and then together they would sit on their matching mats and eat the supper she had cooked. Sometimes, after the meal, he would take her chin in his hand, or touch her cheek. He would stare into her eyes as if they were a treasure he had never heard about across the sea. Then he would stand and leave, and return to the slave quarters where he continued to spend each night. Not until the fifth day, when he brought with him seeds and with a pointed stick planted them row after row, straight and true behind the hut, not till then, after he had taken his bath, after she had bathed from gourds, did they, banking the fire after their meal, lie on their mats together.

I closed my eyes.

It must have gone well for both of them. He never returned to the slave quarters again.

With the mortal practice of keeping slaves I've always had a problem. We gods have assistants, of course, but that's another matter. For one thing, our assistants are never the same species as ourselves. Chac keeps frogs; if my frogs needed assistants (sometimes, in the rainy season, they beg for them) they would not keep other frogs: they'd keep spiders, perhaps, or beetles: something slightly squishier, something more vulnerable, than themselves. Here in the Circle my idiot half-brother is fit to be a beast of burden only, but no one has made a slave of him. He still is one of us, a god, although a fetal accident. A god who retains his own dumb birds.

There's no doubt the mortals seemed content enslaving fellow mortals (those seemed content, that is, who were not the slaves.) But note the premier models of the universe: Time, and Fate. They do not take as slaves other Times, other Fates. They only take as slaves you, and me.

Enough of pale distractions, weak philosophies. Tika and Guerrero became lovers. They did not bother with priests and vows, he simply moved in with her, as man with wife. They worked, they bathed, they ate, they talked a bit, and then a gentle coming together, simple yet profound, no tricks. The artist of the night had disappeared.

Surprisingly, I did not want him dead. I did not want him hacked apart. I did not want his head upon a platter. The only thing I wanted was his place.

Mortal love, too, is weighted with pain, but for that there is a reason. Without the suffering that enmeshes love like iron warp entwined with golden woof, human love would people the earth with creatures who thought they were gods. Who strutted about full-cocked and glorious, fearless and lethargic. What would get accomplished then? What pyramids would be built, what fields would be tilled? Who would bow to Itzamna then?

Mortals need their pain, even in love, just as they need their shit: to remind them of who they are. It anchors them with solid identity, without which they would float away. It's not at all like the suffering of gods, which is a pointless mistake.

11.

Enough of pain. Enough, too, of love. I want to speak of horses. Of one horse in particular, the horse that belonged to the one they called Cortez the Conqueror. It's the Spaniard's story, really, but I don't think he would mind my repeating it.

Night after night as they lay together in the dark, he regaled Tika with stories from lands and worlds that she would never see, that she could hardly even imagine: stories of the great cities of Spain, stories of kings and queens as grand as the Lord Maya, of pirates on the high seas and battles fought in armed sloops, of long voyages across the ocean, on one of which he'd been with this Cortez: journeys whose purpose was to bring back precious metals for the king and queen, and to lay claim to all these lands in the name of Spain (with his tone the Spaniard was mocking, I think, his native land) and to 'convert the heathens' — his very phrase, rich with sarcasm — to the one loving god of the Spanish motherland. All these stories Tika heard with amusement or fascination or incomprehension, depending on the Spaniard's narrative skill that night, or on how restless Tika was. But the one story she enjoyed the most, and which she asked him to tell many times, on nights when she was dreamy with the deepening of his love, was a story that was close to Mayadom, a story he had told the priests and the Lord Maya as well: the story of Cortez the Conqueror's horse.

This Cortez was a particular bully, it seemed, who had made many voyages from Spain to the New World, as the Spaniard ironically called it (realizing , I think, that it was a thousand bakuns older than the Old.) He came with armies and horses and dogs, with jugglers and buffoons, with herds of pigs to sustain them, and he slashed a trail of blood the length of Mexico, subduing village after village, tribe after tribe, in the name of the king of Spain and his alien god. (What the king and the god would want with these distant tribes the Spaniard could never explain convincingly.) Tribes that resisted were slaughtered, their leaders executed. With each new battle the fear of this Cortez spread like a bloody ghost across the land.

Most of his conquests were Mexican, not Maya. The jungle cities of the Maya, which did not rest on precious metals, were the last to attract his notice. In time, when he was getting on in years, this Cortez mounted one last expedition against a tribe far to the south. Along the way he came to the village of a small and unresisting group of Mayas. Ahead lay a march of hundreds of miles through the jungle. Cortez befriended the leader of the small tribe. He asked if, as a favor, he could leave his famous horse with the tribe, to be cared for until he returned from the jungle. The Mayas agreed; they were impressed by this signal of friendship and trust by the great warrior.

With Cortez in the lead the army marched off into the jungle, leaving the horse behind. The Mayas were struck with awe. They had heard tales of the horsebeasts of the Spaniards, but had never seen one before. They viewed it with veneration, as befits such a powerful creature. They treated it, in fact, as they did their own leader: offering it balche to drink, turkey to eat, their spiciest delicacies on which to sup.

In two weeks the poor horse died.

The Mayas were horrified. They didn't understand what they'd done wrong. They were terrified as well, fearing not only the rage of Cortez when he returned but the vengeful spirit of the dead horse itself. The priests conferred and decided that something must be done at once. The tribe's best artists were put to work, and quickly completed their task: the creation in stone of a replica of the dead horse. They named him Tziminchac, after the god of thunder (a distant cousin) and they placed him in the village's main temple. The veneration increased now that the horse was a god. Offerings of flowers and corn alcohol were laid before him daily. Unlike the real horse, the stone horse didn't die.

The wrath of Cortez did not befall the village. The conqueror contracted malaria in the jungle, returned to Spain by another route, and died not long after. He never learned the fate of his horse.

The story of the stone horse god emerged several years later, when two Spanish friars, traveling hither and yon to 'convert the heathens,' arrived at the little village. They were welcomed peacefully, given food and drink and a place to rest. They were allowed to roam freely through the village. The visiting priests were particularly interested in the temples — there were twenty-one in all — wanting to understand the religion of the Mayas, the religion they had come to change. At first they found nothing unexpected. But when they entered the main temple, and saw the stone beast on his haunches in the place of honor, they were stunned. The villagers were worshipping a horse! In a fit of righteousness one of the priests rushed at the idol, flung himself upon it, tried to hurl it from its pedestal down into the dust. Seeing this, the Mayas were at first bewildered, then outraged at this attack on Tziminchac. They dragged the priests away to be sacrificed.

Luckily for them, the priests were good talkers, as most priests are. They convinced the Mayas they meant no harm. They were allowed to go free into the jungle, from which they eventually were rescued by another friendly tribe, and lived to tell the tale of the stone horse.

In the village, however, the attack on Tziminchac was viewed like this: the white man hated him more than any other god; he needed to be protected, lest the Spaniards return with a party of warriors bent on destroying him. So a contingent of strong men removed the stone horse from the temple, where he was too exposed, and loaded him onto a pirogue in a nearby lake. In the center of the lake was a thickly wooded island; there they would place the horse god, far from the eyes of treacherous whites.

The men made one fatal error, however. The statue was heavy, the pirogue rode low in the water. When they were half way to the island a sudden rain storm fell, the lake began to roll with waves, the craft tipped slightly, the great stone horse wavered, tilted, then with a roaring splash fell into the lake. In a twinkling the horse god was gone, deep into the night-black water. It was never seen again.

That's how the Spaniard finished his tale each time. It always left Tika in a humorous mood, more so than his stories of kings and pirates and wars. What lesson she found in it, if any, I never heard her say.

By drowning their hunk of stone, I hoped to teach the silly mortals a lesson: you can't beat a dead horse into a living god. But even the priests and the Lord Maya didn't grasp it. Which led in time to the darkest depths of all.

It was the day the village was to dedicate the great new pyramid, twenty years in the making, to Itzamna. The Chief was feeling so good he declared a holiday. The Circle, myself included, dressed in all our finery to help him celebrate. (We indulged him that way; it was a harmless charade.)

The villagers had crowded into the plaza fronting the pyramid and spilled into the surrounding fields. All of them were there, every last one: nobles, lower men, slaves, even women. Tika, I'm sure, was among them, with the Spaniard at her side, though I couldn't find them in the crowd. On the steep, imposing pyramid steps that led to the temple in the sky the priests, the nacom and the mighty Lord Maya had been joined by their counterparts from all the nearby villages. Some had traveled as far as a hundred miles. So many quetzal headdresses had never before come together in all the years of the Mayas; they looked from above like a glittering field of radiant birds.

Itzamna was nervous and delighted as a child as we watched the rhythmic dancers on the plaza, as we listened to the music. When the opening speeches began, the names of many of us gods were mentioned. The artists had carved the images of every one of us along the pyramid's huge, square base — even the grinning face of Chac-Mool. As the speeches droned on, gourds of balche were passed from hand to hand and mouth to mouth in the crowd.

More music, more dancing; many in the throng were getting drunk. Then, by unseen signal, a silence fell over the plaza, the village, even, it seemed, the surrounding jungle, as the Lord Maya rose to speak.

—We are gathered here today, he began, from every temple and hut in the village, from every village in the region, to dedicate this largest of all the pyramids, this most beautiful and wondrous of all the temples, to the mightiest of the gods.

I was watching Itzamna's face. He tried to repress a smile, but couldn't. Technically, as I've mentioned, he's no mightier than the rest of us, but I suppose that's quibbling.

—We implore the gods to look with favor on this offering of our labor, our love, our humble obedience.

The Lord Maya was ranting on and on; his speech was less artful than his hat. I don't remember it all, I tend to doze during mortal politics. But I bolted awake at the unexpected end.

—And so, in the sight of all the gods, with the hope that they will bless us with their bounty through all the given years, we dedicate this grandest of pyramids to the foremost of the gods: to Kukulcan!

Scores of musicians blasted their conches, banged away at their drums. Thousands of villagers — men, women, children — raised their voices, their faces, toward the sky and shouted over and over, as if with a single throat: —Kukulcan! Kukulcan! Kukulcan!

Covies of birds were released from nets to soar into the air over the pyramid and thence out over the jungle.

It was the most humiliating display any of us gods had ever seen.

As loud as was the noise in the plaza, so dense was the silence in the Circle. No one spoke. Itzamna flushed redder than his reddest sun. Then all color fled from his face. I looked away. Everyone looked away. We all looked down at our feet. I felt sorry for him, all of us did, even though he'd sort of been asking for it.

—To Kukulcan! he muttered. He said it softly, but he was controlling great rage. I would have thought the whole thing funny myself, if he weren't so upset.

Slowly the color returned to his face; he was biting his thick lips, his eyes were beginning to close, to turn inward. It was easy to see what he was thinking: the mortals had gone too far: they would pay.

I suppose I need to explain about Kukulcan. He was a warrior, a mortal, who had lived in the region several bakuns before. He was a fierce fighter, who had defended the villages many times against invading tribes that swarmed over the mountains. When he died he was buried in the jungle, with great oration and ceremony.

In the years after his death, the tales of his accomplishments grew with exaggeration, as often happens with military men. His personal shield had been painted with the head of a quetzal bird and the body of a snake, and this became a popular symbol. Little girls would draw it on the ground, grown men would tattoo it on their chests. Small boys would want to be Kukulcan.

With each generation his so-called miracles grew in the stories of the people. Soon blasphemies began to be heard. It was said by some that he had not been a man but a god; that there was no body buried in the jungle, that he had ascended as a god to the Circle. It was nonsense, of course. A man cannot become a god, any more than a god can become a man. But the cult of Kukulcan spread.

A wise Lord Maya began to fear that the real gods would be offended. To put a stop to the blasphemies, he sent an expedition into the jungle, to open the grave and bring back the decayed body. To prove to the people that Kukulcan had been mortal. But this turned into a mistake. Three bakuns had passed since his burial; the searchers in the sprawling jungle couldn't find his grave. When they came back without his skeleton, the cultists jumped on the news. They said it proved they were right —that Kukulcan had ascended to the Circle. Worship of this dead mortal spread even further.

We didn't pay much heed. It was all talk, funny and also sad. When one god wanted to threaten another, he'd say, 'Beware of Kukulcan!' It was always good for a laugh.

Words didn't matter, you see. Words of prayer are the cheapest things in all creation. But this new offense was something else. This was solid stone, this was architecture, a pyramid, the largest in Mayadom; men had given up lives for this. This was a temple, the highest in the sky. Women soon would lose their daughters here.

To Kukulcan!

Personally, I didn't give a crap. The mortals could worship their own buttocks for all I cared. I alone could keep them alive, with my rain. It's all a matter of confidence. But to Itzamna it was a mighty affront. His powers as god of the sky were mostly symbolic: sunsets he controlled, and starry nights. They're beautiful, but not vital, not matters of life or death. Deep down, Itzamna knew this. He had no base of power. So he had to insist on respect, or he was doomed.

We all knew the unspoken truth of it. But we would go along with him, to maintain the hierarchy, the status quo. Itzamna *represents* the Circle, after all.

The meeting was held at twilight the following day. The Circle was filled to capacity, every place taken. At Itzamna's orders, hundreds of assistants, who normally were not permitted to hear the secret deliberations, were allowed to fill the upper strata in every direction. It was a sight to remember, a sight never before witnessed in the Circle: gaggles of colorful godly assistants crowding in: frogs, lizards, green and yellow parrots, spider monkeys, proud spotted jaguars, toothy crocodiles, bullnecked snakes, antlered deer, crabs, snails, spheroid mollusks, even Chac-Mool's ravens (though my idiot half-brother himself was asleep in the mist, as usual.) The decision we took at the meeting, Itzamna had said, could be so far-reaching as to affect not only the mortals but the gods and assistants as well. As backdrop, as a reminder of his talent, he'd concocted as resonant a sunset as he'd come up with in hundreds of bakuns, a dark and brooding affair that utilized every rainbow color, with deep red dominating, a sure sign he was out for blood. The reds and purples clashing through the strata suggested a vast conflagration, the beginning of worlds, or the endings, another fierce sign of his mood. He had taken the pyramid insult even harder than I had imagined.

He began the meeting by recounting the obscene recent events (his words) — the construction of the epochal temple, and its scurrilous dedication to the false god Kukulcan. Since Itzamna was the offended party, normally he would have relinquished the chairing of the meeting to the god who sits on his right. Which is I. (Or do you say me?) But in this instance the matter was delicate. The mortals had never actually stated that their grandest temple, so long in the making, would hail the glory of Itzamna. That had merely been his assumption. For Itzamna to admit being the offended party would have been an acute embarrassment, an admission of his dashed expectations, and no major concern of the Circle's. Had the temple been named for me, for instance, for Ahpuch, for any of the other gods, Iztamna would have been furious, but there would have been no punishable offense. It was only by invoking the mortal Kukulcan that they apparently insulted us all. So Itzamna remained in his chair, in theory no more affronted than the rest of us, and the case against the Mayas was this: they had honored with their largest temple, and had hailed as the mightiest of the gods, the worm-eaten corpse of a centuries-dead mortal, who was no closer to being a god than the maggots who infested him.

—By their actions, Itzamna intoned from his grand chair (his tone more modulated than the severity of his words might suggest) the mortals have sinned against the Circle with a gravity that we have never seen before. (The word 'sin' alone showed how hurt he was; it's not a word the Circle uses lightly.) They have taken this food for worms, this. . . (he could hardly force himself to pronounce the name) . . .this Kukulcan, and hurled his rotted bones in the face of every god in the Circle. That eyesore of a temple blotting the village is an insult to every god and goddess seated here. It will remain such an insult, day after day, through all the given years.

—I look to my left, to the places of our worthy goddesses. Ixchel I see, (Itzamna bowed his head slightly, and smiled) Ixtab I see, Ixchel Yaac I see, all your worthy gentle faces I see, too numerous to mention. I hope you will forgive me. But whose face don't I see? This Kukulcan! I look to my right. The mighty Chac I see (nodding at me, an attempt at flattery, though it was only truth), Ahpuch I see, Yum Kaax, all the rest of you honored gods I see, on around the Circle. But whose face is absent, who face don't I see? This Kukulcan! Worse yet, I look to the packed galleries of the rear strata, filled today with my invited guests, with hundreds of our illustrious godly assistants. Surely among the lovely parrots and fierce jaguars, among the frogs and the spider monkeys, surely, somewhere among our hardworking friends, there at least I will find him. But I peer through all the strata — look about if you like — and what do I find? Even there I find no Kukulcan!.

At this point I thought he was about to overdo it. But he reigned in his rising rhetoric just in time, his voice, which had been beginning to boom like my thunder, dropped to normal tones again.

—And yet there in the village, towering over the jungle that gives the mortals their sustenance, what do I see? I see a great monstrous pyramid, a temple in the sky, to Kukulcan. He paused to let the weight of his words sink in. The assistants in the galleries were beginning to buzz with rage — perhaps that's why, in his sly wisdom, he had invited them — though most of the gods themselves remained impassive. Sensing that his outrage was far outstripping that of the Circle, where his votes would have to lie, he resumed his speech in more clinical tones.

—The offense of the mortals is clear, he said. It is a grave and outrageous offense, and must be punished. (To Itzamna that was not an opinion, merely a statement of fact.) The questions I wish to put before this great Circle today are two: what form should that punishment take, and how severe should it be?

He paused. I thought he was done, that he would throw the questions to the Circle for suggestions. But Itzamna is a tactician, a marvel at influencing the supposedly independent actions of the gods.

—If the chair may put forth its own view, he said, as a basis on which to begin the discussion, it is this: that to pay for their blasphemy — a blasphemy of enduring stone, no idle thought but twenty years in the making — the mortals should be visited with the deadliest kind of plague, a terrible, painful disease that will wipe out ninety percent of the population of every village in Mayadom, leaving only enough mortals alive to begin their society anew, with a newfound respect for the nature of the gods. Let them pray for relief to Kukulcan, and see what help they get!

He stopped.

The entire Circle was stunned into a sickly silence.

A plague? Ninety percent dead? For a lousy pyramid?

The proposal was so unexpectedly drastic it forced everyone to rethink their positions. Some had come to the meeting feeling the offense was laughable, others that some symbolic slap on the kub would suffice: an eclipse of the sun to re-instill mortal fear, a hurricane that claimed some scattered lives, at worst a below-normal harvest of corn. That was roughly my position, something along those lines. But with Itzamna's drastic proposal I could see all around the Circle a furrowing of visages. Each and every one was thinking the same: if Itzamna had not gone mad — and clearly he had not — then perhaps they had underestimated the offense; perhaps in his broad wisdom he saw implications that they with their more restricted views could not. It was a classic case of authority wielding a mighty scepter, with no firmer underpinning than its presumed but unproven wisdom. Before anyone else had spoken, Itzamna had managed to escalate the forthcoming punishment far beyond what anyone would have predicted.

—Why make this sound so evil? Itzamna said. It goes with the territory. And by the way, if this is what you call 'my big scene,' why keep sticking your long nose in?

I suppose he's right. It was a grand speech he had made, one of the most effective ever heard in the Circle, if you overlook the overkill. In all the prior bakuns only one could compare with it — the speech of the former god of intelligence (I forget his name) nearly six hundred years earlier. The problem back then was that the Mayans were getting too big for their sloping brain pans. They were figuring out too much, setting it all down on their stone stellae, for anyone else who came along to decipher. They had figured out the stars and the planets, the most complex mathematics of the universe, the invisible cone of waves by which the earth is suspended in the galaxy. They had imagined that all would change in the year 2012, when the last bakun ends. But they did not know in what way.

—The next thing they will figure out is what happens after that, the god of intelligence warned the Circle back then. Which was particularly frightening, even we gods didn't know what would happen. If the mortals figured that out, they might abandon us altogether.

We snickered at the thought. We decided that both we and the Mayas could do without a god of intelligence. Shunned, then exiled, he left the Circle in search of another People to serve. I have seen no evidence that he found one.

All this I recalled — no doubt others recalled it as well — during the long silence that followed Itzamna's words. None dared second his proposal, so drastic was the course he'd suggested. Yet none dared oppose him openly, lest his wrath be turned on them.

Unwittingly, Menzabac came to our aid. He is the god of fever and disease, a pimply fellow prone to moaning and groaning, not well respected in the Circle. He rarely had anything constructive to offer, but now, as if goosed from somnolent slumber by Itzamna's words, he leaped to his feet to second the chief's idea.

—A thoroughly excellent choice, Menzabac said. A plague would put the mortals in their place. A nice malaria I would suggest, just the thing to enliven the rainy season. Although yellow fever, with its bloody vomit, also has aesthetic appeal.

He looked about, in search of nods of affirmation. He was too puffed up with momentary self-importance to notice the looks of horror scooting like lizards across the Circle.

—Pneumonia is effective, too, he continued, and almost impossible for the mortals to contain. But if that's too common an approach, the exotic possibilities are limitless. A wonderful dysentery, with diarrhea covering the land like dew. Stomach worms add a nice homely touch. Jaundice would help mute their painted temples. Epilepsy — now there's a thought! A plague of epilepsy would be something different, and great fun to watch: see them falling with comic expressions from the steps of the offending edifice. But if that seems too frivolous a sight, there are always cancers and tumors in endless combinations with which to do the job. In short, the methodology is no problem, no problem at all. I heartily agree with the chief, and am prepared to take charge of the operation at once.

His right hand began to saw the air with disembodied obsequies, as if he were overcome by the huge responsibility about to be offered him. Then, as if suddenly aware that he was the focus of an embarrassed silence, he nodded curtly to the left and right and resumed his seat.

If Menzabac has grace — and I must assume that all gods have grace, that even Chac-Mool has grace — then his horrifying performance at that moment was the essence of a saving grace. A shudder like a running rat caressed the Circle. Most of us remembered the last time, how efficient he had been, but his present outburst had been so lugubrious, so disgusting, that not even the lowliest and newest of the assistants present, if they were allowed to vote, would have cast his marker to place the Mayas — and indirectly, the fate of us all — in the sweaty, boil-covered hands of such as him. They would sooner face the wrath of Itzamna. How to express our revulsion was a problem that hung in the air for a moment, until Ixchel, with her perfect tact, understood that not a word need be spoken, that all we had to do was ignore him.

—I suggest, she said, with her quiet dignity, with all due respect to Itzamna, that other punishments be considered beside those of plague and disease.

—I agree, said Ahcancum, the hunting god.

—Here, here! added Hobnil, god of the bees.

Once the subject had been broadened by dear Ixchel, plague and disease were never mentioned again.

I winked with appreciation at Ixchel, and my old love, now Itzamna's wife, smiled back. She could not know how grateful I was. The thought of Menzabac let loose indiscriminately on the mortals, the thought of what terrible plight might strike my Tika at his hands, was enough to turn my god blood into ice.

So the question remained before us: how to punish the mortals. Kaak, the fire god, suggested that a nice conflagration was in order. But others pointed out that, being spring, it had been raining on and off for weeks, that the jungle, the corn fields, even the thatched roofs of the huts, were thoroughly soaked, so that fire would be mostly smoke just now. Kaak resumed his place with his usual elan, persuaded by the argument. He's a methodical, businesslike god, almost, indeed, a prude. Not at all the wanton hellcat people think.

Kak Ne Xoc, the god of fishing, spoke next. He suggested that a decimation of the fish population in the surrounding seas would cut painfully into the mortal diet. It amused me to see how each god in turn desired to be the instrument of revenge, though most could not have cared a whit about the offending pyramid until Itzamna's speech. As for the fish notion, Itzamna muttered, almost below his breath, but loud enough to be heard: —a trifle! And that was the doom of that.

The next suggestion came from Cit Chac Coh (no relation), the god of war, and had a certain exhilarating logic, as do most arguments in favor of war. (It could also have unspeakable consequences, as most wars do.) Towering above the sacred table, his face painted bright, leaning on his lance as if it were no more than a farmer's hoe, Cit Chac Coh seemed likely to carry the Circle on the strength of his presentation, which he put forth with military directness.

—This false god, he began, this Kukulcan, was a warrior. He defended the mortals many times in battles with their enemies. For this reason they have tried to twist and pervert him into a god. For the Mayas to see clearly their error — and what else is punishment for? — it seems to me that deadly warfare is the logical approach. Let the Mayas be attacked by an overwhelming hostile force. Let them turn to this Kukulcan to preserve them. They will see soon enough what a powerless 'god' he is. The lesson will be swift and direct.

The approach had a certain appealing logic, there was no denying that.

—As it happens, he continued, the perfect instrument for this warfare is at hand. As we all know, these outlanders who call themselves Spaniards have been marauding closer and closer along the coast. A concerted attack by these troops, armed as they are with horses and dogs and cannons, would decorate the jungle with Maya entrails, would cover the limestone temples with Maya blood. With their dying breaths they will appeal to this Kukulcan. Let Kukulcan save them then!

Imposingly the war god sat. Applause burst forth from parts of the Circle, and from the galleries as well.

Itzamna looked about, to see who wanted to respond to Cit Chac Coh. When none requested the floor, he looked at me. I shrugged, and stood at my place.

—And then? I asked

They waited for my speech. I sat. Frowns were visible on many faces. Buzzing could be heard throughout the strata.

—What does he mean, and then?

Itzamna waited for silence. This time it was he who shrugged, and nodded to me again. With a great show of reluctance I stood once more, and scratched the side of my nose. This took some time.

—As you all know, I began, I am a great admirer of the illustrious god of war. (A small but necessary fib.) His brilliant talk just now was perfect logic, perfect sense. For that I join in the applause that greeted it. I paused.

They were clearly puzzled.

I scratched my nose again, this time only the very tip. It's a useful prop sometimes.

—I have no problem at all with mortal wars. Let them tear each other limb from limb if that's their pleasure — which it often is. It's no concern of Chac's. But I am speaking about village against village, tribe against tribe, Maya versus Mexican: the usual three-day skirmishes that take place every year when the harvesting is done. A few dead, a few captured as slaves, no big deal. Nice little limited wars. That, however, is not what we are discussing here. Such commonplace battles would not be seen by the Mayas as punishment. No, what the war god has proposed is a wholesale slaughter by the Spaniards. That would be effective punishment, no doubt. But of whom? We have seen the Spaniards operate down the coast. Those who they do not kill, they torture into submission. They force them to abandon us gods. They bend them to the worship of their one outlandish deity, which their priests have dragged across the seas like a stinking fish. Like a stone horse. What then? When the last conquered Maya has been forced to give up us gods, where will the Circle be? For one false god, this Kukulcan, we shall have lost a pantheon. Fraud will replace the circle — fraud in the name of yet another dead human, whom they are already being told was kin to Kukulcan, or Kukulcan to him. The savage cultists will have the victory. Will that be our revenge?

I paused. I realized I'd begun to shout. Like Itzamna, I was getting carried away. A drop of perspiration hung from the end of my nose. I wiped it away with my sleeve.

There was more I'd planned to say. I'd planned to confront the war god directly. I'd planned to ask him whether, once the Spaniards were unleashed, he had any way of controlling them, of limiting their total victory. Since these invaders did not believe in our war god, what power would he have over events? It's a sticky question, of the type that never has been answered definitively in the Circle. But from the deathly quiet around me I realized I need not proceed. I need not give the war god a chance to fuzz the issue with philosophical speculation. Already I'd turned the Circle into frost.

The god of war stood slowly at his place.

—I withdraw my suggestion, he said.

He's not really a bad god, deep down.

So we were back at the starting point, with no good suggestion on the table. Consternation circled the Circle like baffled butterflies.

—Economics! said a voice from one side. It was Ek Chuah, the merchant god, the god of cacao, rising to speak, stooped under the pack on his back.

—I could destroy the cacao crop. Throw their monetary system, their trade, into chaos. Cause consternation in the marketplace. Not to mention withholding their favorite drink.

Frowns and shrugs greeted him. No one was in the mood for economics. We rarely were.

—Just a thought, Ex Chuah said, and resumed his place.

Then, almost unnoticed, Ixtab stood, sylph-like, at her spot. She did not speak until little by little her black-draped figure was the focus of every eye. Her voice, though firm, was soft. Those in the galleries had to lean forward to hear. I was tense with strained emotions. I had neither seen her nor heard her voice since the day I found her on Chac-Mool's lap and hurled her from the mist.

—I am disturbed by what I have witnessed here, she began, direct, as usual. God after god has put forth remedies that would vindicate, would show off, his own powers. Such was not the purpose of this meeting. We are here to punish the mortals. We should stick to the point.

The goddess of suicide looked around the Circle, from one god to the next, with clear, cold eyes. Only once did I detect a flicker of softening: when her eyes met those of Kai Yum, the golden-locked god of music, a handsome, curly haired god only half her age. He was her new love, I'd heard.

—We must return to tradition, Ixtab said. Without tradition the Circle itself is nothing.

Again she met every eye that would meet hers.

—For thousands of bakuns there has been one punishment, one calamity, that the mortals have feared the most. It is time-honored in its implications. It is direct in its approach. It is easily containable, its consequences can be as drastic or as mild as we desire. I am speaking, of course — at this point her eyes met mine, smoldering, dark, fierce or fond, I couldn't really tell in the sunset glare — I am speaking of course — she repeated, as if she too had lost her thought for a moment — of drought. A cessation of rainfall — at once, right now, during the rainy season. It would be an occurrence so inexplicable that the mortals would have to associate it with their behavior. It would strike terror into their hearts, because they know the havoc it can cause, to their crops, to their thirst, to their very lives. They are all aware of the droughts of bakuns past. None wants to suffer another, not a prolonged dryness that threatens their existence. Drought, it seems to me, is the traditional favored weapon of the Circle. I agree with the mighty Itzamna that the offense of the mortals was grave. None is more qualified to supervise the punishment then the great god Chac.

She bowed her head humbly in my direction. I felt flattered by her words. I wondered if I'd been hasty in throwing her out. The undertones were not lost, either, on those in the Circle who were in the know. The rift between us was no secret. Ixtab's words were balm on a public wound.

—I hereby make a formal motion, she continued, that the Circle instruct the rain god Chac to begin a drought at once, and to continue it in dropless totality . . . Until in his wisdom he sees fit to call it off, I expected her to say. But that was not what she said.

—To continue it in dropless totality until the Circle in solemn conclave shall instruct him to end such drought.

A part of me was stricken by her words. The warm flush I had felt in her confidence in me, her suggestion of drought, was chilled by this lack of faith in my discretion. I thought of protesting, of reminding them that Chac and Chac alone is the arbiter of rain and drought, that Chac alone must decide when a drought should end. But I knew that would have sounded self-serving, as petty and narcissistic as the suggestions of the other gods we'd heard. This would not really be my drought in any case, I reasoned. The call for punishment had come from Itzamna. The vote for drought would come from the entire Circle. If the Circle began it, then the Circle, it seemed logical enough, should have the responsibility of ending it.

Such did I tell myself. I did not protest. I preserved my reputation for modesty.

Thus can the fate of gods and men alike depend on subordinate clauses.

Ixtab's speech was greeted with the graceful dignity it deserved. There were several seconding speeches. As the others spoke, my eyes roamed the Circle. I noticed Kai Yum, the god of music, gazing adoringly at Ixtab with the possessive pride of ludicrous first love. Suddenly I intuited what I had not realized before: that Ixtab's sitting on the lap of Chac-Mool had not been a matter of boredom, but was a ruse for me to discover, that already by then she was adored by the music god and was responding to his youthful and innocent ardor, that giving me reason to throw her from the mist was her way of leaving me. Anger flared in my chest. I'd been had for a fool.

But my anger cooled in a moment. I was obsessed with Tika, and Ixtab surely knew it. If she was by then entranced by the music god, our coupling had to end. She could have simply left; instead she gave me a way to save face, to be the wronged party. It could be argued that she acted out of kindness, that only Chac-Mool got used, and him only for a moment, a moment he would cherish till the end of days. In any case it didn't matter now. Ixtab had her golden-lyred god, I had Tika (more or less). No one had gotten hurt. (I didn't think just then of little Enik. In matters of love someone always gets hurt.)

The vote on the drought was approaching, and my thoughts were below with Tika, with how it might affect her. With an effort I refocused my attention — and caught a knowing glance passing between Ixtab and Itzamna. I realized then what I should have understood at once. I couldn't believe my obtuseness! The drought had been Itzamna's idea from the start!

A deadly plague, my nose. Itzamna is the very repository of the Circle's tradition. The speech from Ixtab's lips had been his creation! He'd suggested outrageous disease in order to be overruled, in order to create once more the illusion of democracy in the Circle. It was all a playlet we had witnessed, with Ixchel and Ixtab the leading players, and Itzamna the secret scribe. I'd overlooked a fundamental truth: there are always circles within Circles.

I marveled once more at his skill. Yet they had omitted me, the drought-maker, from their confidences. This I would have to ponder. This was a puzzlement.

As I plumbed the political thickets, the vote was taken: a drought to begin at sunrise, and to continue until such time as the Circle in its collective wisdom voted that it should end.

The tally was unanimous, with one abstention: Menzabac. He pretended to be asleep, but he was gazing wistfully, I think, at a fantasy of his own: at bloody vomit and running sores that got away.

12.

In 3,000 bakuns I had never had a dream, not me nor any god I know. But the night after the vote I had a dream. In the dream I was adrift in the mist. Pale ribbons of haze floated about in the shape of fuzzy circles, gentle ovals, S-shaped curves. Out of this evanescence a form appeared, a creature like an elderly man. He had a long nose and stringy gray hair and bore a certain resemblance to the outcast chilan of the mortals. It was

Time in disguise, I knew; or else it was Fate, got up in the garments of a man.

—I have come to show you the future, this apparition said.

His words put me on guard. Why bother me with the future? The future was no concern of mine.

He was up to no good, this prophet. I was about to turn from him, to hear no more, when with a wave of his arm the drifting mists parted, revealing against a dark blue sky a tableau of wondrous beauty. The scene was of a clearing in the jungle, a thick soft bed of the petals of jungle flowers. Most of them were orchid petals, pink and white. On all sides tall trees blocked out the world, except for dappled sunlight that fell like rain. In the center of the bed of petals were two figures, languid, intertwined. One of them was Tika, nude and resplendent, a white orchid firing her black hair. The other figure, naked as well, had the body of a quetzal bird — but it was me.

I gasped at the perfection of the scene. I watched in breathless joy as the two figures twined and glided in and among each other, limbs, feathers, lips, beaks, caresses interwoven in a sultry mingling. I became inflamed with the sight of their splendor, their harmony, their silent passion play. It was the stuff of dreams, this dream.

With a jolt, in my dream, I recalled what the prophet had said. My trembling lips could barely form the words.

—This is the future? I asked.

—Till the end of your days, the sly creature said.

I looked again at the lovers in the clearing. They still were lost to the world in their languid games. Agitation and frantic eagerness whirled like a waterfall in my chest.

—When? I cried out. When will this future begin?

The old creature smiled like a friend.

—At the break of dawn, he replied. If you choose.

—Done! I exclaimed. At the break of dawn!

The prophet smiled again.

—To last till the end of your days.

—Till the end of my days, I repeated, joy beating like a bird trapped in my chest. And noticed a certain crookedness to his grin, an evil twist that gave me pause.

—A figure of speech of course, I said. Me being a god, my days shall have no end.

At first he did not respond. He seemed to be watching his own nose growing longer in the mist. Then he said, It is no figure of speech.

I looked at the clearing, afraid the lovers would be gone. They were still at their lovers' games, fragrant and delicate. I didn't understand. I told him so.

—Come, come, the prophet said. You know the rules. A god and a mortal cannot mate.

—I know, I shrieked. I know it cannot be! So why do you torment me with this gentle scene? With this false prophecy?

The prophet touched my sleeve, a friend again.

—The future lies there before you, on a bed of orchid scent, he said. I've come to give you a chance.

—A chance? My heart was flapping as if it would fly from my chest.

—A chance. The future is there as you see it. All you have to do is become mortal.

—All I have to do . . . My voice broke off, my throat was dry as sand.

—Relinquish your godhood, he said. Then you can truly love your mortal Tika. Fulfill your passion. His eyes flashed like bits of sun off the sea. Make love till the end of your days.

I covered my eyes with my hands, to hide the scene in the clearing. My chest now howled like a storm.

—Beast, I muttered softly. Vile, foul, deceitful creature! To offer such a deal!

—Don't be angry, Time or Fate in their disguise said. It's nothing lost if you decline.

Through my fingers I peeked at the clearing. Tika was beneath me, my quetzal feathers were gone, I was in human form, perspiring with passion.

—Nothing lost! I wailed into the mist. Nothing lost! he says.

The prophet drifted silent at my side. I stared near the flowered bed. The petals themselves seemed to shimmer with ecstasy. My voice was shaky as I spoke.

—How many?

The creature merely shrugged.

—How many? I demanded again. I grabbed him by the cloth at his shoulders. How many days? How many days would there be until the end of my days?

He grinned. His teeth were rotting, but maybe that was mere illusion.

—How many? he echoed. How many days? A thousand perhaps. Ten thousand, perhaps. A week, perhaps. He shrugged again. One day, perhaps. Or one hour. You will be a mortal like any other. Who is to say?

—There will be no assurance? No minimum?

He gazed at me with disdain.

—Mortals get no guarantees.

I looked away from him. In the fragrant clearing the lovers in their final ecstasy were quivering, a drawn bow, an arrow poised for flight.

—How soon? I blurted. How soon must I decide?

Mocking me, he plucked a whisker from his beard.

—You have until the break of dawn.

—You will wait for my answer?

—I will be nearby.

I looked at the night sky. Dotted through the dark, the stars were ticking. Ticking off the passage of time. When I looked down again this insinuating prophet was gone. But not the gentle lovers, now asleep, her head on his chest. How can I describe the hours that followed? I cannot. Half a second. Ten thousand years. Torment carved a stela in my chest, my gut. Gray hairs whitening like a badge. Or a betrayal. A simple choice that stabbed me like a sharpened stone. While high above, the bright stars ticked.

I was sheeted with cold sweat. Boiled in warm.

And then dawn broke, like a mango thrown by a child.

Chac still reigned, the rain god of the Mayas.

The lovers were gone, and the clearing, too.

I never made a choice. I merely let time run out.

A dream, it was, my very first dream. I tremble at the memory. I pray that I shall never have another.

That is my one consolation: it was only a dream. No such tormenting choice was ever offered.

—Gods don't dream, Itzamna says.

And so, a drought. Ordered by the Circle, for as long as the Circle deemed it should last. I summoned my frogs. Jag and Ahau had attended the meeting; to Ben and Cib it was news.

—But how can we have a drought? Cib asked. It's the middle of the rainy season.

—Fine drought you would create, Ben replied. Just in the dry months.

Ahau and Jag seemed not to be paying attention. Ahau and Jag, frog and turtle, were in love. And coping quite nicely, it seemed. How they were doing so I could not imagine. I had too much pride to ask.

—It starts today, I told them.

Heavy rains were scheduled for that afternoon, just as they had been poured down every afternoon for the past three weeks, just as they were scheduled every day for the next two months — rain the mortals depended on to fatten their corn, to fill their wells, to feed the jungle and the myriad useful plants and animals he harbored in his chest. There would be no more rain for some time, I suspected. Itzamna and the Circle were serious.

—How do we do it? Jag asked. In love or not she was always alert.

—We don't do anything, Cib said, a trifle condescending. That's the point.

—We go on holiday, Ahau said.

I think he winked at her. Ben and Cib must have seen it, too. They glared, not at her but at him. Winks between lovers can break lonely hearts.

Tension was building in the house of Chac. Perhaps the drought had come at a useful time. Let them go their separate ways. Though where they went on holiday I had no idea. I don't like to pry.

—It may be a long one, I said. The Circle will decide. This they already had heard.

—That's all. You can leave whenever you like.

It didn't matter where they went, how far they went; they would be back faster than lightning could flash, pouring their gourds, the instant I gave the command.

But instead of rushing off, they stood about, uncomfortable. I wasn't sure what was wrong, in the old days they'd have been scampering away with glee, Ahau in the lead, Ben and Cib hurrying after, little Enik , dragging his lame leg, following in the rear, noisy in their unexpected freedom, like children let loose to play. But now, embarrassed, none would be the first to leave. Cib looked at Ben, who stood stubbornly in place. Jag and Ahau kept their eyes toward the ground. It was a new configuration.

Ahau's cheeks began to puff.

—Ah, the hell with it, he said. He reached out and took Jag's hand, and without another word he led her out of the mist. Cib stood glaring at Ben. Then those two left, sullenly, in the opposite direction. I refused to trouble myself with frogly rifts. Let them work it out themselves when they returned. Assistants are there to serve you, nothing more. You can't get personally involved. Yet their leave-taking left me unaccountably sad, until I realized why. Caught up in their own emotional business, not one of them had bothered to say goodbye.

No sooner had I realized this when the blushing faces of Jag and Ahau — frogs and turtles blush yellow — peered in at me through the mist. Jag waved happily.

—See you soon, Papa Chac, she said. Ahau winked at me, broadly this time.

—Love to Tika, he said.

Then they were gone.

I bowed to the vacant air.

—Love to Tika.

Rueful, I suppose I felt at the words, but I knew he had meant them well. Their goodbyes, his and Jag's, restored my spirits. I hadn't yet considered what I myself would do during the drought — it had come up so unexpectedly. But I imagined I would find some diversion. Love to Tika, indeed.

It would be nice to have the mist all to myself for a while, I thought. Then, in the gray gloom, I saw my half-brother, risen from his slumber, slouching in my direction. His paws were raised above him, as if he would beat his breast like a giant ape. But all he managed to do was claw his chest.

—Drou . . . he said. Drou . . .

It was the only word, or partial word, he knew.

He repeated it several times, seeming pleased. He grinned his stupid grin.

The ceremonies surrounding the dedication of the new temple lasted for days. Which is to say that drunken mortals sprawled motionless on the ground or were propped against huts, walls and sacred stones in colorful disarray, others guzzling drink near the vaunted tabernacle in a frenzied effort to join them.

Like most days during the rainy season, the morning after the meeting of the Circle had broken blue and washed with sun. Around noon clouds would gather over the distant highlands, it was assumed, and by mid-afternoon the sky would be almost black, the clouds would open (actually, my gourds, of course), and heavy rains would drive the people indoors, rousing even the deadest of the drunks, ripping petals from jungle flowers, drumming marching tunes on thatched roofs. But this day it didn't happen. The sky over the highlands remained clear. The afternoon darkness did not crawl in like a snake. The afternoon rains didn't come. To most of the villagers this was a welcome respite from the preceding weeks of rain, a happy break before the months of rain to come. It was welcome to all, it appeared, except to the outcast chilan, who stood near his stela at the side of the main road, looking first to the Temple of Kukulcan, then to the clear skies above, and wailing in a terrible voice, to anyone who passed nearby.

—Beware the wrath of the gods!

It was his typical doomsday manner, of which the village had long since stopped taking note, except for the children, who gathered nearby to laugh.

When the next day also remained clear, the chilan repeated his litany. One who heard him in passing was the Spaniard, who was curious about everything.

—Why do you say this, old man? he asked.

—You're new here, the chilan replied from within his matted hair. He seemed not at all surprised to be addressed.

—You do not know. The others should know, but they wish to be blind. A terrible drought is upon us. It is the wrath of the gods.

—But there's only been two clear days, the Spaniard said.

—It is the season of rain, the chilan replied.

Not knowing what else to say, the Spaniard nodded uncertainly and continued on his way, toward the hut

at the edge of the jungle, where Tika had his supper
waiting. Understandably, he had missed the subtlety
that struck me immediately: that the chilan was blaming
the wrath of the gods, and not, as would be expected,
the wrath of Chac. Sometimes it seemed as if he had his
own secret source within the Circle.

When the dry spell, as the mortals began calling
it, entered its second week, panic had not yet set in.
The wells still were full, the jungle was heavy with fruit
and plump with game, the earth between the rows of
corn and beans, of squash and pumpkins, was only
beginning to show faint signs of drying. A good rain
within the next few days and nothing would be lost.
There was occasional talk among the lower men as they
weeded the drying fields that Chac must be upset about
something, but this was not the official version. The
learned nobles, making their nightly calculations from
the round observatory, concluded that the planet Venus
was in a rare state of retrograde, a circumstance that
may have distracted Chac from his normal routine. The
rains would resume within the next three days, they
predicted, and all would be well. (The mortals always
placed great importance on this Venus, charting her
comings and goings with pompous precision. In truth,
she's just a bit of celestial fluff, no more significant
than an orchid in heat.) When, three days later, Venus
was back in step with the rest of the sky, and still the
rains didn't come, the noble astronomers asserted
that while their calculations were indubitably correct,
such retrogrades can sometimes trail a longer wake
than expected. The farmers in the fields listened to
the learned astronomers, nodded sagely, looked at the
cracks beginning to appear in the earth, and began
singing songs and offering prayers to Chac.

I wasn't moved. Prayers are only talk, and just as
cheap.

—In any case, it was out of your hands, Itzamna says, drily.

While the nobles fulminated and the lower men prayed and the chilan wailed his warnings like an old dog baying at the moon, more fateful events were taking place in the chambers of the Lord Maya, who was nobody's fool. He didn't need a buzzard to shit on his hat to recognize the start of a drought. This he explained, with more or less elegance, to the nacom and the High Priest, both of whom were seated at his feet. These two worthies were quick to agree; few mortals ever disagreed with the Lord about anything — certainly not to his slope-headed, tattooed, ear-ringed, nose-ringed face.

—It appears that a drought is upon us, the Lord Maya said. It appears that Chac is offended. We shall take the usual steps to appease him: prayers, dances, offerings. Presumably these will suffice to regain his favor. But if not, we must prepare other steps.

The priest and the nacom nodded with understanding.

—We are low on slaves, the Lord Maya continued. Many lost their lives during the building of the Temple of Kukulcan. But it would be unfortunate to sacrifice villagers if slaves could be offered instead. Therefore, while the High Priest begins the prayers, the nacom shall gather a force of lower men and strike across the jungle at our friends to the west. Aided by the weapon of surprise, he shall bring back enough slaves to satisfy Chac, should blood be Chac's desire.

I didn't listen to the rest. I was too perturbed. You live with people for three thousand years, you'd think they'd know what you like.

Blood. When had I ever asked them for blood?

When had I ever asked them for anything?

I turned my back and left them, the three wise men of the village in their silly hats, planning their stupid war.

The hairs around me are thick and wiry, short, curled, shining, bending back upon themselves, a black-brambled self-containing brush, a nest, guarding, beckoning: a dense yet penetrable jungle in miniature. The lips around me are reddening pink, moistening pink, parting, widening, opening, calling, calling with a pulsing private voice, asking, beseeching, tingling like a pure silent bell in the night, calling, calling . . . the fire-hot blood-red water-cold water-black jungle-sound of gem-laden orchid skins. The utmost private part of Tika. While deep in the center the center awaits, circles within circles, hidden white berry seed of Tika.

I am. . .

Thou art. . .

I am. . .

I was fantasizing again.

I suppose you guessed.

13.

Shimmering with dry heat, the village burned as well with a high fever. The prospect of a war, especially an aggressive attack against a weaker enemy, always makes mortal blood tingle. The nacom had laid in a full supply of spears, clubs, lances, bows, arrows, slings, and flint knives for close encounters. The most fit of the lower men were being conscripted for the expeditionary force. A short battle was envisioned: a sudden strike at the target village, a roundup of prisoners to be brought back as slaves and sacrifices, a quick retreat. The difference between this and other Maya battles would be the timing. Wars usually were held in the autumn, after the corn was harvested, when the farmers had time to fight. A reasonable arrangement. But with the drought in its fourth week — it was acknowledged by all now to be a drought — and the corn beginning to wilt in the fields like babies flaccid before their time, the need for a successful raid was on nearly everyone's lips. Little bloodshed was anticipated, since the purpose of the raid was slaves, not slaughter. As always in Maya battles, the fighting would cease when the nacom on one side or the other was captured or killed. At that moment the soldiers, being farmers at heart, would drop their spears, shift their hardened vests from front to back, and disappear into the jungle, emerging eventually where they'd begun, to plant another crop, alive to fight another day. It was a nice arrangement, except perhaps for the nacom. But that was his job; more than that, it was his purpose in life. It is no small thing to have a purpose in life.

The Spaniard, of course, would be among those going off to fight. Tall, strong, experienced, he was one of the first ones chosen by the nacom. Tika knew it would be so, and offered no objection; no woman could. Her demeanor did not change. She continued her daily routine, tending as best she could the browning field behind the hut, cooking with less water than usual, bathing less often, weaving mats and kubs to trade in the marketplace, sleeping securely beside her man. I noticed only one small change. Since the coming of the Spaniard she had seemed less overtly tender to the slave girl Tel, who now slept in the cooking half of the two-room hut, or outside on certain nights. But with the battle due to begin any day, Tika seemed to move closer to Tel again, to oversee her actions, to confide however obliquely her inner feelings, to reestablish in her quiet way a sisterly affection for the rapidly maturing girl. Without realizing it, it seemed to me, Tika was preparing herself for widowhood. As if she perceived her own role in life to be the successive loss of her men.

The night before the force was to depart, Tika and the Spaniard made love. It was quiet and strong and almost orderly, but all through the gentle passion tears fell from Tika's eyes. And when, in the morning gray, the entire village lined up to watch and cheer the panoply of men departing, Tika stayed behind in the hut, far from the noise of the drums, rolling tortillas for Ixtel's lunch.

The spectacle of the warriors going off to fight was impressive, particularly the costume of the nacom. Towering over his shield and breastplates was his enormous wooden hat, half again as tall as he, festooned with feathers of the quetzal and the parrot that snaked down over his shoulders. His face was painted in the brightest of hues, and he was hung with bracelets and necklaces of jade that glinted in the sun. Standing at the head of the column of men, ready to lead them into battle, he looked like some magnificent beast the gods had neglected to invent. I think that's when mortals most get themselves into trouble: when they try to rectify the oversights of gods.

The lower men were more soberly attired. Their faces were painted, but the rest was merely dull brown shields and breechclouts, and woven vests that had been toughened to armor by being soaked in brine. In every hand, of course, were weapons of war. If the strategy were mine, I'd have dressed the nacom that way, too. Why plume him out like a peacock, crying out to be captured or killed, the most visible target in the fray? Why not force the enemy to search for him among the others? Curious, I inquired about this of Cit Chac Coh, the god of war.

—It's a matter of honor, he said. Of spirit. Of bravery. Of manly self-importance. That's what wars are about. Surely you don't think they truly fight for slaves, or land, or goods.

I didn't reply. That's really what I thought they were fighting for.

On later reflection, I think I was right after all. The war god had to cloak his battlefields in the bright plumes of glory to justify his own insouciance. But it wasn't honor they were fighting for, not really. The tunes and plumes of glory were deceptions, scarecrows, to frighten away their fear of death. Any mortal will gladly die for honor, village, glory. Few would leap open-eyed into the pit in praise of economics.

The jungle beasts don't deceive themselves that way. That's why they die more content.

Vibrant in his plumage, the nacom stood tall and proud at the head of his men. Behind him in a double column stood the raiding party of forty warriors, the Spaniard among them, his wavy blonde hair visible, almost like the nacom's feathers, above the dark heads of the others. Arrayed around and behind the fighters were the musicians, beating drums of animal skin and blasting conch-shell trumpets, to send the men off in triumph, to honor the god of war. (As you might guess, he actually liked that stuff.) Behind the musicians stood the other villagers, men, women and children, shouting their encouragement as on command the nacom led his men from the village, down the long broad road to the west.

The tribe they'd be raiding was an old adversary, which they fought almost every year. It was a full day's march away. As usual they'd spend half the day making good time on the open road; then, when the sun grew hotter, they'd veer off into the jungle and hack their way through the shade, in the hope of gaining the advantage of surprise. (Since it was always done this way, it rarely was a surprise.) Nearing the enemy village at dusk, the nacom bedded his men in the jungle, to sleep before the dawn attack.

While the warriors rested, I stooped to something far below the dignity of Chac. I spied on my friends. I sought out the whereabouts of Ahau and Jag, to see what they were up to on holiday.

I'm ashamed of my motivation, but there it was. I hoped to discover if they were making love. Because if turtle and frog could do it, perhaps there was a way for mortal and god.

I spotted them at the edge of the sea, deep in a rocky cove, where tongues of white water licked at protruding stones. (All the world is sex when you're obsessed.) Jag was edging slowly toward the sea while Ahau remained behind, snuggled in a watery cave. The sea licked and retreated, licked and retreated, carrying away plumes of sand, hurling up shells of creatures alive or dead, the broken homes of creatures in her path. Like the jungle, the sea, too, could have been a god to the mortals, so central was she to their life — the fish she provided, the essential salt, the transport she offered on her back. But like the jungle she was palpable, visible, easily touched, often mastered. And so like him they never exalted her. (Of the sea I wasn't jealous, the sea had no designs on Tika.) At first I didn't understand why Jag walked alone while Ahau stayed behind. But soon I understood. It was her first visit home since she'd become ambassador to my court.

It was twilight gray in the cove, the stateliest time of day. The giant turtles were below the surface, partaking of their evening meal. Jag sat patiently on the shore, her cute shell glistening, not wishing to disturb them, awaiting their return. When one by one they broke the surface and lumbered onto the beach, their reunions with Jag were warm or proper, depending on how well they knew her. In time there were a hundred giant turtles on the beach, welcoming their ambassador, listening to what I assumed were her favorable reports of life at the court of Chac. In the deep purple dusk they were an image of dignity. I wondered again if I had made a mistake in turning them down.

In time, Jag and two of the other turtles moved off to one side. From the warmth with which they conversed it was clear they were parents to her. I did not pay attention to their chatter until a catch in Jag's tone caught my ear.

—I've brought a friend I'd like you to meet, she said.

—Oh? her mother said.

—Well, where is she? her father asked.

—He, not she, the mother said.

—What do you mean, he? the father said. Do you know him?

—Close your mouth and look at your daughter, the wise mother said.

Jag was blushing pale yellow and staring at the sand. I think she knew there was worse to come.

—He's waiting by the rocks, she said.

—Well, go on and bring him over, the mother said. That's no way to treat your friend. Your boyfriend especially.

—Boyfriend? the father said. Oh, boyfriend! Yes, of course. Don't leave a boyfriend in the rocks. Where did you meet him, anyway? I thought you were the only turtle in the mist.

Jag's blush burned warm and paler still, like a yellow flame. I had the feeling she wanted to flee just then — as fast as giant turtles could flee — be anywhere but home. But her voice was firm when she spoke.

—He's not a turtle, father. He's a frog.

She kept her eyes cast down, as if waiting for an earthquake to rock the beach. But there was no explosion. Giant turtles are far too dignified for that. What happened was more like a disintegration of personality, strength ebbing away like the beach itself in the outgoing tide.

—A frog? the mother said, in a small turtle voice.

—What do you mean, a frog? the father said.

—A frog, a frog! Jag said, irritated. He's not just any frog. His name is Ahau. He's one of Chac's assistants. He's the smartest and wisest and nicest of them. But he's a frog nevertheless.

I could see her lower jaw quivering as she hurled defiance at them.

—A frog, the father repeated. His voice was defeated and angry at once. We send her off to commune with the gods, and she comes home with a frog.

The beach was dark now, peppered with the flashes of fireflies. The turtle voices flared and died as quickly as the lights.

—I think I'll be going now, Jag said.

—Going? the mother asked. You only just arrived.

—Look, the father said. Go bring your frog out from the rocks. Lets have a look at this wonderful boyfriend of yours.

—Sure, the mother said. Bring him over. Make him welcome. We won't bite his head off. We understand the phase you're going through.

—Good-bye, Jag said, and she turned to leave.

—Jag, the father said. Don't go.

She stopped and looked back at them. The moon had risen, a long, wavy reptilian stripe on the sea. By its light I could see the glint of her small, raging eyes. Then she was gone, out of the path of the moon, toward the dark of the rocks. No doubt she found Ahau, told him what had transpired, returned with him to wherever they had been. I didn't have the heart to follow.

Their happiness, I was sure, would survive. As for my quest — to discover if they made love together, and how — I never pursued it again. It was their own private business.

For my curiosity I had been amply punished. I'd lost the last of my illusions about the dignity and grace of the turtles. Their bigotry had been sad to behold. They were as flawed a race as the over-prideful jaguars, as the silken deer who flee from the slightest intimacy, as the soaring ravens who stupidly act superior because they feast on the flesh of mortals. I had believed the turtles were different. Live for 3,000 years and every last illusion gets shattered.

I returned my attention to the scene of the impending battle — the warriors asleep in the jungle (while nervous monkeys peered down from the trees), lookouts posted on all sides, the nacom, too excited to sleep, idly fingering the point of his new invention: a traditional wooden lance to which he had affixed a deadly point of flint. For centuries the mortals had fought with wooden lances carved from trees, tapered to sturdy points. Such lances had served them well, doing sufficient damage to many an enemy caught by the point in the eye, face, neck, groin or any other sensitive spot. If the point caught their hardened cloth armor, however, or their limbs, the lance tended to glance away, or the point to break off, not doing much harm and rendering the lance itself useless. Pondering this problem some moons before, the nacom experienced one of those moments of temporary insanity the mortals call inspiration. Comparing the wooden lances with the sharp flint knives his warriors carried for close combat, he reasoned: why not affix one to the other? After experimenting by tying actual knives to existing lances with hemp, he soon developed a lance with a point of flint. Testing the weapon on animals in the jungle, he discovered that even a glancing blow with the flint-tipped lance could create such enormous bloodletting as to render the victim useless for further combat, and in some cases could even cause death. Amid great secrecy he demonstrated the new weapon to the leading nobles, to the High Priest, eventually to the Lord Maya himself. All were impressed by the potency of the weapon, but a bitter debate ensued about whether such a deadly instrument should actually be produced in quantity, should actually be used in warfare against other humans. To the nacom and his supporters there was no question that it should; it could mean certain victory over an enemy armed only with wooden lances. Others argued, however, that the weapon would be counter-productive; it would produce much more killing, they agreed, but since the main object of combat was not to kill the adversaries but to capture them to use as slaves, it would be self-defeating. In addition, they pointed out, once the weapon was used it would quickly be copied; before long every village would stockpile flint-tipped lances; the end result in future wars would be an escalation in blood and death, a consequent diminution of available slaves, but no real advantage to either side. The Lord Maya let the debate rage hotly, but ultimately came down on the side of the nacom. The nacom was responsible for the defense of the village, he ruled. The nacom would have his way. (Nacoms usually do.)

The plan for this battle was for the warriors to capture as many men and woman as they could before any defense was mobilized, and quickly retreat through the jungle with their prize. With any luck the nacom's new weapon would not be used at all; there would be little actual combat. But that's not how things transpired.

As I've indicated, a midsummer attack, in the midst of the growing season, was unheard of; that was the key to the nacom's plan. But the drought was causing distress through all of Mayadom. If it lasted much longer, slaves for sacrifice would be as scarce as quetzals in the sea. Such was the reasoning of the nacom of the target village, and to guard against surprise attack he had for several days posted lookouts in every direction. The lookouts had sent back word of the approaching force. So it was that when the warriors of Tika's village crept from the jungle at dawn, they found themselves trapped in ambush. Spears, arrows and lances flew in every direction. Part of the attacking force broke through and entered the village; the rest was trapped in a jungle battle that lasted most of the day.

Of the details of the brief war, of the running and creeping of all these smear-faced mortals, I can give no more accurate account than I could of a covey of herons taking flight from a beach. Suffice it to say only this: men died that day with arrows in their eyes; men died from spears that carried off their groins; men died from flint knives plunged into their necks, or slashed through their throats. Men bled to death through holes in their bellies ripped by the nacom's flint-tipped lances, or died from the shock of seeing their arms or legs carried away by the same efficient weapon. They died shouting defiance, or screaming in pain, or gurgling blood with rattling in their throats to the tune of Ahpuch's bells, or silently, face down in the jungle earth. I thought: there are so many terrible ways in which mortals can die, it's a wonder they do not die from that knowledge alone. Perhaps some of them do.

The battle surged in and around the village and the moisture-starved jungle for much of the day. Despite the ambush, by late afternoon the warriors from Tika's village seemed to be gaining the advantage. A small band had gathered together a number of captives, and was preparing to depart with them. But suddenly the most feared cry of the mortals rang through the air and echoed off the nearby temples:

—The nacom is slain! Flee, the nacom is dead!

It was true. The green and gold quetzal and parrot headdress of the nacom of Tika's village hung askew from a soapberry bush. Below it on the bloody earth sprawled the lifeless body of the nacom, half his painted face, half his skull, torn away by the force of a flint-tipped lance, one of his own weapons hurled back at him. Poetic justice, I suppose you could say, though his torn body did not look like poetry.

As news of the nacom's death rang through the battle, the warriors of Tika's village did as expected: they dropped their weapons and began to retreat. It was the only way they knew how to fight a war. How else, indeed, would a battle ever end? The one exception was the Spaniard. Though he knew of the tradition, he'd been trained quite differently, and now, in the clamor of battle, his soldier's instincts gained sway.

—Don't run! Bring home the slaves! he shouted, running hither and thither among the men. But they scarcely heard him; they didn't care to listen; they continued to fade into the jungle. Till the Spaniard, seeing the dead nacom's headdress hanging from the bush, ran to it, yanked it free, held it aloft. He dared not put it on his head — that would be sacrilege — but he ran to and fro among the remnants of the battle with the headdress held high in the air, shouting encouragement, particularly to those with the captives. The green and gold feathers, waving above the battle like a flag, caused enough confusion about whether the nacom was really dead to slow the retreat. The captives were herded toward home by warriors thinking the nacom was still alive. Seeing this accomplished the Spaniard gave up the day, dropped the nacom's hat, ran like the others into the brush. The local warriors, after token pursuit, returned to their women and children, to their wounded and their dead. The warriors of Tika's village — the roughly half who were still alive — straggled through the jungle toward home in ones and twos, a small group leading four bound prisoners in tow. Leaving scores on the ground, bleeding or lifeless.

Such were the first mortal deaths caused by the drought.

But not the last.

14.

The Mayas were sore obsessed with time. With their stone calendars — they had three different kinds, which intersected with precision — they could calculate ninety million years into the past and many bakuns — those are each 59 years to you— into the future. They built their temples and their observatory in accord with the stars, the better to watch the ticking. They understood the broad sweep of the galaxy, with all its conflicting waves, its fierce field of force. What they never seemed to grasp, however — it is a difficult concept even for me — is that all time is simultaneous, that everything happens at once. It is not a straight road that that points like an arrow to the future. Time (if he will excuse the metaphor) operates rather like the belly of a snake, coiling and looping back upon itself, and it works the same way. Forward motion is an illusion; its digestive power is the one reality.

So here is Tika, weaving in her hut, Tel by her side, awaiting the news she is certain will come — news of the Spaniard's death in battle. There is the Spaniard, at the very same moment, tired but unscathed, hacking his way home through the jungle. Two separate realities, simultaneous. That much the mortals understood. But consider: here is Tika, waiting for the news, more mature than before, her face leaner, the beginnings of dark hollows under her eyes, the cares of life and death beginning to cast their shadows on her face, however faint. And here is a child of seven, talking of immortality, offering her little hand to Kel to cut, to mingle their blood before the gods. And here is Tika taking her bath, rubbing herself with my rain. Wearing a mask, grinding under the weight of sweating men. Holding a mango, playing with a monkey. Eating butterflies. All at once, all of it circling in the coils of time.

I know. If all the past is simultaneous, the future must be, too. What did I see there, you want to know. Especially after your year 2012, when our current cycle ends and a new one begins, much like your millennium. Alas, I could not see it back then. The future has already happened, it is happening even now, yet it remains invisible, curled up inside us, poised, precipitate, but not yet ready to be unrolled. A fleeting image we are allowed sometimes, but mostly not. Only Time himself can see the future, and Fate. When they are not too busy fucking.

So there is Tika in her hut, grimly rolling tortillas, flecks of ground corn dropping to the earthen floor. And there is her man, emerging from the jungle, smeared with paint and crushed berries, bits of earth and leaves clinging to his sweat. Tired, he approaches the hut, stands in the glare of the entryway, Tika turning at the sudden graying of the room, seeing only a dark apparition. HIs ghost? A messenger of death? Her eyes adjust, the shadows fall from her face, she drops the tortilla she is rolling, wipes her hands on her kub, rushes to him as she used to run on the beach, hurls herself into his arms. Together they stand, cling, silent, motionless. A resurrection. I didn't know why she believed he was dead.

That night she explained. The Spaniard had bathed, they had eaten, had stretched out on their mats together, Tika's face on his chest. Outside, the last bit of orange was fading from Itzamna's sky.

—I had a terrible dream, she said. In the dream I was talking to the chilan. He was sitting on his broken stela. He reached out with his withered hand, he touched my hair, as if I were a child and he was comforting me. Then he said, You will not lie with the Spaniard again.

When she did not continue, the Spaniard asked, Why would he say that?

—I don't know. That's what I kept asking myself when I awakened. There was only one answer I could think of: that you would be killed in battle.

—But here I am. It was only a bad dream.

She shuddered, he could feel it when she spoke again into his chest.

—The chilan knows things, she said.

—He does, the Spaniard said. But this wasn't the chilan speaking. This was a dream. This was your fear speaking.

—I suppose, she murmured. But she did not sound convinced.

For a long time they breathed softly in silence. Gently Tika's mood turned to love. But when she stirred against him she discovered that, weary from the battle and the long march home, he had fallen asleep. Quietly she left her mat and went outside and sat on the dry earth. She began to stare at a single white star that gazed back at her like a lonely eye, a star whose ticking she imagined she could decipher.

I couldn't tell if the distant star was within or without the net. Time has a net, like a fisherman's, in which the world hangs as in a great, loose sack. The net gives shape to the world without excluding light. Beyond the net is space without time. The interstices in the net are wide, it is possible for mortals to drift away through an opening, to become infinitesimal moons, never to return inside. These are the ones they refer to as lunatics.

Though Time's net is invisible, most mortals wear it heavily, like fishermen just home from the sea, thick hemp nets dragging with flotsam and kelp draped around their necks and shoulders, hanging in thick strands to the earth, hiding their bodies, revealing only their worn faces, their phlegmy eyes. We gods, being immortal, do not bear the burden of Time's net. And yet, so large is our conceit, we cannot slip out through the interstices. We are denied the freedom of insanity.

I think now I understand their dreaming. In dreams the mortals briefly slip through the net. That's why logic loses shape. The act of waking catches them back, like a fish. And makes them wriggle.

A pristine day of azure sky that matched precisely the water lapping the beach. One of Itzamna's artsy effects. Not even the faintest swirl of cloud textured his blue silk reaches. The parched mortals cursed mightily, then lowered their voices lest we gods take offense. Their frustration with the drought had metamorphosed into anger, intensified by the casualties of war. Soon I knew it would turn to fear, even as the corn turned to rope, the squash to turds, the avocados to dried gonads, the jungle himself to a useless burial ground. They had tried many dances. Pageants to Chac on the Platform of the Skulls. Music and masked mimes. Drums and conch trumpets pouring forth a pregnant howl for rain. Every instruction that had been passed on by teacher priests from one generation to the next. Unlike us gods, the Mayas were perfectionists. The wrong word would spoil a prayer, they thought, a misstep by a dancer, the slip of a single foot, and it wouldn't rain. Drummers in the past had been stoned to death for missing a beat. A curious intensity, if misguided. I never cared much for dancing, I couldn't tell one tune from the next.

Soon, if it did not rain, they would panic. They would throw those slaves they'd captured into the well.

But first, the day after the battle, they had other business. This did not become clear until late afternoon, when the Spaniard returned to the hut. Tika, still delighted, amazed that he was still alive, ran out to greet him on the path, as if somehow her life had begun anew, as if the carefree laughing girl would return. I was happy to see her that way, even though it was the Spaniard's arms to which she ran.

It lasted ten steps, this freshet, this mental spring, and then, seeing something dark in his eyes, she stopped. She waited until he approached her. He kissed her cheek — a formal greeting, he should have gathered her into his arms — and he led her soberly into the hut. I studied him as they sat cross-legged on their mats. In his eyes along with love was a desperate hurt. I'd heard him tell Tika tales from his native land of men and women burned alive for their beliefs; such mortals, I thought, as the fires were lighted that would consume them, must have appeared much like he did now. Tika saw it too, and blanched.

—What has happened? she asked.

Her question drew the Spaniard from an inner crevice, like a spider from a gourd. He rose slowly and paced the hut, as he must have paced the decks of ships on his voyages across the sea. He seemed weary as one sickened by the sea, though I doubt in truth that he was one of those. He seemed to be reaching out to choose his words one by one, as if he were picking fruit and setting aside the rotten ones. When he had plucked enough he sat on the mat again, and spoke.

—I was summoned from the fields today by a priestly guard. He escorted me into the presence of the High Priest, who in turn led me to the Lord Maya himself, and left me there. Alone with him.

I watched Tika's face. Her shaking had calmed. He'd been to the Lord Maya many times, to tell his foreign tales. The Lord Maya liked him, would cause him no harm.

—The high Lord studied me for a long time. When finally he spoke, he insulted me. Your people continue to maraud along the coast, he said. If your people attacked this village, on which side would you fight? My face burned at the question. I think it glowed red as fire. How could he ask me such a thing? Had it been anyone else I might have cut his throat. But it was the Lord Maya. I clenched my fists and took deep breaths.

—My people do not maraud along the coasts, I said. My people live here, in the village. The Lord looked at me without humanity, as he can. He spoke almost the same question again. If the Spaniards attacked the village, on which side would I fight? Again my eyes grew fierce. I struggled not to shout at him. I thought to say: I work in the fields. My woman is here. My home is here. But he knows all that. Instead I spoke the same four words I had spoken the day he set me free.

—I am Maya now.

—The Lord considered my words. He squinted beneath his high hat, as if he were taking my measure, his long lips pressed together in his crocodile way. Finally he resumed his throne, and motioned to me to sit at his feet.

All this time I was watching Tika. I expected her to smile. At the Lord Maya's feet! Surely there was no danger there. But she did not. She had guessed more than I had. She seemed to crunch her teeth, folded her fingers together as the Spaniard continued.

—The Lord Maya's face was friendlier when he spoke again. We know of your actions in the battle yesterday, he said. Raising the nacom's hat. It was very unorthodox. A questionable example at best. He seemed to be criticizing. I was very confused.

—On the other hand, he said, we now have four slaves to give to Chac. Slaves we would not otherwise have had. But that is a trifle, he said. I will come directly to the point. The nacom was killed in the battle. We live in perilous times. Every village must have a nacom. The priests and the nobles met this afternoon. They have elected a new nacom, to serve for three years.

—He was speaking over my head. I still did not understand why I was there. Coughing falsely, he lowered his face toward mine.

—The priests and the nobles, he said, in their collective wisdom, with the approval of the Lord Maya, have chosen you.

Watching from the mist, I gasped, coughed a real cough. The Spaniard, the former slave, become the nacom? It was without precedent in all the bakuns gone by. It was unheard of, unthinkable — though he could fight, there was no denying that. Tika's face was opaque, without expression, as the Spaniard continued.

—You are acquainted with the burdens, the Lord said. Do you accept the position?'

—Imagine! Do I accept? With all humility, I said. And I kissed the hem of his kub.

Tika kept her eyes on his face; they seemed to be aflame with black fire; then they softened to smoke. She waited for him to continue. But he was through. With a grace that stiffened into dignity she rose from the mat, walked to the entrance to the hut, stared out into the falling night. When she spoke it was into the air, but he heard.

—How long until the ceremony?

—Fourteen days.

She looked up at the stars, then turned and walked behind him where he sat. With the slim fingers of both hands she gripped his curly hair from above. —Fourteen days, she said. Fourteen nights. And then we have none.

She continued tugging lightly at his hair, like a child and a lover both. —The nacom cannot touch a woman, she said. Did they tell you that?

He reached up his arm and took hers, and guided her down to the mat beside him. The pain in his eyes that had diminished as he spoke was back again.

—Tika, he said. A helpless agony was slicing his voice like flint through a sacrificial throat.

—Don't she said. It is a great honor.

—Yes, but . . .

—You are a warrior, she said.

—Yes.

For a moment he seemed comforted by her understanding.

—But that's not the point. Tika, listen to me.

How could she do anything else?

—What? Can there be more? At least we have . . .

—The public ceremony is in fourteen days. But that is mere formality, the Lord Maya said. He raised his scepter high above me, with much huffing and puffing. Then he set it down, and placed a tall feathered hat on my head. I am now the nacom, he said. The village cannot go a day without one.

Fleeing across Tika's lips was the tail of a rueful smile; that was all. The room was silent as a temple. In a tree at the jungle's edge a spider monkey screeched a curdling laugh in the night. At least that's what it sounded like. Then there was silence again.

In the west the sun had completed his daily dive into the ocean. Tika walked from the hut, past her dead garden, the dying fields, through the brown brush, into the jungle's parched body. Aimlessly she seemed to stroll, but her aim was unerring. She came soon to a tattered bush, some of whose brown leaves had been replaced by butterflies. With a hand swift and merciless she caught one, let it flutter in the loose cage of her fingers. She peered at its trembling wings. It was more a dusty brown than burnished gold. I had the notion she was studying less the butterfly than her own agile fingers in which it was trapped. She murmured aloud, as if speaking a private poetry.

—Fingers are the tools of the soul, she said. (There's that soul again.) Fingers are the authors of beauty. It's fingers that make music, make art, that carve gods. Lovers may touch through the eyes, but it's fingers that caress. Villages are built by broad backs, strong arms, thick thighs, but it's fingers that weave mats, shape pots, cook food. It's fingers that catch beauty on the wing.

This she murmured as if speaking to the butterfly she would soon devour. But something seemed different this time. It was as if she was the one who was trapped, not the butterfly. As if understanding this, she spread her hands and let the brown wings fly erratically away.

Perhaps I am too romantic. Perhaps under the dust the butterfly was not the black-tipped, gold-winged type she preferred. Perhaps the dust was unappealing. Or perhaps she merely was not hungry then. The news she had heard from the Spaniard could easily have stolen her appetite. In any case, the butterfly, freed, doubled back from a few feet away and did a curious thing. It circled twice in the air, as if to test its wings, then landed, soft as a flea, on Tika's unrestrained hair. It clung there like a fallen leaf, unnoticed by her. She had become distracted by a black hole beyond the bush, below an outcropping of rock. The entrance to an underground cave. She seemed drawn to it, wanted to explore this cave. But night was beginning to fall. She memorized where she was, in case she wanted to return another day.

As she wended her way back through the jungle, toward home, the lone butterfly accompanied her. Not till she reached the jungle's edge did it lift in flight and twist in a querulous line back into the cover of the thirsty trees. Back toward the hidden cave.

When she reached the hut the Spaniard had not moved. He still sat upright on his mat, as if in contemplation of his new responsibilities. Tika entered so quietly he did not hear her. She sat beside him. She was careful not to touch him. It was as if nothing had changed between them. It was as if everything had changed between them.

The Spaniard crossed his arms on his drawn-up knees.

—We shall live in the nacom's house, he said. The great stone house near the temples.

Tika pulled both her hands through her tangled hair.

—You will live in the great stone house, she said, not looking at him. I will remain here.

I think he expected that answer.

—You are no longer my woman?

It was she who looked at him. She wondered why her men never seemed to understand.

—I am still your woman, she said.

She told him a meal would be waiting for him in her hut each night, before he returned to the nacom's stone house. In three years, she said, if they both should live, his mat would still be there beside hers, if he wanted to return.

—But I don't think that will happen, she said.

The new nacom looked off into the night-falling gloom. No fire had been built.

—Why do you say such a thing? he asked.

—Because of the words of the chilan in my dream: You shall not lie with the Spaniard again.

—Perhaps he meant something else. Perhaps he foresaw what I told the Lord Maya. I am no longer a Spaniard. I am Maya now.

Pulling her hair together behind her head, Tika tied it with a small piece of hemp that she took from the pocket of her kub. Stretched tight that way the hair revealed the bones of her cheeks, made her look severe, like a widow not to be touched. Her empty hands fell into her lap. Her voice, dry and controlled, seemed to come from far away, perhaps from Cozumel.

—The chilan knows things, she said.

15.

The chilan this, the chilan that, the chilan knows things. The phrase began to irritate, as the faults of even your beloved can irritate once the initial ecstasy has passed. The chilan didn't know that much. To choose a subject at random, what did he know about rain, the sustainer of mortal life? The chilan looked at rain — when there was rain — and he knew it was good for the crops, good for the animals; no more. He called it a drizzle or a downpour, a shower or a storm, like any other mortal, never penetrating to the liquid center, never understanding a single drop. The fact is, there are more kinds of rain than there are fears in the mortal brain. And all of them are controlled by Chac. Each with its own source, its own purpose, its own smell, its own taste. You've heard people speak of the wondrous smell of grass after the rain? There is no such aroma. It is not the grass but the rain itself that smells.

Any mortal could distinguish between rains, if only he or she paid attention. They're not at all alike. There is the Rain of Blood, which disintegrates mortal bodies in the earth, turns them into blood-gorged worms, makes room for mortal bodies yet to come, lest the earth become a platform of their bones. There is the Rain of Love, in which the mortals like to frolic, not realizing it makes them blind, and can leave them haunted by terror once it stops; you've seen them many times, no doubt, walking hand in hand in this rain, oblivious to the depressions that lie in wait. (Perhaps you've walked in it yourself.) There is the Rain of Tears, which often follows soft upon the other; in this rain, dense growth sprouts between lovers, till the lovers can no longer touch, can no longer see one another, can no longer hear each other's cries. There is the Rain of Seed, distilled from the semen of the gods; it is this that makes the corn grow tall, that makes trees stretch erections toward the sky. There is the Rain of Power, which uproots trees, swells rivers, carves new canyons through the land. (That one is mostly me, showing off.) There is the Rain of Doubt, which batters down on human enterprise until it forces the mortals to huddle indoors for protection, peering out, uncertain, hesitant, expending their energy on wondering. There is the Rain of Illusion, the only rain that makes flowers bloom. And the Rain of Reality, which rips pretty petals from their stems. There is the Rain of Memory, which falls alike on monkeys, mangos, children. And the Rain of Forgetting, which makes those little indentations you often see in the softening, balding skulls of older men.

The mortals look at rain and see what? Tender droplets kissing the summer dust. Fat heavy liquid needles spawning rivulets. But nothing more. They never distinguish among the Thousand Rains. They hardly ever try. They act as if they're all the same. The Rain of Consolation, which tries to convince the lonely they're not alone (that one's a tricky one, it hasn't been perfected yet.) The Rain of Monsters, which leaves dark stains on the walls of temples, and crawls on flimsy roofs in flashing nights. (A harmless sort of rain, but lots of fun; it often leaves the mortals baggy-eyed.) The Rain of Exaltation (it lasts for days) which makes them ponder great imponderables (to no avail, of course.) It's also known as the Rain of Suicide. Each rain with its own special aroma, its own secret formula, brewing in the vats beside the gourds. The Rain of Promises, the sweetest rain of all, though it often leaves a foul aftertaste (it has to do with evaporation time.) The Rain of Joy, which falls from a clear blue sky, more a passing shower than a rain. The Rain of Fantasy, a special favorite of mine (perhaps you're not surprised), a happy pitter-patter of a rain that dances across the land like tulip buds. And her stupid half-brother, the Rain of Expectation, which falls in ugly clumps of mud.

You've seen them, all, I'm sure, at one time or another, and never tried to make distinctions. The Rain of Innocence, a gentle rain of brief duration (though some would say it's quite insidious), often followed by a precise Hail of Pain. I didn't invent these, I'm only their guardian, the executor, so to speak, of the estate. The Rain of Mercy, always rare. And the Rain of Endurance, in somewhat greater supply, although its gourd, too, occasionally runs dry. The Rain of Laughter, a cleansing rain that sweeps clean the air, the ground and all it touches. And the Rain of Truth, which is invisible: another name for drought.

They're all listed, and hundreds more, in The Book of the Thousand Rains, carried in my head and in the heads of my assistants, along with all the formulas. Does the chilan know any of that? Of course not!

—Of course he doesn't, Itzamna says. Because it's all a crock!

Even the great Itzamna doesn't know. Even he ignores the subtleties, sees all the myriad rains as merely wet. How they underestimate my task. (It's a function of my humility.)

But let the secret of the Thousand Rains get out and your busybodies would swarm like rats, grabbing up pots of rain, studying, testing, dissecting it with their beady little brains, perverting every rain to their own end, to see if they could copy it, bottle it, to see if they could peddle it like balche. A rain for every mood, as near as the marketplace. Better to keep the secret. Pretend it's all a crock, as Itzamna says.

But getting back to the chilan. The chilan knew nothing useful; he couldn't even end the drought.

—Neither can you, Itzamna said back then. To flout a decree of the Circle is a god's ultimate sin.

I knew that, of course.

—You're talking morally, I said. I'm talking technically. Technically I could end it in an instant. Whistle up my frogs and let 'er rip.

—Technically is for the busybodies, Itzamna said. To quote the illustrious Chac.

He had a point. It led my mind to a question. If Technically rules the world — which it does — than what's Morality for? Is it merely to make the Technical feel guilty? What's the advantage in that? Things are either Useful or Beautiful. Where does Morality fit in?

It's a question would arise again.

Rain comes in many colors. Drought is white. If it lasts for a time, it touches with its whiteness all below, until beast and bird and brazen building seem to shimmer with the dying whiteness of Ahpuch's bells. So it was in Tika's village and the surrounding villages that year. So it was in all of Mayadom. The proud painted temples began to fade in the ceaseless stare of the sun, and the dyes with which to repaint them didn't grow. The rich red earth turned brown, then sand, then yellow, then gray, then ashen white. Beasts of every shape, parched and starving, ribs protruding in their skins, crawled with their last strength toward a bit of jungle shade in which to die. Ravens cleaned bones to match the earth. Brush and bush, starving, lost their leaves, giving up this last illusion, shade. Naked bones bordered every path, the only memorials to those who had lived. Even the jungle began to age, topmost leaves of trees turning white like the hair of old men.

It was all quite beautiful.

There were no convulsions in the village. Life went on much as before, if at a paler, slower pace. Dances were danced to Chac with hope and futility, until habit replaced passion. One by one the four captured slaves were tossed with ceremony into the sacred well. The only result was the predictable one — the deaths of the four slaves. These were hardly reckoned by the mortals, as death slowly invaded the village itself. Water in the drinking well was low. The fields of corn, pumpkins, beans and squash were barren mockeries. Half-grown dried-out stalks were the tombstones of shriveled birds. The fish in the sea, discomfited by uncooled waters, floated up dead on the beach, like auguries, or vanished to distant shoals. Elderly mortals folded up like empty kubs and were buried in common graves. Infants, crying for the milk of empty mothers, were tossed away. The priests proclaimed it was a test by the gods, a weeding out of the race, that the weak would perish but the strong would survive. Then they returned to their temples and ate from their secret stores.

Pageantry didn't cease, it soon increased, to take collective minds off the drought. On the appointed day the Spaniard was installed as the new nacom in a ceremony off the central plaza, in front of the gigantic new temple. In a rare departure, not the High Priest but the Lord Maya himself publicly placed the sacred hat of quetzals on the blond nacom's head. At the edge of the crowd some could see the Spaniard's woman watching from afar, her hair tied neat and close. Elbow nudged elbow to point her out.

—The nacom's wife, the admiring whispered.

—The nacom's widow, others said, and smirked, and hefted their balls beneath their cloths.

Tika's life continued as before. She was accorded new respect by much of the village, but as always the people kept their distance, as she kept hers. The nacom came to sup with her each evening, bringing with him the extra food that was due such a high official. Tika, growing lean, served only the minimum they needed for themselves and for Ixtel, storing what could be stored in case the drought continued. The rest, known only to the nacom, she distributed to the neediest families in the village, moving about in the dark of night, leaving pots of meal and clusters of mangos at the huts of those whom during the day she observed were suffering most. It was as if Tika, after loss, must always find restoration in the night.

The nacom, needless to say, kept his vows. After supper he returned to his quiet stone house and slept alone. By day he did whatever the warrior nacoms do in times of peace, which is mostly, I think, to prepare for war. Rumors had spread that a new group of Spanish sloops had been sighted off the southern coasts, that a major invasion was possible. The nacom began to train the able-bodied men in the Spanish ways of war, so they'd know how to defend themselves. Some took it seriously, believing the village faced a deadly peril. Others scoffed and jeered, saying the rumors were merely another priestly diversion to take people's minds off the drought.

Amid the thirst, doubt, confusion and spreading death there was one bright surprise for the villagers, a mystery as inexplicable to me as it was to them. They called it 'the miracle of the mangos.' In all directions the green world was turning white — except the mango trees. Wherever such trees stood, alone or in clusters at the edge of the village or out in the jungle amid the sturdier growths, the mangos alone seemed immune to the drought. They retained their leafy green, their limbs hung heavy with fruit, like the gonads of a lover left. Of all the creatures that walked or crawled or flew or rooted long toes in the earth, only the mangos seemed to have their own water, hidden and sustaining life. In the worsening drought the mangos alone sustained the life of the village. And this was a further miracle: no matter how many mangos were picked in a day, fresh lush fruit reappeared in the night.

No one could explain this mystery. (The stupid among them gave credit to Kukulcan!) But one day, watching Tika eyeing the chilan from afar, I understood what she had realized: that this odd fellow, a hundred years old, wiry as a sapling but tough as rock, had for as far back as anyone could remember lived on a diet of mangos alone.

The question of loyalty was beginning to interest me. The reports of a new Spanish threat were no idle rumors. A fleet had indeed anchored off the southern coast, replete with the usual circus — man-eating dogs, gallant horses, gun-toting warriors. The distant king of Spain and his god of love, having subdued all the Aztecs and all the Mexicans, had turned their full attention to the Mayas, whose peaceful but separate existence seemed to irritate them like a thorn in their shoes. The Spanish warriors were marching from village to village, bringing the spiritual blessings of torture, death and subjugation. Would the new nacom, faced with this opportunity of personal rescue, of safe passage home to his native land, leap to embrace it? '

—I am Maya now, he'd said. But he'd said it when there were no sloops around. When the fire grew hot, which way would he jump?

Pondering this loyalty notion more and more, I realized it wasn't the Spaniard I was thinking about. The drought was closing in on the life of these Mayas just as palpably as the Spanish soldiers were. It began to seem like a race as to which would destroy them first. And if their survival in the first instance depended in large measure on the skill of the warrior nacom, their survival in the second depended largely on Chac. To end the drought on my own, to break the decree of the Circle, was unthinkable. And yet to let the village die — to let Tika die — from want of water, from want of Chac — this prospect began to infuse me with horror. Being mortal, she would die in due course. But not at my own hands. For me to be responsible for her death

— to carry that burden to the end of time — seemed more despicable than even inventive Fate should ask.

The issue was not yet pressing. Any day, any hour, Itzamna could decide that the mortals had suffered enough. He could summon a meeting of the Circle, and with the wisdom and mercy of gods we could end the drought. The rain would come pouring down — any of the Thousand Rains that seemed appropriate. White fields could turn again to the brown of mud, then to the green of life. The fish could return to the shores, the crops could rise from the earth. The Mayas once more would grow strong, strong enough to repel the outer world. And Chac would not be burdened by divided loyalty, the Circle on one side, lovely Tika on the other.

All surcease would take was the mercy and wisdom of the gods. In the meantime, Tika and the nacom remained strong, were among those in the village who, like the mangos, were thriving despite the drought. So the question of Chac's loyalty for the moment remained abstract, turn and turn though it did in my brain.

To my surprise I found myself feeling sorry for my old rival, the jungle. He suffered as much from the drought as the mortals did. As he paled under the daily sun, hanging vines brittled and broke, beasts in his innards died shriveling deaths, leaving their corpses to rot. He was in no danger of death himself, underground rivers fed his larger roots, but his old elan, his old cockiness, was gone. When Tika walked within him now, as she did more and more once the Spaniard became nacom, to eat a butterfly or two, the jungle watched with tired lids. He hadn't even the strength to swat her rear.

His weakness left a void in my being — in the place where jealousy roots. Like all true lovers I could conjure jealousy from the perfume of a passing breeze. With the jungle no longer a threat, I found myself inventing another one — the sly old chilan by his stone. As the drought continued, the chilan's prestige climbed. The villagers recalled his recent warning words:

—The end of the world is at hand.

He was still an outcast, but some began to wonder if he was right.

For Tika, who used to watch him from afar, listening to his predictions, one too many had come true. Kel shall neither win nor lose the games. You shall not lie with the Spaniard again. His uncanny wisdom attracted her. (It wasn't his stringy hair, his elongated nose.) One day she approached his stela, holding in both hands before her a mango, like an offering to a god. The chilan took it without a word. Tika, also silent, sat at his feet. The chilan split the mango with a rock, sat on his stone, slightly higher than Tika, and gave her half. In the quiet of some unspoken communion they drank its juice and ate its pulp.

The next day she did this again, and the day after that. They began to converse. Passersby stared at the sight. Soon it was the gossip of the village — strange Tika was entranced with the chilan; the nacom's poor wife, once a laughing girl, had become a madwoman again.

Now I envy the chilan, dried out codger that he is. Though he does not lust for her (I think), he daily hears her voice beside him. His paper skin is warmed by her eyes. The smell of her must surely recall remembrances of youth, like a dying jaguar smelling a fawn. Given a second chance, I'd give up my godhood (I think) for such proximity.

But that might be worse — to be so close and be too old to touch. To be so close and talk philosophy. I think I'd want to scream.

Mostly I want to scream anyway.

I do not do it. Screaming isn't seemly for a god.

Sometimes I wish I'd been born like Chac-Mool. I could scream all I wanted and no one would pay any mind. But I am a true god. Glory personified. So I suffer in silence.

Each day I see Tika bathing before her daily visit to the chilan. I watch her sponge her thighs. . .

But enough of pain.

—He doesn't like to speak of pain, Itzamna says.

What did they have in common, what did they talk about?

Long before anyone else alive in the village had been born, the chilan had been an up-and-coming young priest, known for his sharp mind and his quick wit. Then he began to expound a revolutionary theory of his, which did not sit well with the other priests, or with the existing Lord Maya. He was told that his theory was not only wrong but blasphemous, and a threat to the very core of Maya life. He was told to give up these views, and all would be forgiven. But the young priest was both clever and strong of will. He knew that he would never be truly forgiven, that his judgment thenceforth would always be suspect. And he was convinced, besides, that he was right. When he disregarded orders and continued to expound his theory, the priests and nobles banded against him. While they did not have him put to death — a curious act of mercy — they stripped him of his priesthood and they banished him from the temples. Undaunted, he set up shop, so to speak, on the road outside the village, beside a blank stela that had toppled and fallen and broken in half. Beside this broken stela, for seventy-five years, he had slept every night in dry weather and wet, he had eaten his mangos, he had expounded his radical theories to anyone who deigned to listen. With the passing years he'd become, as I've said, a village character, an object of pity to some, of comedy to others. None seemed to ponder why the chilan still dwelled beside his stela long after all who'd banished him had died.

The view that had gotten the chilan banished was this: that no more temples should be built for the gods.

This was unthinkable to the priests and the nobles and the existing Lord Maya. The proud painted temples were considered the apex of Maya achievement. They reflected glory not only on the gods but on the Lord Maya, the priests, and on down the line to the nameless lower men who built them, and sometimes gave their lives, their bones crushed under the weight of heavy stones. Not build temples to the gods? Why, what then was a civilization to do? What was its ultimate function? The chilan's view was a challenge to all the bakuns of Mayadom that had gone before, and to all the temples then being planned. Take away the temples and there would be an emptiness in Maya life that nothing would be able to fill. So the high priests had said.

—What's wrong with temples to the gods? Tika asked him one day, sucking a mango pit. It was one of their conversations I chose to listen to.

—Nothing, child, the chilan replied. There is nothing wrong with temples to the gods. But they need not be built by men. If a god is a true god, does he need piles of stone to hail his glory? If the gods want temples, aren't they capable of creating their own? And they have, they have. The temples of the gods are everywhere. It is the function of men and women to seek them out. To discover the temples that the gods themselves have created. And there to do obeisance, to give thanks. There are temples of the gods in rock quarries by the sea. There are temples of the gods in jungle caves. There are temples of the gods in the highland range. There are temples of the gods in the minds of men. Yes, and women, too. These it is our task to discover in all their glory. Building false temples is too easy. It's searching out the real ones that's the point of mortal life.

It was an interesting theory.

—Harumph, Itzamna says.

He wasn't understanding. By the chilan's theory each of his stunning sunsets was a temple.

—But if these temples are everywhere, Tika said, how shall we know where to look? How will we know when we've discovered one?

The chilan ran a crooked finger across his cracking lips. He withdrew a pebble of wax from his ear.

—We shall know them by the light, he said. A soft, calm light that pervades. We shall know them by the dark. A soft, calm dark that pervades. We shall know them by the peace. A soft, calm peace that pervades.

—Have you ever found one? Tika asked.

—Many, the chilan said. In many places. Mostly inside my head. Hatching like ducks from eggs placed by the gods. The eggs of understanding. Of ideas.

—Does everyone have these eggs in their heads?

—I would have to think so, the chilan said. I am not so different as they make me out to be.

—And what of the other temples? In the jungle. By the sea.

—You come upon them every so often, the chilan said. A certain time, a certain mood. A feeling that comes over you. A kind of cosmic love.

A grown woman, Tika felt now like a little girl again, looking at her mother's pots before they were broken, before they were swept away, all but those shards she still kept hidden in the hem of her kub.

—Then why don't we go to these places, she asked, and honor the gods there?

—Because they move about, the chilan said. You cannot pilgrimage. One place, one time, then they're gone. The best trick is to catch them on the wing. To try to hold them fast, imbibe them into your belly, absorb them into your soul before they fade. They always do, of course; then you've got to search again.

An intensity flashed in her eyes, like Chac's lightning. Just for a moment. Then it passed.

—But the temples that men build, they stay, Tika said. Forever.

—And bring no peace, the chilan replied.

They talked like that for many days. After each talk, Tika stood to stretch her legs, and wandered into the jungle, in search of butterflies. At first she did what she had usually done, trapped them on a browning bush. But little by little she did it differently. Little by little she caught them on the wing.

16.

The Spaniard came to sup with Tika less and less frequently. He loved her no less, he told her, but his nacom duties were keeping him away. With reports that the Spanish warriors were moving closer up the coast, destroying all who would not submit, he was trying to devise a strategy to save the village.

With the nacom not appearing for supper, Tika stayed longer each day in the jungle. Her walks took on the nature of searches, as if she had some inner need to know if the chilan was correct. As if she needed to find a temple herself. It would be a substitute, perhaps, for her frustrated desire to carve gods. As she moved without direction through the white lianas, she feared that even if she came upon a temple she would not know it, would pass it by. Also I think there was this. In her heart she'd already found a temple, which had been ripped away by Fate. Her temple was the Spaniard's arms. She was trying to become a creature of the spirit, but her body yearned for the weight of him.

That same day, a secret meeting was held in the quarters of the Lord Maya, attended by the two nacoms and the High Priest. The Lord, wearing his highest hat, told the others that between the drought and the approaching warriors he feared catastrophe. Action must be taken soon, he said. If they waited for the Spaniards to attack, and in the meantime grew weaker from the drought, there would be no hope of victory.

The Lord, the High Priest and the priestly nacom had already been conferring when the blond warrior nacom arrived. They turned to him for advice. He gave an account of his readiness, and of the latest reports of the enemy advance. As for new advice, however, he had none. Hearing this, the Lord Maya gave instructions of his own.

—You will take a scouting party to discover the exact location of the enemy. Then we will know how much time we have, and prepare the best defense.

—I'll dispatch such a party at once, the Spaniard replied.

—That is not my wish, the Lord Maya said, pursing his protruding lips. You will head the scouting party yourself. You will leave at dawn.

The warrior nacom rubbed his mouth. It was not normal for a nacom to act as a scout, other eyes were as good as his. He was restless for action, however, and decided not to question the word of the Lord. Orders were orders, in any case.

—I will depart at dawn, he said.

The Lord gave the nacom his blessing and sent him on his way. The High Priest and the priestly nacom remained behind. If the Spaniard felt that something mysterious was going on behind his back, he did not show it.

The night is a restless one, for the nacom, for Tika, for me. And also for the stars. One of those nights when the ticking lights are all at play, shimmering with expectation. As if forces set in motion long ago will soon collide.

Even Time was paying attention, I think. And Fate.

The Spaniard, after choosing his scouts, slept little. Long before dawn he woke the others, and they left in the cool of dark. There had been no time to say goodbye to Tika. If she inquired she'd be told where he was. He expected to return in six days.

Tika, too, was a long time finding sleep that night. Her eyes, open or closed, recalled the mouth of a jungle cave near a rock outcropping, which she had seen that afternoon in her wanderings. It called to her in her vision like an unknown destiny, a resolution. It was a temple of the kind the chilan had described, she felt certain of that. She would explore it the next day. She knew she would get no rest until she did.

At last she fell asleep. From high in the mist above the jungle I watched them both. There was a meaning to the moment I could not fathom. In the hut Tika's breasts rose and fell, arousing my desire. On the road leading south the nacom moved away, leaving her vulnerable.

The space between I filled with fantasies.

Her face that morning had an urgent youthfulness, a glee that had vanished long ago. Although alone in the room — Tel had already gone out — she smiled a sheepish smile. Her kub had slipped to her waist when she awoke and sat. She stripped it off and stepped outside and let the sun's eye warm her breasts, her thighs. She rubbed her nose in a childish way, as if it were tickling her.

She seemed to busy herself longer than usual with household tasks. She swept from the hut with a broom of tied branches the drought's ubiquitous dust. She ground a bit of meal, enough for just two tortillas, one for her and one for Tel; this would be their breakfast, with the fleshy pulp of a mango replacing drink. She lifted the mats from the floor, carried them outside, beat the dust from them. All morning she fussed with such domestic chores, as if she needed to affirm her womanliness before setting forth in search of the jungle cave. Or as if she wanted to leave a good opinion, in case she did not return.

When she had finished this ritual — that's what I think it was — she fingered the hem of her kub, the shards of her mother's pots. Then, instead of visiting with the chilan, which she'd been doing every day, she walked the other way, to the center of the village.

Here the spoilage from the drought was worst. Huts stood abandoned and needing repair, their former occupants dead from lack of food. Children sat listless in what shade they could find, ribs showing like branches through their skin, only their oversized eyes retaining promise. The carcasses of dead animals littered the ground, awaiting the patrols of able-bodied women assigned to carry them away, to burn them in distant quarries, the only place where fires were still allowed. In the marketplace a residue of trade continued, more to keep people busy than for anything else. Many of the adults had vanished in search of food and drink in distant lands, more often to the burial grounds. Grown men sprawled beside the Temple of Kukulcan, where daily offerings had failed to end the drought, wondering where they'd find strength to fight the invaders when that day came.

Idle eyes watched without expression as the nacom's wife moved about. Their owners had no use for her. No mortal had use for any other. They felt abandoned by the gods. They stared at the sky, accusingly. In the sky there was not a cloud.

Having seen whatever she needed to see, Tika turned and left the village. Her sandals raising dust with each step, she walked back toward her hut, and then past it, out to the jungle's edge, and then into the jungle himself, as she had done so many times before. By now the drought had whitened not only the jungle's thatch but the hair of his chest. Lianas that used to curl with lust hung straight and dry, brittle as prayers. Bleached cedars stood silent as sages, sages speechless not from wisdom but from senility. Sapodillas surrendered toward the sky, dried chicle useless and painful inside them, like still-born ideas. Copal, which the mortals burned at sacred festivals, drooped blanched and lusterless, priests without faith. Every few minutes a bird or monkey, ceasing to struggle, let go a branch and dropped like a soft stone to the ground. Thick-necked snakes converged to devour the spoils, not slithering silently as once they did but rustling awkwardly, dead leaves chafing dried skin. I've seen the gray splattered brains of mortals whose skulls had been smashed by heavy lances, grayness splattered beyond even dreams and fears, stray images rising from the dead in search of a second life. Like them the jungle seemed this day. Walking through this land of ghosts, Tika, her copper skin still healthy, her black hair hanging loose, her every movement a charm, seemed the embodiment of life itself — beautiful, heaving, untamed. The only creatures her match were the mango trees, leaves yet thick and green, purple fruit hanging ripe as breasts.

The cave lay beneath a tongue of rock that protruded from the jungle floor. Around its mouth, wild bushes curled brown, stripped by the drought, missing the leaves that till now must have hidden the cave from view. Its face indeed looked like a temple, a stone facade of eyes and lips and noses, mostly noses, carved through the bakuns by the hands of the underground rivers, by clever rivulets of runoff rain. Approaching by indirection, Tika returning in search of the cave found herself almost at its mouth. Half-swooning, she reached out for support, clung to a promontory that jutted from the face. Then, before fear could overcome her, she thrust herself through the mouth and into the darkness.

The floor was strewn with rocks. She turned an ankle on one of them, stumbled forward blindly, fell forward faster as the floor sloped sharply away. Propelled by this momentum, putting one foot in front of the other simply to keep from falling, losing first one sandal then the other to the jagged bottom, she found herself stumbling deeper and lower through a natural passageway, till the floor dropped sharply again and losing her balance completely she fell to her knees, expecting as she did painful scrapes, finding herself instead on a carpet of moss. She thrust her hands down in front of her to hold her balance, to feel the soft carpet. Hands and knees on the moss, wild hair falling over her face, eyes closed, she resembled an untamed beast waiting to be assaulted. Only for an instant. Then she fell to her side, fingers clutching deep into the moss as if to keep her in touch with reality.

When her breath slowed she opened her eyes. At first all was dark, as before. Then she saw, high above, an opening no bigger than a star. Through it streamed a narrow fall of light. Her eyes followed the light down into the cave, till it shed itself on a raised platform several feet in front of her. The passageway had widened into an underground room, with a large flat stone in the center. Rising slowly, she started toward it. Then, frightened, she fell again to her knees. She had seen something move up ahead. She couldn't tell what it was, there was no sense of solid shape, only an abstract whirring, like a breeze made visible.

Fearful of moving toward it, she nonetheless was enticed by a pale shimmering. Slowly, so as not to provoke whatever it was, she stood again, began to advance, pausing after each uncertain step. Soon she began to discern a clearer sound, a sound not unfamiliar, though she did not know what it was. And beneath the rustling she could see a solid shape, this, too, familiar yet unknown, because the color, and the substance, were wrong. The thing seemed to be fashioned of bright green eyes. She sunk to her knees to control her fear. She inched forward that way for a closer look. Atop the level stone, illumined by the shaft of light, was a mortal skull — man or woman, she could not tell. The skull was studded with turquoise stones, which she'd mistaken for eyes. Above the skull, golden breath spun. Now she could see what it was. It was swarms of golden black-tipped butterflies, the very kind she liked to eat. Around and above the turquoise skull they swarmed in golden bands, in circles, ovals, S-shaped curves. They appeared to be in perpetual motion, ordained flutter, never alighting, never breaking rank, around and above the skull.

It seemed like an altar of sorts, and she stared as if hypnotized. She felt stripped naked, stripped to her soul, before two jade stones that glittered from the eye sockets, although her kub, stained from the moss, still covered her. She felt strange stirrings within, alternating currents of hunger and fulfillment, the twin feelings flowing outward in widening circles to embrace the world, the galaxy, the universe, currents heated she thought by lust, a lust that she could taste, a taste she already knew.

I could tell by the look on her face what she wanted to do. She wanted with violent sacrilege to reach out, to pluck a butterfly from the golden breath, to eat it on the wing.

She didn't do it. But as if reading her thoughts, a single butterfly, with great struggle, as if defying some unearthly gravity, detached itself from the swirling mass, fluttered crazily away, looped about in the air, alighted then as if with growing purpose on her finger. She didn't stir, but simply looked at it. Soon another broke free. This one lighted not on her hand but on her hair. Others began to come, alone, in twos and threes, most not landing on her, content to flutter around her face. More and more broke free, as if some spell had vanished, or some curse. Abandoning the turquoise-studded skull they flew to her and circled around her hair, more and more till thick golden bands wrapped her upper body in whispering veils of sun.

Her beauty at that moment reached its apex, and so did my desire. In retrospect it was the watershed of passion, when Heaven's bells have not yet turned to Hell's.

—It's the one moment she even caught my eye, Itzamna says.

When at last she stood to leave the cave, she expected — I expected — that the butterflies would abandon her, would return in a golden stream to their previous orbits around the turquoise skull with its fierce jade eyes. But they did not. As she picked her way along the rock-strewn bed of the cave, barefoot now, the butterflies remained in motion around her hair, thick bands of living halo, tilted, like Saturn's rings. As she ducked under the overhanging lip, as she emerged once more into the half-light of the jungle, they stayed with her. Unafraid of the light, they moved with Tika, leaving the skull staring harshly, silently, in the abandoned cave.

As if in a dream she knelt to smell a dead white orchid, its aroma somehow finding her in the pungent jungle air. The whirring, whirling butterflies rose and dipped with her every motion. Idly she moved among the trees, stalks, vines, snapping dry lianas, peeling with her fingernails a loose piece of bark. The butterflies did not obscure her vision, they moved in circles above her hair, trailed with it behind her head in a black and golden train. From a low-hanging tree she plucked a mango, soft and overripe. She did not eat it, merely held it like a ball, a talisman, half forgotten, as she moved among the dusty trees, thousands of butterflies still swirling and following in circles, in ovals, in S-shaped curves. She walked as if unaware of their presence, as if such obeisance happened every day.

For several hours she moved that way, roundabout, circling, in the vague direction of the village, in no swift hurry to arrive. Twigs and brambles crunches under her feet, and unseen insects. Spider monkeys, quieted by the stunning sight, looked down from trees at the pageant of her passing, and squealed.

Her revery was not broken until she emerged from the jungle behind her hut. Mortal voices. At first she couldn't make out words. Then with a crash of bodies the brush in front of her parted and a tall guard of the priests, carrying a spear, was blocking her path. He shouted something and two more guards crashed through. Startled by the voices and the men, the butterflies rose higher in the air. They did not desert her, merely began to swirl in a golden cloud out of the reach of the men.

Tika, who had seemed in some kind of trance, saw the spears and flushed with anger.

—What do you want? she demanded.

The priestly guards, rather young, seemed awed by her. She was the nacom's wife. They looked with puzzlement at the masses of butterflies hovering tightly in the air. They had never seen such a sight. No one had ever seen such a sight. Still, they had a duty.

—You are Ixtika Chel Chek? the first guard inquired.

—Yes.

Her voice was gentler now as she realized that whatever this was about was not the doing of the guards.

—We have been sent by the High Priest, to escort you back to the village.

—Escort me back? What for?

—The priests don't confide in us. Our instructions were to find you and to bring you back.

She was puzzled. Her first thought was that the High Priest had somehow learned of the jungle cave, and wanted her to take him there.

—How did you know where I was? she asked.

—We didn't. They're looking everywhere.

—Who is looking everywhere?

—Twenty-four guards of the priest.

Sudden fear quickened Tika's breast. She didn't know what this meant. She had never heard of such a search before. She looked about, in case she needed a route of escape. But one of the guards sensed her thinking. Before she could turn he grabbed her wrist. Roughly she wrenched it away. As she did, the forgotten mango fell from her grasp, dropped toward the barren earth, broke into three parts as it struck a rock.

—Don't touch me, Tika said, flashing with anger. I can find the village myself.

—We have our orders, the first guard said.

Eyes raging, she looked from one to the other. They were merely boys.

—Well, lead, then, she said. Don't worry, I'll come with you. Let's find out what the High Priest wants.

I didn't know what it meant, any more than she. I was curious, at that moment, about the myriad butterflies. Afraid of the men and the spears, it appeared, they hung back near the trees. They did not follow her as she moved off toward the village, a guard on each side, the third guard following behind. They hung in place for a time, as if awaiting her return. When she disappeared from view behind her hut, when it seemed she would not be back, the swirling butterflies, as if by some invisible command, swooped low. They dropped toward the earth, to the spot where the shattered mango lay. One butterfly landed on each of the three shards of pulp. The others at once began to swirl just above, in thick golden circles, in ovals, in S-shaped curves. Around and around they swirled above the broken mango, in a low, fixed orbit, paying homage to their new leader. I had the quivering sensation that something of importance had just occurred, some critical transition that extended beyond the mortals, a moment when myths die and new ones are born. It is not easy to catch such a moment on the wing, as the old chilan might have said. I was convinced I had just witnessed one.

I tried to see the events through the eyes of a butterfly: to adopt their short life-span, the emergence from cocoons, the fragile life of beauty, the too-easy death that waited at every pause for rest. In this way I worked it out. To the black-tipped golden butterflies, at that moment in their history — brief to gods, brief even to mortals, but the eternal present to them — the universe itself had the shape of a beautiful woman. The universe had infinite strands of long, black hair on which a butterfly could rest; short, wiry nether hair in which to nestle; sloping shoulders that offered solid purchase; perfumed breasts; soft, protective thighs. But no universe is completely safe. Their womanworld also had snatching fingers greatly to be feared: the fingers of mortality, which snatched golden butterflies — the innocent and the guilty — into the mouth of death, gateway to the afterlife. There the trapped, frightened butterfly met one of two fates. It was transformed to womanflesh, the place of all salvation, and became one with the universe; or it was transmuted into excrement, was flung away to the place of everlasting stench.

That was how it must have been to them. But it was not always thus. They had tales of previous worlds, passed down from cocoon to cocoon. Their prior world had been one of darkness, an eternal-seeming cave, shaped like the empty skull of a man, the center of this universe a turquoise-covered smaller skull of a man, with jade eyes, silent, inscrutable, offering no instruction, no pleasure, no way to the light, no matter how much they beseeched. Some butterfly philosophers argued that the skull at the center of the universe was not covered with turquoise, did not peer with jade eyes, but was covered with jade, and peered with turquoise eyes. This debate went on unceasingly in learned circles, causing great strife, but still offered no way to the light. Until, in a gradual transformation, a major evolution of butterfly perception, womanflesh came and showed the way to a new world of freedom and delicacy.

That was how it must have been to them — an evolution of the universe. But soon another transition took place. Religion gave way to myth. Womanworld receded into the past, a tale of times gone by. The new reality of the universe was clear to all. The universe is shaped like three pulpy pieces of fruit, jagged and juicy, set around a central stone.

Already, I imagine, their philosophers are debating. Some say this evolved universe is clearly an improvement — so streamlined, so simple. Others are horrified, they find it barren, sterile, static, an absence of beauty compared to the previous luscious world of womanflesh. I suppose one could argue either way.

This theory of mine is correct. I believe it still. But only later did I understand what I had done. By focusing on the butterflies — as if my calling were scholarship — I missed the essential truth of what had occurred. I missed the golden opportunity (as it were) to fulfill my passion. I missed the chance to avoid all that came after.

Then!

During those golden hours when Tika walked in the jungle with the butterflies swirling obeisance around her head in circles, ovals, S-shaped curves! Then we could have loved! Then, had I invited her into the mist instead of watching dumbly, she could have come! Then in passion's arms we could have consummated every fantasy. Then we could have become lovers worthy of all the Codices, lovers till the end of days! Chac and Tika! Tika and Chac!

Then! When Tika was their universe.

Then! When Tika was a god!

This it had all been leading to, though she may not have known it herself. The years of trapping their bodies in her fingers, the years of crunching them in her teeth, the years of eating beauty on the wing: to the moment when they would make a goddess of her. To the moment when we would be equals, she and I. To the moment when, with neither opprobrium nor prohibition, we could have loved! God to god, and smiles all around! Hand in hand and leg to leg we could have shared a perfect bliss until the end of days — the rain god of the Mayas and the goddess of the golden butterflies. A legendary match.

A child, a monkey, a mango, playing on the ground. That one, Fate says to Time, let's do something special with that one!

If only I had understood. Before the guards came to take her away. Before the butterflies lost their faith in her. Before they dropped to the mango shards.

During all the bakuns since, I have mourned the waste of it. I have tried to seize again the moment, to reclaim those golden hours. I have made the best of pleadings.

—I didn't understand. Just give me another chance, is all I ask.

But Time, eternal creep, refuses to run in reverse. Time, with snickering Fate astride him in his bed, does not care. Time, eternal fuck, says no.

Whether Tika comprehended what had taken place — whether in her meandering through the jungle, with the butterflies in abject flutter around her, she was waiting — waiting for me — waiting for me to invite her into the mist — waiting to say yes! — that I do not know.

That I do not like to think about.

17.

Of her arrest, of her audience with the High Priest, you've already guessed. Perhaps you've seen it coming all along. Tika was to be killed.

The guards left her alone with the priest in a dark stone chamber. The faces of the two of them, priest and woman, danced black and orange beneath the flickering torches on the walls. On a stone lectern a secret Maya Codex lay, open to a certain page.

—Ixtika Chel Chek, the High Priest said, you have been selected by the priests for a great honor. You will forfeit your life to save your entire people. (He didn't waste words.) To end the drought that threatens all, you will be thrown into the sacred cenote, as an offering to almighty Chac. So great Chac will be merciful. This message you will carry beyond the horizon of death, on behalf of all the people. You will ask Chac to give us rain.

Hearing his idiot words, I was apoplectic. Tika, in contrast, was calm.

—Is it because I have befriended the chilan?

—Of course not, the priest said.

He moved closer to her, as if he would touch her cheek. But he didn't. I think he liked her, anyway.

—The chilan is merely a flea, of little consequence. We allow him to make us itch, so we can have the pleasure of scratching. Your fate, your honor, is of a much higher order. It is written in the sacred books.

I didn't know what he was talking about.

He moved to the stone lectern, ran his hand idly along the open page. Tika couldn't read, in any case. Only the priests and nobles could read.

—Twelve bakuns ago, he said, our people suffered an awful time. The Terrible Seven-Years Drought. I'm sure you've heard it spoken of. Many people died. The village itself almost died. Many sacrifices were made to the gods. None seemed to satisfy them. Until, one happy morning, a maiden named Ixki Chel was hurled into the cenote. This Ixki Chel was very pleasing to Chac, for that very afternoon it rained. The rain fell for many days, watering the fields and the jungle. It saved the very existence of our people.

The priest was out of his mind! A careless oversight that had been, nothing more. The rain had nothing to do with the girl!

—Ever since then, the priest continued, the names of the blood kin of the hallowed Ixki Chel have been recorded in a Sacred Codex, against the time when their tasty blood should be desired again by the gods. The names of all of them are written here. Your mother, Ixlu Chel, who died when you were born, is the next to last. Your name is the last. You are the only living descendant of the hallowed Ixki Chel.

Getting his drift, I wanted to scream at him.

—Fools, I wanted to shout. Touch a hair on her lovely head and I'll kill you all!

I didn't shout. He wouldn't have heard me anyway. They never do.

—The drought that plagues us now, though not yet seven years, is severe, the priest told her. You have seen the dead and the dying all around. It's made more difficult by the approach of a powerful enemy come to enslave us. We have offered up many sacrifices to the gods — first slaves, then our own. The gods do not respond. Chac does not respond. This time we cannot wait seven years. Our warriors grow weak, we shall perish as a people unless the great Chac gives us rain. The priests have decided, therefore, that we can wait no longer. I explain all this because you are the woman of our honored nacom. But we are certain he will understand. The drought must come to an end. Chac must have the blood he wants.'

—Blood! I shrieked. That's all you mortals think about!

He didn't hear.

—The Spaniard, Tika said, calmly. Where is he?

—Today he is out on patrol, scouting the enemy.

—The nacom become a scout? You sent him away because he will understand?

The priest didn't reply, but turned his attention to the book, as if to say the matter was out of his hands.

I saw again the child, the monkey, the mango. I heard again whispering in my ears the sultry voice of Fate beguiling Time. This time my visage was skyward when I screamed.

They wouldn't kill her for twenty-eight days, the needed time of purity. She'd be kept under guard, her only companion the slave girl Tel.

A single moon.

It will never happen, I told myself. The Spaniard will return and save her life.

If not him, me. I couldn't let her die — not in such a useless cause.

Tika remained calm. Perhaps because in such a circumstance a moon is an eternity. Perhaps because, like me, she was convinced the Spaniard would save her when he returned. But I think it was something else. I think that somehow, through the varied phases of her life, she had reached a serenity that few mortals achieve: an inner strength, the wisdom of a living stone. Or it may have come from the teachings of the chilan — or from her experience that very day in the jungle cave: the strength of being, for a brief afternoon, a goddess, if only to crazy butterflies. Or perhaps it was an accumulation of sorrows that led her to accept her fate. Whatever the reasons, Tika did not protest. Escorted away, she did not seem to suffer in her loose captivity.

Instead it was I who suffered. Mortals can endure much if gods agree to suffer in their place.

It's a blessing they cannot count on often. We do not suffer suffering well.

I thought of going to Itzamna, of asking him to help, to call a meeting of the Circle at once: to end the drought.

—The mortals have suffered enough, I envisioned myself saying. It is time to be merciful. And I could hear his reply:

—Suffered? They haven't even accepted the cause of it all. The offending temple still stands — to Kukulcan.

What could I say to that?

—This girl, this woman, Tika, they are going to kill her. A sacrifice, in a useless cause. And he would say,

—They have killed many. What's another one to us?

Pretending not to know. What could I say then?

—I love this mortal woman. Now they would kill her — for me! There are limits to acceptable irony!

All of this I imagined. None of it could I say. Forbidden passions are laughable (except to the passionate one.)

There was another choice. I could make it rain, on my own. Whistle up my frogs and let 'er rip. Violate the Circle's decree. Commit the unthinkable. No one could prevent me, if that was the course I chose. I didn't know what would happen if I did. No one had ever done so before. There was no precedent. The consequences, though surely dire, were unknown.

Even to think that way was traitorous. I put it from my mind. Time enough to ponder it again if the fatal day drew close.

Besides, I thought, if I broke the decree, if I made it rain and saved their butts, the mortals might kill Tika anyway. In gratitude. A way of saying thanks. Sometimes mortals think that way, ignorant as they are. Then I'd be in a double bind.

I decided to watch and wait. To hope she would be saved. To hope the problem would go away with no interference from me. In short, to be a god.

I think I've solved the mystery of souls. There are no souls.

Some mortals claimed they had seen souls rising from the bodies of the dead. This was their only evidence. But now I understand what they saw, what I, too, have seen, rising like frail smoke from brains darkened beyond even dreams and fears. What they have seen are stray images seeking livelier haunts. Leftover imaginings. Terrors that have not yet terrified. Unloved loves, the wrappings still intact. All the unripe nonsense of mortal life. These are what flee when a mortal dies, lest they be trapped inside and rot. They flee to the nearest living thing, and climb aboard, and cling like parasites. Even as orchids do. That's the surviving mess they call a soul. A glob of unspent images, which has an elusive property. Unless it lights in someone else's living brain, it soon disintegrates.

Why they think this glob is important remains obscure.

Her hut became her prison. Guards were stationed front and rear to make certain that no man entered. This seemed an unnecessary precaution, because other than young Tel and the Spaniard no one had entered the hut for years. If she walked through the village for exercise, a guard followed discreetly some distance behind. Glassy eyes watched, but there was little gossip about the arrest of the nacom's wife. Beaten down by the drought, the mortals were trying to survive, each in his own way. They had little concern to spare for the fate of others, certainly not for the fate of a madwoman.

She was not permitted to visit with the chilan. She could speak to no man until the day of her death. She was not permitted to walk in the jungle, they feared she might try to hide, to escape, or to kill herself in his grasp before the priests could do it properly. Most of the time she remained alone in the hut, reviving a childhood interest — making pots from clay. She had an idea that now they might turn out as beautiful as her mother's. I thought that might happen, too. But it did not. Her pots turned out clumsy, clunky. Undeterred, she kept on making them.

Tel became her eyes and ears in the village. Tika sent her with a message to the chilan — that she had found a temple of the gods. The chilan nodded, as if he already knew, Tel said. But he sent no message back. Of his speech that day to the roadside loiterers, of which there were many now with no work to be done in the fields, there was only one warning that Tel understood: The end of the world is at hand. Tika was beginning to accept, I think, that the end truly was near for her. For the rest there was the obvious choice: universal death by drought, or massacre by the invaders with their horsebeasts and their dogs and their shooting sticks. She wondered if the chilan knew which.

She sent Tel to inquire of the priests when the Spaniard was to return from his scouting. Any day now, was the word. Whether Tika was hoping for rescue, or merely for the forbidden chance to talk with him, I couldn't tell.

One day Tika sat Tel beside her and showed her how to make a cage of her fingers, how to trap a butterfly inside. She sent her into the jungle to bring back several of the black-tipped, gold-winged type. When the girl returned and they were sitting side by side again on the dirt floor, Tika told Tel to pop one of the butterflies into her mouth, to feel it beating in her cheeks, then to chew and swallow it. Tel smiled. She thought that Tika was teasing her. Tika took one of the butterflies in her hand, dumped it into her mouth, let it flutter inside. Then she chewed it and swallowed. Tel's eyes grew large as she watched.

—Now you do it, Tika instructed.

The slave girl shook her head, then asked, Why?

—Because I want you to.

The slave girl studied her face. Tika was like a god to her, she never disobeyed. Shaking her head again, mystified, she popped a butterfly into her mouth, filling her cheeks with air as she did. As she felt the insect flutter in her mouth, a small grin fought its way to her lips, her dimpled cheeks.

—Now chew it, Tika said.

Tel, still grinning, shook her head.

Do it! Tika ordered.

Tel's eyes grew wild. Choking, she clamped her teeth on the butterfly. Yellow insect guts spurted through her lips. She tried to chew, began to retch. Quickly she stood and ran outside and vomited into the dirt.

After she rinsed the smell from her mouth, and tearfully sat on her mat, Tika said,

—Tomorrow we'll try again.

The Spaniard returned two days later, marching up the dirt road with his scouts, and reported at once to the High Priest. The invaders had conquered several more villages, he said. But in their last battle they had suffered many losses. They were encamped several miles to the south, regrouping, giving their wounded time to recover. They, too, had been weakened by the drought, and spent much time in search of water. But there were no villages for them to conquer between there and here, he said. It was not be long before they would resume their march, before they would attack.

When the priest had absorbed this information, the Spaniard set out for Tika's hut. He had not been told of her arrest. Not until he encountered the spear-carrying guards at her door — tripled in expectation of his return — did he learn of it.

—Out of my way, he said to the guards.

—No man may enter here, the senior guard said.

—I am the nacom, the Spaniard said, grabbing the guard by the throat. Let me pass.

The other guards surrounded him, their flint-tipped spears lowered toward his loins.

—No man may enter, the chief guard said again. By order of the High Priest.

The Spaniard was outnumbered. In a rage he spun about and strode with long strides back to the central plaza, to the dark rooms of the High Priest, where he'd been only minutes before. He demanded an explanation. The priest, who apparently had hoped to avoid this — I can't imagine how — repeated what he had told Tika: how one Ixki Chel had ended the terrible drought of bygone day, how Tika was her last descendant, how Chac wanted Tika's blood before he would make it rain.

The Spaniard tried to control his anger.

—How do you know this? he said.

—We have tried everything else. This is what Chac wants.

—Have you talked to Chac? Are you sure that's what he wants?

The priest did not deign to answer such an absurdity. I thought it was a pretty good question, myself.

The nacom was beginning to lose control.

—Have you ever seen Chac? he demanded. How do you know he even exists? How do you know it isn't the clouds themselves that make it rain? Brainless, mechanical clouds!

I thought the priest would have a fit. Now the Spaniard truly was being absurd. But the priest remained calm, except for the brittle malice in his words.

—I thought you were Maya now.

—I am Maya, the Spaniard shouted. I am the nacom who defends this village! That is my woman you are planning to kill.

—To sacrifice, the priest corrected. There are other women to take to your bed. Which you cannot do while remaining nacom, in any case.

—To you they may be all alike, the Spaniard whispered fiercely (perhaps not the best thing to say to a priest.) But there is only one Tika!

—Apparently, the priest said, with icy precision. Apparently Chac thinks so, too. And he wants her blood.

How close he was to the truth! And how far away!

The Spaniard's face was flaming the color of his red-blond hair. He drew his knife and advanced on the High Priest. It was some kind of reflex, I don't know what he thought he could accomplish. Before he took two strides he was seized by priestly guards who stepped quickly from behind decorative mats hanging on two sides of the room, where they had been concealed for this very purpose. They disarmed the Spaniard and held him fast.

—Take him to the cave, the high priest ordered. (It was not really a cave, but a stone room deep below the Nunnery.)

—You will be held there until the sacrifice is done. Upon reflection, when the rains begin to fall, you will understand that this was necessary, for the survival of the village. You will resume your rightful role as the warrior nacom, and help us repel the intruders. But the drought must be ended first.

He waved his hand to the guards, began to turn away, then turned back again.

—When you are truly Maya, he said, you will understand that the gods demand much of men. Sometimes they demand all that we have to give.

What, I asked myself, has this priest given?

The Spaniard may have thought the same, but he knew not to say it. He let himself be led away by the guards.

He has a plan, I told myself. Surely he has a plan.

18.

One bright and sunny and very dry morning, in a lonely corner of the aerie, I heard over the snoring of Chac-Mool a curious sound, the arrival of chirpers, tiptoed, first one set of four, then another. I went out to look and confronted Ahau and Jag, returning together from I knew not where.

—What are you doing here? I said, trying without success to sound stern.

—We got bored, Ahau said.

—Lonely, Jag added.

—We missed the lovely mist.

I was about to reply when another set of chirpers came clod-toeing into view. Ben and Cib, apparently friends again.

—What is this, a family reunion? I asked.

—Ben and Cib looked at one another.

—We got bored, Ben said.

—Lonely, Cib added.

—We missed the lovely mist.

I looked at each of them. Script by Ahau, of course. He was blushing bright yellow.

—We thought it might be time for rain, Ahau said.

—I'll whistle when it's time for rain, I said, with a hint of anger.

They looked at their frog and turtle feet.

—Meanwhile, don't expect me to entertain you.

With that, I turned and hurried away to my private niche, before my emotions showed. Blood is thicker than drought.

That thought calls to mind Tika's father, with whom she had not spoken in years. I did not explain it earlier, it was private stuff. Now I suppose I should, to help to justify my fatal actions. The split occurred after she left his house, after that athlete she liked had died, when night after night in the brothel she worked off some imagined debt. When she was the artist of the night. When behind her suicide mask she was the talk of the village. When even married men came to see.

One who came to see was her father. Naked and glorious in her mask in the corner of her room, turning toward her next client, Tika was aghast to see her father standing there. Horror filled her eyes inside the mask. Wild thoughts careened in her brain like trapped birds. She didn't know what to do. To admit she recognized him would cause him shame. Worse, it would reveal herself. His outrage at finding her here would be uncontrollable. He might beat her to death at once, and be justified.

But if she did not . . .

Tika screamed, grabbed her kub, fled past her father, out of the steamy brothel hut, into the forest night. I do not know if he recognized her. Only this I know: in the ensuing years, father and daughter passed one another as strangers. They never spoke again.

—It happens in the best of families, Itzamna says.

—Stupid female, drooling Zeus intones. Why ruin a good party?

Despite the strange morals of the mortals, her father had come that close to having her. Would Tika have run if instead of her father Chac had appeared? I do not know. The trickster Fate chose not to make it so.

And so I debated.

Though it was less a debate, I suppose, than an entertainment in my brain, borderline insanity, two monkeys chasing each other's tails. I began to envy Chac-Mool, to long for peaceful imbecility, to be freed from responsibility for my actions. I began to notice in Chac-Mool's grin an inspired malice I had never seen before. As if this imbecile, of all the gods, could see what lay ahead.

The Spaniard, imprisoned underground, could not save Tika. Only Chac could save her. And only by breaking the Circle's decree. By making it rain.

What would be the harm, one of the brain-monkeys asked as he grabbed a tail. What was the point of this bond called loyalty? Invisible, ephemeral, a mere conceit. What high purpose did it serve?

It is a principle, the other monkey whined. Without principles men are as low as worms. What, then, shall we say of gods?

But she will die, the first monkey screamed. She whom you claim to love. Is that your godly wisdom? The blood of the one you love on your own hands? When it is in your power — and yours alone — to set her free?

The second monkey bit a revolving tail. Let her die, he spouted. You know you cannot possess her, no matter how long she lives. Her death will set you free.

For a moment I was swayed. I'd never thought of it that way. If I was passion's slave, then Tika's death would loose the shackles. It might be for the best.

But the first monkey wouldn't quit. How high-minded, he mocked. How godlike! To idly witness the death of the one you profess to love, for the expedient purpose of easing your own pain. Because to save her you'd have to break a principle! Time and Fate forfend!

How nice it is when our principles coincide with the easy way. Besides, he added, how do you know that with Tika's death your pain would be less? Picture the vast universe, with not a single life in it for you to love. Is that your idea of pleasure?

Around and around the monkeys spun, biting and scratching within my brain. I would have given anything to make them stop. But they refused. Together they paralyzed my will. They made me powerless to act. All I could do, like a coward, was listen to the night stars tick.

Not long before he was eaten by Chac-Mool, my favorite frog Enik had approached me with a painful look. He had been teased by the servants of some of the other gods, he said. They told him there was a new way to make rain, which did not require frogs, or even Chac. The sun could raise water from the oceans and the lakes, they had told him. The water would rise in the sky with a will of its own. It would gather inside the clouds, and these clouds, without the help of frogs, could burst and let loose rain. It was all mechanical, this system, they had said, with no need for a brain, with no need for a heart, with no need for desire. With no need for Chac.

—Tell me it isn't so, Enik had pleaded.

What was I to say? I hate to lie, the feelings of guilt aren't worth it. I picked Enik up and sat him on my nose. I stroked his green pate.

—There's more than one way to kill a jaguar, I said.

It was a bad metaphor, and the wrong thing to admit. I didn't make myself clear. Though this system recently had been invented across the seas, it would never be installed here. Not as long as a single Maya lived. But in my distraction with Tika I neglected to add that. I left the wrong impression. He limped away, hopeless and distraught. An easy prey. I think that killed him more than Chac-Mool's teeth.

How I wished that would happen now! For rain to fall without the aid of Chac. And save Tika's life. Without heart. Without desire. Without the need for a godly brain to decide.

Fat chance.

With the passing days Tika spent more and more time in her hut, confined not by the guards but by her own lack of will, her own dwindling interest in life. She had heard the shouting outside the hut when the Spaniard was denied entry. She had heard, through Tel's acute ears, of his arrest. She knew now that he could not save her. But I don't think she expected him to. I think she'd merely hoped for a chance to talk with him again.

Frustrated, she became disconsolate. Her food — she received special rations as a pending sacrifice — she barely tasted. She rarely spoke, even to Tel. She continued to make pots, each one uglier than the one before, as if she were mocking her mother's legacy, her mother whose bloodline had marked the path to her death. As if she were mocking the very notion of beauty. As if she were saying that beauty unseen, like Codices unread, might as well not exist. It was not a valid thesis, I think, but a product of her hopelessness. Beauty, where it exists, exists even in a void, if only in the mind of its creator, be that creator mortal or god. It's one of the twin muses of life, the orphaned ward of Time. The other muse being Love, the orphaned ward of Fate.

One evening, the hut dark except for one corner where light from the moon reflected off the sea. Tika, feeling expectant, not knowing why, watched the illumination begin to move, to carve a shape, at first indecipherable, then ghostlike, the shape of a young woman like herself. She seemed not surprised to see it, or to hear it speak. The voice was disembodied but distinct, like the sound of waves on the beach.

—Why do you fret, sister? Why do you mourn?

She had never seen a ghost before, but she was not afraid. She answered directly, as if it were Tel who had asked.

—Because I am going to die.

—Everyone is going to die, the voice said.

—Not like this. Not murdered before their time.

—Who can rightly know the proper time?

Tika did not like the conversation. She drew her knees to her chin and turned away. The moonlight followed into her line of sight. Tika brushed in front of her face, as if at the web of a spider. The moon ghost remained.

—Do you know who I am? the ghost asked.

—No.

—Don't you care?

—No.

The light seemed to glare, as if angered by her apathy. It flickered like a fire. Then it calmed.

—I am Ixki Chel. I am your great great great aunt. Returned from the waters.

Tika's eyes, glazed over, glanced at the vision with only vague interest. —The priests sent you, she said. To convince me to die willingly. The priests. The Lord Maya.

—You are wrong, the ghost said. I was sent to you by the gods.

(A lie! A fib, at the least. A fibbing reflection of moonlight!)

—Why do the gods want me? Tika said.

—They have heard your talk. They have heard your wishes. You wished to be a man, so you could build temples that will last through time. So you could carve their images, which will be admired through time. It is worthless being a woman, you said, to grind tortillas and spread your legs until you die.

—That was a long time ago. I was young. The gods have good ears.

—What about making babies?

—It's all the same.

—Perhaps. But why, then, are you sad? You have been chosen for a woman's highest honor. You shall be sacrificed to the gods. If Chac is pleased, if he ends the drought, your name will be honored until the end of days. Even as mine is honored. Your name will live in the Sacred Codices. And your soul will dwell forever in the harem of Chac.

I nearly fell headlong out of the mist. Harem? I peered closer at this moonlight, this alleged ghost. I'd never seen her before.

—Perhaps, Tika said.

She sighed a disconsolate sigh, and lowered her gaze to the ground. She blew cold breath into her hands. When she looked up again, the imposter ghost was gone.

It was a magic trick of that High Priest, I'd bet. He was pretty clever, for a mortal. Him and the chilan both. On the opposing sides of wisdom.

I hoped Tika wouldn't fall for it. Why would we send a ghost to do a god's work? Do you want to know the most dangerous words in every language on earth? 'It Is God's Will.'

Yet the visit of the ghost did seem to calm Tika's fears. She appeared to put aside her thoughts of death, to lose herself in fantasies. Perhaps, I thought, she has joined the harem of Chac.

I snorted at the thought, before Itzamna could.

Day ran into day and night to night while I waited for Itzamna to summon a meeting of the Circle, while I waited for the order to make it rain. And dared not whistle up my frogs. Monkey chasing monkey in my brain, and

Chac refuses to act. Refuses to pit his godhood against the will of the Circle. Furrows his brow in the shape of thunder clouds. But nothing more. Sees the gray ends of his hair turn white, as if the drought is bleaching him, too, as it has bleached the vistas below.

The world is awry, as if the waves that hold the earth fixed firmly in the galaxy have lost their grip. In a cave in the jungle a lonely skull waits naked and afraid. At the jungle's edge a myriad of golden butterflies importune a foul and decaying mango shell. A scout runs breathless into the village — the Spanish are on the march, they're coming here. In five days time there will be war.

The chilan by the blank stela no longer warns that the end of the world is near. The chilan is dead. Of natural causes, the High Priest says. Not revealing to the lower men the back of the chilan's skull, nor the bloody rock that crushed it.

The Spaniard, the warrior nacom, chafes in his cave of darkness, unable to escape, unable to save his woman, unable to prepare for the war to come. He thinks of Esmerelda, the girl he was engaged to marry back in Spain. He wonders what has become of her.

The starving mortals groan in their huts. The drinking well is almost dry, the only remaining water, untouchable, is in the sacred cenote, the province of the gods. The fires grow higher in the funeral pyres in the rock quarry near the sea.

The frogs grow irritated with the inaction of their master. Ben and Cib quarrel. Ahau and Jag quarrel. Jag says Ahau doesn't love her, that he wishes she were a frog. Ahau casts his eyes to the skies.

From the blooming mango trees a single mango falls, as if in remembrance of the chilan. At night the observatory stands empty, the nobles no longer watching the skies. They have lost the strength and the will to predict.

Tika's father would like to rescue her. Also to kill her. He knows he cannot do either. But he no longer is able to bear his guilt, now that she's to be a gift to the gods. Calmly sharpening his favorite flint knife, he lies on his mat and cuts his throat.

Dust lies thick on the village. Chac-Mool snickers in the mist, his fingernails sharp as claws. And Chac? Chac sleeps. Chac tries to dream of Tika, but cannot dream. Chac wishes he were mortal, so he could die.

Something is going on. I rouse myself. A procession of guards is moving toward Tika's hut. Tel has just rushed in. On Tika's face is the calm of resignation. It is the only peaceful face in the village, among the living.

Tel shows Tika her hands, cupped in a loose cage. She shows Tika what's inside: a black-tipped, gold-winged butterfly. Tika nods but shakes her head. She doesn't want to eat it now.

Tel smiles. With a sudden swift motion she pops the butterfly into her own mouth. She closes her eyes and feels the wings beating inside her cheeks. Her thin chest is heaving. She crunches with her teeth. She chews. She swallows. She waits, then opens her eyes and grins. Tika smiles, too, leans over and kisses Tel's cheek. Then with sudden passion she kisses her full on the lips.

For the first time I notice how Tel has grown. She's quite a dark young beauty.

Tika and Tel, looking deep into each other's eyes, move apart at a noise outside the door. The procession of guards has arrived. Tika will be escorted to the ceremonial waiting room, beside the main temple, where she will spend her final night. Tomorrow she'll be hurled into the well.

And still I dared not act.

Tossing and turning in our private mist, I lay awake all night, trying to imagine what punishment could be inflicted on me if I should make it rain. How do you torture a god? How, indeed, except by letting him love a mortal girl and not letting him possess her? We are immune to physical pain, we gods. We are immune to disease, to dismemberment, to death. Mental anguish is the only kind we suffer.

So my fruitless thoughts darted about that night, in circles, ovals, S-shaped curves. You can't control your thoughts, any more than you can control your destiny. Take her away, then! Let her die, let me exist in peace.

19.

Before I describe the events of the last day — while I've still got your attention — I would like to raise a metaphysical point. The philosophers among you may well be questioning whether I, Chac, still exist, in the absence of any believing Maya minds. Most likely, you were unaware of my existence until I began to tell my tale. If you believe in my existence now, then my decision to speak out has been rewarded. For this reason: I have new reason to hope. I have new hope for all of us abandoned gods. I haven't said a word to the others, I don't want to raise expectations. But I have developed a compelling thesis. The absurd one-god fad, so prevalent among mortals today, cannot last much longer, for this reason: it doesn't work.

Consider. The mortals have been traipsing around for thousands of years, in cold climates and warm, on many parts of the earth, in deserts and by the sea: hunters, gatherers, farmers, builders. All had one essential belief in common — a community of gods which they served, and who served them in return. It doesn't matter where you look, or how far back in mortal history — at the flatbrowed dwellers in caves, at the sharp-toothed tribes of the jungles, at the worldly Greeks and Romans, at the proud, classic Mayas. All had their rain gods and their sun gods, their gods of fertility and their gods of sustenance, of lightning and disease, of war and of death. Gods for every circumstance. The need for these gods, the existence of these gods, identical everywhere, in function if not in form, they discovered independently, each tribe on its own, on every face of the earth. What does this indicate? It suggests that we are necessary. That we fill a critical place in the mortal psyche. Else why would we have been ubiquitous?

So what happened? You know as well as I. Along came Yahveh, a minor god at best — some called him the God of Broken Promises. But he pulled

off a fearsome stunt. He huffed and puffed and threatened, and convinced a tribe called Hebrews, a tiny minority of mortals, that they must worship him alone. And how long did this Yahveh survive by himself? Just a few thousand years, when along came a usurper, Jesus, to sit beside him. They believe in one god, the mortals say, but if there is Yahveh, and there is his son Jesus, you don't have to count like a Maya to know that there are two. Not to mention their Holy Ghost, who muddles things altogether. So even these mortals who have spread their strange cult across the earth believe in two, or three. Clearly it did not take them long to discover that one god is insufficient, and unnatural — as unnatural as monogamy.

How long, then, before you turn again to the rest of us?

For your own mental health, it can't be soon enough. You mortals fared so much better before. Did you have a problem with your crops? All you did was spread a bit of pollen in the name of Yum Kaax (or whomever) and you were confident he would take care of it. Were you setting out to do battle? A nice burnt offering to the

war god would prepare you for victory. Or at least for
survival. And the war god did not hold it against you
if you masturbated the night before. That was not his
province. Were you threatened by a drought? A dance to
the rain god, a little water poured over a nubile adolescent
girl, perhaps in extreme cases a throbbing human
heart, and you regained peace of mind, convinced that
the drought would soon end. The result didn't matter.
Gods don't have to produce, not in the short term. The
mortals knew they'd done what they could, and felt
better. The system was compartmentalized, specialized,
an efficient delegation of authority,

Under the one-god myth, the responsibility is much
too great, both on the god and on the mortal. The
pressure often builds to levels intolerable, and grave
mistakes occur. Witness your Holocaust, your other
genocides.

Consider an analogy with mortal economics. If
a man has many creditors, it's easy enough to pacify
them in turn, first one with a small token payment,
then another. No one creditor has a large enough stake
to make a fuss, to make real trouble. But if the man
goes to an aptly named loan shark, borrows to pay off
all his small debts, thinking it will be easier to deal with
a single creditor, then he is finished. Then he is owned
by the shark, body and mind. Then he must do the big
shark's bidding at every turn, or risk his wrath. The
interest piles up at an outrageous rate. He knows he
can never get even. He is no longer a free man (insofar
as any of us are ever free of Time, or Fate.)

So it is with this one-god idea. Whatever name he
goes by, he's a shark. You mortals owe him so much
(or he makes you believe you do) that he owns you.
You fear you must constantly do his bidding, or face
dire consequences. And the interest, forever growing in
your psyches, is guilt. Thus does he control you further.
Your lives are circumscribed by guilt and fear. By

accepting the myth of one god, you have relinquished all tranquility.

The consequences are visible everywhere among you mortals of today — depression, alienation, frustration, unhappiness, greed. You have relinquished your birthright of pleasure for a mess of insecurity. To put the best mask on it, you could call it a worthy experiment that failed. But fail it has. It's only a matter of time before the cleverer of you mortals come to realize this — to abandon the current jargon, to return to the tested ways of old, to the proven beliefs of your forebears everywhere. To resurrect the colorful pantheon. To readmit into your lives the community of gods. To rediscover us, like lost loves. To spread the authority around.

That's my hypothesis. I haven't told the others, because even if I'm right not all of us will be summoned. There are so many sun gods, rain gods, war gods here in the asylum, there's no way of knowing which ones you mortals will once again take into your hearts. Not being Mayas, you may not even choose Chac.

Still, for the first time in many bakuns, I have hope. Hope that redemption is not far off. That's why I am venting this confession. Though it's out of character for humble Chac, a bit of publicity might prove helpful just now. A bit of visibility, to let you know I'm around. Me and my frogs both.

How I wish crippled Enik were alive. How the crowds would love him!

—A vote for Chac is a vote for Itzamna, Itzamna says. Maybe yes, maybe no.

But enough of politicking. I must complete my tale.

20.

Even the hairy jungle knew that something was amiss. His shriveled gonads tightened, the frightened woodland shivered like a bride. Creatures of the night were prowling in the sun's first rays. Instead of sleeping, spotted jaguars stole through leafless brush in search of vanished shade. Stilted deer descended from whitened highlands to nibble the jungle's toes. Hungry pumas sniffed at stricken deer but didn't eat. Warblers high in lifeless trees, who should have welcomed the dawn with gentle songs, screeched instead from roughened throats. Secret snakes, shy iguanas exposed themselves to the light. Golden butterflies impaled their wings on the pointed beaks of birds. All seemed to understand, except me: when the sky darkened again, all would be lost.

The High Priest feared that Guerrero would manage to escape and rescue his woman. He ordered the guards — six of them, well-armed — to bury the prisoner alive. He was only a Spaniard, after all.

Tika, who had slept alone in the ceremonial hut, as was the mandate, knew nothing of this, and did not say a word when she was awakened by Tel. To cover her nakedness she pulled over her head the brown kub she had used for a blanket in the night. She cleansed her face with cold water from a pot that had been lifted from the dregs of the drinking well. While Tel watched, she washed her hair with soapberry root and the last of the precious water.

She sat in the sun to dry it in the small, walled yard behind the hut. Tel brought her a breakfast of tortillas and warm chocolate. She drank the chocolate, sipping it slowly, but left the tortillas untouched. When she was done with breakfast she walked into the main room. On a stone in the center the ceremonial kub lay flat and beautiful in its terrifying way, a white kub painted richly with figures intertwined — snakes, jaguars, serpents with feathered heads, all of them painted in blue, the color of sacrifice.

Mute and unresisting, she stood motionless while Tel pulled her brown kub off. Her nakedness filled the hut like beams from the sun. Obediently, though neither had spoken, she raised her arms and let the sacrificial kub fall over her. She seemed to have abandoned herself to her fate. She tied her hair behind her with a hemp braid. Tel, watching, began to cry. Tika hugged her close. The girl sniffled. Tika sat on the stone in the center. From across the village they could hear the sound of drums, like morbid thunder. Young Tel sobbed again.

—Tell them I'm ready, Tika said.

Reluctantly the servant left the hut. For a few moments Tika was alone. I wished she would run, climb the rear wall, vanish into the jungle. But she made no move. Perhaps she knew there were guards with spears all around.

A short time later the High Priest's assistant entered the hut. In his hand was a small earthen jar. He approached Tika, and without a word, using dye from the jar, he painted her face blue. He paid her no more heed than he would a doomed chicken. He had done this many times before. When he left, two guards entered the hut, carrying ropes. Tika, seeing the ropes, asked,

—Is that necessary?

She knew one of the guards. A neighbor's son. They had played together as children.

—Orders, he said. His face reddened in spite of his will.

With a short rope they bound her wrists behind her back. With a longer one they tied her ankles together, loosely, so she could walk without discomfort. The neighbor's son, standing before her, parted his lips slightly, as if to say something. But he couldn't speak, any more than I could. Reddening again, he turned quickly and left the hut, followed by the other.

When they were gone, Tika walked to the sleeping room, where men were forbidden to enter. On a high ledge Tel had propped a small polished flat of obsidian. Mirrors were forbidden here, but Tika had entreated her to smuggle one in, her last request of the girl. The servant would remove it unnoticed during the ceremony, and would come to no harm. Hands bound behind her, Tika looked for the last time at her image shining back from the stone. The blue paint lost itself in the slate, only the whites of her eyes stared back.

A large rock on which the water jug had rested stood against the wall below the ledge. I noticed Tika gazing at this rock. Calculating. I knew what she was thinking. If she stood on the stone, her hands tied behind her, one hand could clutch the slate mirror. Holding it tight, she could slice her opposite wrist with the sharp edge. Switching hands, she could cut the other wrist, deep into the veins. She could stand there, collapse there, her blood mocking the sacrificial gown. She could thwart their plan, give herself not to Chac in supplication but to Ixtab in pride. To the goddess of suicide. She looked from stone to slate and back. She looked at the roof, trying to look through it. She spoke aloud.

—Do you want me?

Frantic, I looked about for Ixtab, to urge her not to answer. Usually she didn't, she ignored such entreaties, she took who came but tempted none. I was relieved that she was not about. She was off with Kai Yum, no doubt, he of the music and the golden curls.

Looking down, I saw that Tika had moved away from the stone, away from the slate with its hard white eyes. She would not give them the satisfaction. Not the laughing girl. Not the artist of the night. Not the Spaniard's woman. Not her mother's daughter. She would shame them instead with her grace.

The drummers were lined up in a double row in the plaza. At both ends arrays of trumpeters began to blow on conch shells, long, wavering notes that summoned all the males in hearing to come and witness the sacrifice. All across the village the remaining starving men summoned their strength to leave their huts, and began to flow like slow, drying fish toward the plaza — lower men, artisans, traders, nobles, some solemn, moving in stately procession, others trying to joke despite their hunger. From every direction for half an hour they flowed into the plaza, the vast offending plaza of Kukulcan.

When the trumpets had sounded twenty minutes there was a commotion outside the hut. Tika, feeling faint, pale beneath the blue on her face, clutched at the mud wall. But when the two guards entered the room the sickness passed. She stood erect, shook off the hands of the guards, walked easily between them toward the entrance, out into the ravenous sun. A full retinue of guards was waiting. At their head stood the High Priest, dressed in his finest blue breechclout, his gaudiest hat, replete with the green and gold feathers of the quetzal. At the sight of him Tika turned her head and said something to the tall guard beside her, the neighbor's son. The entire array of guards saw this, wondered what solemn epigram she had chosen to utter. The High Priest would ask the guard later. What she had said to him was,

—How is your mother?

At which the guard flushed, but did not respond.

When the trumpets stopped, the High Priest began to walk up the sloping path to the plaza. Behind him were a double row of guards, carrying spears. Behind them walked Tika, flanked by four guards on each side. Behind her marched another double row, as if they were expecting someone to attempt to rescue her. As if they expected the Spaniard to escape from under the earth, or the athlete Ahkel to return from his grave beneath the sea.

Perhaps I was wrong to drown that boy. Perhaps he might have done something.

Probably not. He would have stood there beaming, proud as a mango tree that his beloved had been chosen for the honor. Secure in his unquestioned loyalty to the village. The picture of mental health.

It's just as well he drowned. I couldn't have borne that smug face.

The Lord Maya himself, in a prescribed display of humility, brought up the rear. As if to say, if the sacrifice did not work it was not his doing.

The procession moved toward the plaza. Skeletal women, bloated children, watched its passing. Women hugged the boney shoulders of their adolescent daughters, a gesture easily understood: there but for the grace of Chac go you!

With each passing minute, strange things happened in the dust-coated jungle: jaguars sodomized coati mundi; pumas lay down with snakes; owls made off with serpent eggs; the few remaining white and purple orchids wept. (The word 'orchid' comes from the Greek word for testicle. So says Zeus. I remember when, in happier times, Tika wore an orchid in her hair.) Brittle vines nibbled by baby deer turned suddenly on their attackers, piercing windpipes; birds and lizards mated, birds crunching in the underbrush, lizards flying high. From the sea, manatees left the too-salty waters and filled the jungle like giant, awkward rabbits; giant turtles fell to their knees and prayed.

Itzamna says it wasn't so. Itzamna says these were frantic illusions, created by the impending loss of my beloved. If so, the golden butterflies must have been frantic, too.

On the plaza the drums resumed, muted now, a low insistent throbbing in the bones. The Lord Maya approached his throne, a swirl of beaded breechclouts, his blue beaded headdress half again as tall as he. Without a glance at Tika he took a place near the priest, half a step in front, and led the march up the broad curving causeway to the sacred well. There they would be joined by the spiritual nacom: the executioner.

They were halfway to the cenote when a green-gold quetzal bird, sacred and rare and terrified this morning of the doings in the jungle, fell from the sky at their feet. Drums and procession stopped at once. A worried look on his tattooed face, the Lord Maya conferred with the priest. What was this sign? he wanted to know. Was it a warning, perhaps, that they should not proceed? The priest bent and lifted the stunned bird. It wriggled from his grasp, flew crazily into the air, away from the jungle toward the sea. On the contrary, the priest told the Lord, See how the bird lives! It is not a warning, it is an urging. They were on the proper course.

The Lord Maya was not convinced, I could tell. But he saw little choice but to resume the march to the well. The drums began again, and the marchers, a long winding column, in which after the priests, the guard and the nobles, hundreds of bedraggled villagers trailed as best they could manage, within a floating ribbon of dust.

A warning, I thought, looking down. If only I could devise a warning to frighten them, perhaps Tika would be spared. I could not think of one.

An hour later, of course, when it was much too late, I thought of plenty — a burning bush, a fiery sword, giant spiders, black horsebeasts racing through the sky. Any one of those might have saved her life. (I always think of excellent warnings an hour late.) But it didn't matter. As god of rain I never learned such tricks; not even Itzamna did. In the sacred school for gods that we attended, those were soft electives, cheap tricks, frowned upon.

In the sky above the marchers, as the leaders arrived at the sacrificial cenote, every last person closed their eyes in obeisance. The quetzal returned at that moment, was flapping madly, screeching raucously. To me it looked and sounded like a warning. But it wasn't one, for who could have sent it, except their false god Kukulcan? And he was not only mortal, he was dead.

The priestly nacom, the official executioner, covered every inch in the same ugly blue as the others, greeted the Lord Maya and the High Priest beside the well. The guards led Tika up beside them. The village stragglers formed a great circle around the circumference of the cenote, which was as wide across as the temple. Below them the smooth stone sides of the well plunged sixty feet to the level of black water. Below the surface the water slept for forty feet more.

—Unbind her, the High Priest ordered.

Two guards removed the ropes from Tika's wrists and from her ankles. They stepped back. Tika stood alone among the High Priest, the priest-nacom and the painted Lord. Looking down, I felt my heart begin to freeze. It was as if until that moment I had not truly accepted the depth of their stupidity, the reality of their intent.

—Ixtika Chel Chek, the Lord Maya intoned, you have been chosen to receive the highest honor our people can bestow. You shall be a messenger to the gods. The great drought has ruined our corn, has left our people hungry. Many have perished. You shall visit the rain god Chac, who lives at the bottom of the cenote. You shall tell him of our plight. You shall beg for rain on behalf of your people, even as your great aunt of sacred memory did many bakuns ago. Will you do that for your people, Ix Tika?

—Turtle shit! I wanted to shout. But I had no voice they could hear. Indeed, not a sound could be heard anywhere near the cenote, not even the buzzing of a fly. All waited mute for Tika's ritual reply.

—No, I will not, she said, in a voice firm as a bell.

All in her hearing gasped. The Lord Maya grew red beneath his blue paint. The purple of rage did not become him.

—Strip her! the nacom ordered.

The appointed guards stepped forward. Tika stood tall but did not resist as they lifted the blue-painted kub over her head. Her burnished body gleamed in the sun with the brilliance of a full moon.

The High Priest stayed the hand of the nacom. He stepped in front of Tika. His voice was unctuous, with a phony sympathy.

—Why do you decline, my child?

Tika seemed to relax from the statuesque; her limbs loosened, she seemed for a moment a carefree young woman about to go for a swim.

—Because Chac doesn't live down there, she said.

The priest shook his head at her unschooled ignorance.

—Of course he does.

—How do you know this? Tika asked.

—Everyone knows this, the priest said. It is the teaching of the ages.

Tika ran her tongue along her sweaty upper lip, where an iconoclastic fly had alighted. The fly buzzed off, dove at the ear of the priest, swirled away.

—The teaching of the ages is wrong, Tika said.

Again those in earshot gasped. The Lord Maya motioned the priest away, and took his place beside her. I wondered if he remembered visiting her, that time when she was little, when she threw a mango at him.

—Why do you say the teaching is false? the Lord Maya asked. Where do you think the god Chac lives?

All this I heard with fascination. I wondered, like them, what she would say. When she spoke it was in firm, strong tones that created the merest hint of an echo within the cenote walls.

—He lives, she said, in the mist above the jungle. In the mist that hangs there even in the drought.

—In the mist? the Lord Maya repeated.

Some around them laughed, mostly the guards. The high priest silenced them.

—Why do you say that? the Lord Maya asked.

Tika looked down at her ankles. Redness flushed her neck, crept down toward her breasts. She had seemed unaware until now of her nakedness. She stood tall again, straight as a stela, and looked at the Lord Maya's eyes as she spoke.

—Because I have lain with him there.

Silence primeval. Like the silence before the world began. Then the noise erupted, the buzz of a thousand flies, as her words were repeated from face to incredulous face around the well. As for myself, there is no other way to put it: I was struck dumb.

—I have lain with Chac many times, Tika said. He lives in the mist that hangs above the trees.

My heart was leaping like my frogs. My fantasies! She knows them! She sees them! She lives them! Then my excitement plummeted. Perhaps she was merely pressing some advantage, to save her life.

And yet she knew!

The sacred ceremony had become a chorus of obscene remarks.

—How does Chac do it? With his nose?

Things like that.

The three top Mayas were conferring. They soon reached agreement: the woman did not seem insane: she was play-acting, sowing confusion, in the hope of being spared; she must be sent to Chac as planned. Once there, she would do what was right for her people; and if, in fact, she was pleasing to Chac, as she claimed, well, that is what they hoped.

The Lord Maya raised his hand for silence. The buzzing stopped.

—The ceremony shall continue, he intoned.

The High Priest and the priest-nacom stepped to the edge of the well. They beckoned to naked Tika, who followed them willingly. A lovely dimple in her buttocks tore my heart.

—Hear, O Chac, the priest implored, with a deep voice and full theatrics. We send you a gift from the people — that you in return may send us rain.

—See, O Chac, the priestly nacom sang out. Accept the treasured gift we send.

The shimmering silence of held breath was like a vast clear bubble of sunlight settling over the cenote. Slowly the nacom reached his blue-painted arm toward Tika. She held up her palm, to stop him. As the nacom paused, she reached both arms behind her head, in a gesture that seemed to expose her even more. She untied the hemp braid from her hair and let it fall. Her wild black hair flowed like dark snakes over her shoulders, half way down her back. She lowered her eyes. The nacom and the priest stepped behind her. I blanched, I felt ill. My face I'm sure had blended with the mist, become one. I couldn't stand their bloody piety! I had to save her life.

They moved toward her. They gripped her arms.

In a moment it was done. In an instant, a mere nothingness in their concept of time, she was falling through the air, tumbling, turning, drifting, head over sex, toward the gleaming black water at the bottom of the well.

At the very same instant, the rains came. I overturned my gourds and let torrents pour down — not on the fields of corn, not on the village, not on the thirsty jungle. Only in one narrow cylinder the waters fell, a cylinder wide as the cenote but no wider, a concentrated deluge pouring into the well. Gourd after gourd I poured.

—Four! I shouted, and my frogs and my adopted turtle, glancing about for only an instant, as if fearing the wrath of Itzamna, quickly obeyed. All of us emptied gourd after gourd from the mist into the well.

Tika, straightening her erratic fall half way down, had turned it into a dive. With arms extended in front of her and legs straight out behind she cut into the water like a spear, disappearing into the depths — unbroken, as many are, by a blunt landing. But there was no way she could climb the sixty feet to the top along the slick cenote walls. She could tread water for as long as possible. Then she would drown.

—Four! I shouted again, and the frogs and the turtle poured. The deluge was unabated. The water in the cenote rose quickly.

From the depths Tika emerged, her wild hair glistening. She felt the rain on her face and she lay on her back and let the cool deliverance fall upon her eyes. She floated without tension as the rising waters bore her up, as the falling waters splashed on belly and breast. Around the cenote the Lord Maya, the priests, the villagers had fallen to their knees. Gone now were their obscenities. They were giving thanks to Chac for saving them. Never before had a sacrificial offering produced such quick results.

Only the priestly nacom scowled. He had wondered at the sun still shining, he had turned away from the cenote to look. He had seen that it was raining nowhere else, not on the village, not on the jungle, not on the wilted corn, not even on the drinking well. He had never seen such a thing.

In the sacred cenote the water continued to rise. When it reached almost the top Tika ceased floating, turned over, swam with graceful strokes to the edge. Half a dozen villagers reached for her, lifted her dripping from from the well, while the people and the nobles cheered, shouted her praises lustily. They thought they had been saved. Only the three officials had their backs to the well: the High Priest, the nacom, the Lord Maya. In every direction they saw that the earth remained parched, that it shimmered, cracked and still, in the baking sun.

I was ecstatic. In the moment of crisis, I had risen to meet the challenge. I had made a miracle. I had saved Tika's life — without breaking the edict of the Circle. The Mayas still had drought.

The frogs and the turtle put down their guards and danced. But even as my chest filled with pleasure, the nacom, eyes red with rage, ordered the guards to seize dripping Tika. The officials put their hats together again. I couldn't imagine what needed discussing, I thought my meaning was clear, clear as the drops of water still clinging to Tika's thighs. She must live, I had showed them. I do not want her blood, her death!

Never underestimate the stupidity of leaders. They read my meaning wrong.

—Chac has rejected this sacrifice, the High Priest said.

—He mocks us with his rain, the Lord Maya said.

—He wants us to do the other, the priestly nacom pronounced.

I am an old god with a long nose and stringy gray hair. I have always looked thus, even when I was young. But perhaps, at that most critical moment, my countless bakuns had affected my brain. Little strokes,

which, unnoticed, kill patches of the mind. Make for
forgetfulness. For dulled response. Or perhaps it was
merely my own ecstasy at saving Tika's life that blinded
me. That made me as stupid as the mortals below.

—Then we must do the other, the nacom had said.

And I scarcely heard, I hardly paid attention, so
smug was I with my deed. Not only had I saved her
life, she had confessed in shameless nakedness before
all the living men of the village her secret longing. Her
secret lust for me!

—I have lain with Chac many times.

Our fantasies entwined in future sheets of heavens
not yet formed. I imagined us together in sacred unions
of our own devising. Coalescing illusions. My years fell
away at the thought.

And with them, perhaps, my good sense.

So filled was I with this imagined future that I barely
recorded the present. Down below I saw the villagers
moving, running despite their weakness, back toward
the plaza — and I didn't grasp the point of it. I had
saved Tika's life, and she knew it had been me. That
was all that mattered just then.

In the midst of the running villagers, I noticed
suddenly, Tika, still dripping. She could not run, she
could not walk. She was being dragged along the dusty
road by whoever's arms could reach her in the throng
— dragged now by an arm, now by a leg, now even by
her hair. She twisted and contorted but couldn't free
herself. Men on the outer rims of the crowd who could
not get near her were finding stones and hurling them at
her. All were screaming epithets at the Whore of Chac,
who indulged her pleasures above the jungle while the
corn in the fields died.

—Stop! I screamed. What are you doing? Let her go!
It was only fantasy. We never touched each other!

But humans cannot hear the voice of gods. Not even
at the end. No matter what their priests pretend. All

they knew was the parched fields around them, and the lingering odor of death, and this shameless harlot who had the ear of Chac and didn't speak.

The angry mob, for that's what it had become, slowed to a congested halt. In the center I could see the bright feathers of the priest, the nacom, the Lord Maya. Even at that moment, perhaps, I could have saved her, and all would have turned out differently. I could have made it rain everywhere, let rain fall on their fields, their jungle, their highlands. Why didn't I? I've asked myself that a thousand times in the bakuns that have passed since. Partly there was the Circle and its decree. Partly there was the fear they would kill her anyway, as a gesture of thanks. Of thanks! So I thought and thought, and didn't act. Rain gods, I realized, are not supposed to think.

—Then we must do the other!

I didn't realize where they had paused, until the center of the mob pulled back, and four guards of the priesthood stood apart. Only then did I see where they were. Only then did I grasp their intent.

—No! I shrieked, in a voice most booming, and filled with awesome command.

They thought it was only thunder. They didn't react.

The four guards surrounded their stupid rock. Not ten feet away was the grinning stone statue of my idiot half-brother Chac-Mool, stretched toward them on the ground like a serpent, his vacant face staring, unblinking, a great stone bowl between his paws. The priest and the nacom were intoning prayers while the Lord Maya watched. Tika, still being held roughly by the crowd, her flesh now scraped and bleeding, was shoved violently toward the rock while the villagers cheered. The guards seized her, lifted her fiercely onto the gritty arch. They sprawled her, face up, over the wedge, forcing her body to arc, pressing her down, each guard holding fast to a limb. Her hair hung wildly, her eyes searched frantically, her breasts beseeched, her sex cried out to the sky. Only her mouth was closed, composed, as if she had determined she would not scream.

It was I who screamed.

—No! I will destroy you all!

In their wildness they didn't hear. Through the mist of my own watery eyes I saw the blue hand of the priestly nacom raised over her, a sharp stone knife in his fist. I felt the moving air of a crowd surround me. Itzamna, Ixtab, a dozen other gods were pressing around to watch.

Perhaps I could implore them now. . .

Like blue lightning the nacom's arm struck. A gasp of bright vermillion spewed across her breast and down her loins. Again he slashed, her eyes still searching, frantic — searching for me? Her mouth somehow still refusing to scream. He struck again, and where a moment before had been the breast I longed to touch there was now only a gaping red cleft. Into this cleft, with a curdling yell, the nacom jammed his hand — the Hand of God, they called it, the ultimate blasphemy — and with a twisting, wrenching, obscene yanking he tore from its mooring of arteries and veins her still-beating heart. He held it aloft for the mob to see.

Cheers and curses rose like a stench from the beastly men. The nacom with the ragged crowd pressed all around strode toward the bowl of Chac-Mool. There, like feeding a scrap of gristle to a mangy dog, he tossed in Tika's heart.

It was then my godliness cracked. No more thoughts, worries, anxious explanations. I leaped. I leaped at the form of Chac-Mool, who was watching with the others. I saw his stupid grin — he was actually going to eat the pulsing heart! — and I went for his eyes. I gouged his eyes and then amid his shrieks I went for his thick and sweaty throat. I squeezed and squeezed with a strength I never had before, until this bastard evil image of my blood fell half-dead and stony through the mist, down to the earth.

I should have calmed then. My rage should have been satisfied. But it was not. The force of it had just begun to build. Guilty of attempted god slaughter, in front of the highest witnesses, I saw nothing to hold me back. I could not have held back in any case.

I made it thunder. I made it lighten. I made it rain. I poured down rain on all the Maya lands with such ferocity as had never been seen before. The fierceness of the deluge drove the mortals to their huts before they could further desecrate the lifeless body of my love. Alone on the sacrificial stone she lay, her eyes no longer frantic but at peace, her still heart lying undevoured in the watery cup of Mool. Her lifeless eyes encouraging me. My rain washing away her blood, as once before it had in gentler times.

How I made it rain! The fabled flood of Noah was a spring shower compared to the rains I made. I filled their huts with rain, and their sacred temples. Of their cornfields I made lakes — nay, oceans. I covered their ball fields, I drowned their remaining athletes as they huddled together like rats, pawing on the walls. My rain tore a thousand mangos from drooping limbs and cracked their shells on the earth. A million golden butterflies went mad, writhing in the mud, trying to define their proper world.

I covered the sun with clouds. I covered their cries with thunder. I covered the earth with a powerful new rain to add to the book of a thousand others: The Killer Rain.

The other gods implored me to stop.

—Enough, they cried. If you won't think of them, think of us!

I was as deaf to their pleas as the Mayas had been to mine.

Even the mighty Itzamna begged me to stop. Him I was reluctant to refuse. And yet I turned my back. My rage still sizzled. I filled their plaza with water. I filled the jungle to the tops of the whitened trees. My floodwaters rose on the pyramid of Kukulcan — where was their mighty mortal warrior to save them now? Until its ugly temple top was no more than a crown of pebbles at the bottom of the ocean deep.

Still my rage poured forth. It was not confined to Tika's village. My vicious rain whipped across the jungle and the woodlands and the mountains, ushering down vast slides of clay, submerging every last Maya village, hamlet, hut. The mortals were no more than insects being swept away. Every last Maya — man, woman, child — paid with their lives for Tika's life that day. Only when the last Maya drowned (I think it was little Tel) did my wild rage slacken. Only then did I call off the frogs. Only then did I stop the rain.

If there are living mortals today who claim to be Maya, it isn't so. They're Mexican, they're Indian. They may follow Maya customs of which they have heard, but no true Maya lives. They may still tell tales of Itzamna, even of Chac. But they worship the one god of the Spaniards — whose own time soon will come.

For weeks, for months, I watched the waters, stinking with death, ever so slowly yield themselves to Itzamna's sun. Beneath them the watery jungle slowly grew thick and tall. As the floodwaters left he quickly usurped the village. Great vines and rapine trees captured and submerged all: huts, temples, pyramids, observatories, sacred stones, carved stelae — everything. All the artistry, all the mathematics of the Maya mind, buried under mounds of earth, shrubs, thickets, mulch, poisoned vines too thick to penetrate.

That way did I leave them. A civilization dead. A playground for your busybodies.

And they have come. They have come with their shovels and their spades and their picks. They have unearthed a smattering of ruins. Much of Tika's village they have unearthed, have cut out from the jungle like a heart retrieved from a breast. They have studied the signs left behind. They have credited the vanished Mayas with artistry, wisdom, sensitivity — but have ignored the brutish evidence all around.

They have made much of the Maya disappearance. What happened, they ask, to those clever people who seemed so fit to survive?

Now you know.

As for myself and the other gods — our destiny I had not considered in my rage. When the last Maya died, we became, all of us, gods without clients, without honor, without subservience. We drift about in the aerie, the asylum, rather aimlessly, trying not to admit our loneliness, trying not to admit how much we miss the little buggers.

We have learned a new equation: religion plus time equals myth.

At a recent reunion of the Circle — many didn't even come — the idea was floated about to sacrifice one of our own members in the temple of a higher god — in the temple of Time, or Fate — in the hope of finding ourselves a purpose again. Maybe we'll try it, maybe we won't. I doubt that it would work.

Not long ago, I peered into that old jungle cave. The butterflies are back where they had been, black-tipped, gold-winged, swarming in thick yellow bands around the turquoise-studded skull (or is it jade?) Around and around they flutter, never stopping, in circles, ovals, S-shaped curves. As if they believe that once again all is right with the world.

As for Tika, what more can I add? Only that, even if she and I had been possible, I suspect it was just a passing fancy. It probably wouldn't have worked, in the end.

Time, in his idleness, has been learning magic tricks. He still lets the weeks and months pass slowly, with laconic ease. But, as you may have noticed, as you live year after year, he creates the illusion of their flitting by with incomprehensible speed. In my dotage, it seems as if the events I have been describing happened only yesterday.

This is so with Itzamna as well. And he thinks something similar could happen again.

—So lock up your pretty ones, he warns.

Fate, listening, says nothing. Fate, listening, smiles. And grinds another butterfly between her teeth.

Other books from Robert Mayer

The Origin of Sorrow

"A Masterpiece"
New York Times contributor
Robert Lipsyte

Robert Mayer

It was a time of love, of struggle, of hope, of worship, of the birth of dynasties and the crushing affliction of hatred...

In the 1770s, the Jews of Frankfurt are trapped, both physically by the walls of the ghetto within which they must dwell, and in a larger sense by the rules of a society in which they are outcasts, legally debased and barely suffered to live.

And yet within those confines they find life, in all its glories and tragedies. This is the story of young Guttle, whose sweet face and curves could win her any man in her little world, but whose keen mind demands the best. It is the tale of Meyer Rothschild, who knows all the ways of the business world but discovers the ways of the heart. It is a tale of love and lust, of murder and betrayal, of holy works and unholy schemes, of bakers and brigands, of hope and of ruin.

"Succeeds while dealing with the question of Jewish identity and survival that is as relevant today as it was in 18th-century Frankfurt." —*Hadassah*

"Brilliantly writtten." —*The New Mexico Jewish Link*

"A masterpiece of story-telling, rich characters, moving scenes, delicious history. I loved reading it the second time, too." —*New York Times* contributor Robert Lipsyte.

The Origin of Sorrow, ISBN: 978-1936404-09-4, 578 pages.

New Orleans,
August 2005.

The lives of a ballet dancer, a reporter, a psychiatrist, and a Voodoo queen intersect and overlap in the shadow of a stalker and a serial killer... and all the while, a bad wind named Katrina is headed their way.

Danse Macabre
ISBN 978-1460973-02-8
232 pages

A tale of the human struggle, of love and war, sorrow and joy, death and renewal, faith and doubt... all seen from the ferret's point of view.

Ezra Wroth is a man of today, a master of science but facing his own mortality, struggling with an array of uncertainties. His children are adults with more exuberance than wisdom, his own past holds dark secrets, and the world around him has plans for him he cannot imagine. Into his life comes Cleo, a ferret who understands him better than he understands himself... or is what is happening not quite what it seems?

The Ferret's Tale, ISBN: 978-1456358-97-6, 334 pages.

**Ask for them where you got this book,
order through your ebook device,
or at www.COMBUSTOICA.com**

www.ingramcontent.com/pod-product-compliance
Lightning Source LLC
Chambersburg PA
CBHW021241260626
47155CB00004BA/1247